For:

Anthony, my one and only Son-shine…

And for My Miguel…El hombre de mis sueños…
(The man of my dreams)

Acknowledgements:

Anthony, my son. Thank you for your patience. Thank you for your encouragement, for critiquing my story, my plots and ideas. Never forget, dreams come true. Thank you for being my biggest fan. I love you with all my heart…

Thank you mom and dad. Mom for encouraging creativity. Dad for his teaching discipline and hard work. I wish my dad were here to see my accomplishment. Without you both, I would not be the person I am today. I love you.

Miguel…My Miguel… Gracias, por inspirarme, por eso pude crear esta historia de amor. Gracias por ser quien eres, por que sin ti, nunca hubiera nacido esta historia. Gracias por creer en mi y por tus consejos y ideas. Y mas por ser el aliento que me hizo volar en las paginas de este libro. Eres unico…eres Mio. Te dedico mi obra de amor. Te quiero mucho. Y te voy a querer Forever…

FOREVER...

His whispers of forever echo through my hallowed soul,
filling it with love of days, now but a memory.
The beat of his heart is the song I will hear until a day past
forever,
filled with lyrics of a love so pure, yet so forbidden.
A love we will long for, until our dying breath...

CHAPTER I

"Could life get any better?" Nicolas asked himself. He leaned back in his chair, crossed his hands behind his neck and he smiled. The Sunday paper was open to the restaurant section on the table in front of him.

Headline: NICO'S II   A taste of Spain in the heart of Miami.

"Wow," he said to himself, slowly lifting his coffee cup to this mouth. He blew on the hot coffee then sipped it slowly while he concentrated on the article written about the restaurant.

When he got to the bottom of the review, there they were. 4 solid gold stars and one hollow star, signifying only 4 out of 5 stars.

"YES!!!!!" he yelled, slamming his hands 4 times onto the table "4 stars!!!!" Again he shouted, "We're a 4 star restaurant, YES!!!" He stood up and raised his hands in the air and yelled "Thank you, Jesus!"

He couldn't believe it. His newly opened restaurant was front page news and included a 4 star rating. "Wow," he said again, with a huge grin on his face, "I knew it!"

He read quickly through the review again. And, although Joseph Martel, the restaurant reviewer, hadn't given the restaurant a 5 star rating, he smiled. He nodded confidently as he thought of the plans he had in store for the restaurant and knew the next rating would be a 5.

Nico's II was the Spanish restaurant Nicolas had opened six months earlier on Miami Beach. It was a sudden decision after Nico's, his first restaurant in South Beach, had been such a success.

Nicolas sat back and reminisced how he came upon the opportunity to open the new restaurant in such a prime location. But, was shaken from deep thought as he heard Mia, in her slippers, shuffling over the wood floor in the hallway.

Mia always dragged her feet when she wore her slippers. Nicolas thought it was funny and once asked why, only in her slippers, did she drag her feet. Confidently, she told him, that in her slippers she could be lazy and in being lazy she was allowed to drag her feet. Nicolas slightly laughed as he remembered her answer. He lifted his head and looked toward the door as Mia walked through the arched doorway.

Mia tied her robe more tightly as she entered the kitchen. She walked toward the table where Nicolas was sitting. As she approached him, she gathered her long black hair and secured it tightly in a bun with a clip she had taken from the pocket of her robe and asked "Baby, what is going on? You scared me. I heard you shouting. Is everything ok?"

Nicolas looked up and smiled coyly and said "Good morning beautiful, and yes, everything is perfect." He stood up and walked quickly toward Mia and picked her up gently then twirled her around. She held on tightly and screamed, "Nico, the baby!" Nico placed her on the floor and grabbed her face in his hands and kissed her lips forcefully.

Mia pulled back, looked at him curiously and asked insistently, "Baby, what is going on?"

Nicolas began to tell Mia about the article. "He gave us a 4! A 4 out of 5 star rating, Mia!"

Mia clapped her hands then threw them in the air and said "Congratulations baby, I knew he would love it, I had no doubt, whatsoever."

Nicolas began to read the article to Mia. Mia, with a smile on her face, watched him as he spoke, then reached for his cup of coffee. Nicolas continued to talk but looked at her curiously as she put the cup toward her mouth.

She knew why he looked at her this way. At her last doctor appointment, her doctor told her to stay away from caffeine while she was pregnant. Mia looked at him and said, "Just a sip baby, just a sip." Feeling a bit guilty, she shyly asked, "May I?" He said, "Sure, just a sip, just a sip" imitating the words she had just uttered. They both laughed and Mia put the cup to her mouth and took just one sip, then placed the cup in front of Nicolas.

"And?" she asked lifting her eyebrows, in a questioning look.

He smiled and continued, "A 4 is all he gave us, but next time, I can guarantee it will be a 5!! Martel says the front display wasn't illuminated enough and it could be a make or break item, as it was hard to see by the passing traffic. But, he loved the food. The way he described the lamb chops made even my mouth water." Nicolas continued, imitating Martel's deep voice and strong New York accent, "And the tomatoes, mouth watering and baked to perfection with just a slight hint of garlic."

Mia laughed at Nicolas' imitation of Martel's comment while she shook her head in disbelief. "One point for display, wow!" she said.

"Mia, we're lucky we got a 4. Martel is not one to ever give a 5. Nothing is ever perfect for him. In fact, I've never seen a 5 since he became head reviewer for Miami News. And the last time I saw a 4 was…" Nicolas stopped and rolled his eyes upward trying to remember when he last saw a 4, then he laughingly said, "I can't remember! But, next time for us, baby, I promise a 5!" Nicolas pursed his lips and nodded his head with conviction as he spoke.

Mia smiled and grabbed his hand. She puckered her lips and blew a kiss and said, "Baby, I am so very proud of you."

He pulled her close and as she fell onto his lap he whispered, "I love you Mia," then winked at her. Mia kissed him and said "I love you too, baby."

Mia ran her fingers slowly through Nicolas' hair as he showed her the pictures that had been taken during the dinner. Nicolas spoke quickly as he turned the pages, pointing out the things Mr. Martel had mentioned in the article. Then he asked Mia, "Do you have a busy day planned?"

"I have some ad writing I have to get done, a few things I thought about last night during the opening. I also have to work on the new display at the shop. Will you be there tomorrow?" she replied.

Mia had opened a small shop in South Beach just a few of blocks away from Nico's. The store carried the line of clothing she had begun designing the year before. She had been very busy stocking it and working on her new designs for the grand opening.

Nicolas pulled her close and pushed his face toward hers. He grabbed her face and opened his mouth, gently sucking her lips into his mouth. She looked into his eyes questioningly, as he kissed her He pulled away and said, "Of course I'll be there, I wouldn't miss it for the world and have you forgotten who's catering the event, my dear?" Mia rolled her eyes and laughed.

Mia nervously rubbed her hands together and said, "I was hoping you wouldn't miss it, I need you there for support." He looked at her with a curious stare and said "Silly, I wouldn't miss it for anything."

Mia smiled at Nicolas then quickly stood up. She placed her hand on her mouth and looked at him wide eyed and ran toward the bathroom, shuffling quickly, in her slippers. He ran after her. She ran to the toilet, lifted the seat quickly and stood over it throwing up the little she had in her stomach.

Nicolas kept his eyes and mouth closed tightly and faced the ceiling. He rubbed her back awkwardly with one hand and held back her hair with the other.

His concentration was more on not throwing up than it was on Mia. He had such a weak stomach, and did not want to end up in the same position as Mia. He felt sick to his stomach. He hated seeing anyone throw up because it always made him sick.

Only two days prior, they found out Mia was pregnant.

Worried, Nicolas stood behind her and asked "Mia, what can I do? I don't like to see you sick!" She shook her head, as she hunched over the toilet, dry heaving. Nicolas ran for water and crackers. He grabbed the small hand towel that hung by the sink and sat on the floor next to her. His head was bent down and his eyes and mouth remained tightly closed.

She took the small towel from his extended hand and cleaned her mouth. When she turned her head she laughed at the expression on his face. His eyes and mouth appeared to be sealed tightly. She wondered how he was breathing, and definitely knew he couldn't see what was going on. She laughed to herself and grabbed his hand and kissed it. He pulled it back instinctively, still thinking of her vomit.

"Baby, I'm ok." Mia said, "I'm only pregnant, remember? You, on the other hand, have no excuse to be so pale! I'm the nauseous one and you are more pale than I am?" She laughed more and kissed him. "Ewww, vomit breath!" Nicolas said with a slight gag.

He relaxed and leaned back against the wall when he realized her nausea had subsided and said "Hey, I've never been around a pregnant woman before, much less my beautiful pregnant wife." Mia stood up and swished her mouth with the water he had given her.

She laughed and shook her head as she reached for her toothbrush and toothpaste. She ran the water over her toothbrush and said, "Baby I'm ok, I'm really ok." She brushed her teeth slowly looking at Nicolas, who was still on the floor.

When she began to brush her tongue, her gag reflex was triggered. She immediately put water in her mouth and let her head hang over the sink. She rinsed her mouth again then reached for Nicolas' hand. He stood up and kissed her on the back of her head. "Not so strong after all?" he teased, then pulled her closely to him. Mia tightened her mouth, then opened her eyes widely and nodded her head in agreement.

They returned to the kitchen and Nicolas finished his coffee as he read the sports section. Mia drank a small glass of milk and ate the crackers Nicolas had given her, as she flipped thru the pages of the fashion section of the paper.

Everything seemed perfect. They knew they couldn't ask for anything more. All they had ever wished for was happening. All the dreams they had talked about were becoming reality. Nicolas was a success in the restaurant business and Mia's clothing line had stirred a lot of interest in the area. Most importantly, they were going to have a baby. What could possibly make it better?

***

Mia's shop named Mia Designs was very popular with the tourists. Most importantly, the locals loved it. It was not a typical South Beach line of clothing, it was tropical and had a touch of Mediterranean flare.

Nico's II was always packed with people, tourists and locals alike. Nicolas was working a lot. Mia spent a lot of time at the store working on displays, and also working on designs in her small office. She walked over to the restaurant daily to have lunch with Nicolas.

Mia's pregnancy was difficult. She was constantly tired. Everything she ate seemed to make her sick. It was hard for her to keep anything down. Her desire for any type of meat had diminished quickly. Now her diet mainly consisted of bread, potatoes, and lots of fruit. She also could not get enough water or liquids in her system.

Mia carried around a book of names and a small journal, where she made notes of her pregnancy and things that came to mind. She did this because lately, she had trouble remembering things. The doctors told her it was natural during pregnancy. Mia thought it was unusual. But, she also knew she didn't want to forget anything important. She also thought the journal of notes could someday be a gift for the baby.

She kept her journal close to jot things down, like names or how she wanted the baby's room decorated. She had always done this for her designs, and now she had two journals to carry around.

Mia had been thinking of names and would run them by Nicolas every night as they lay in bed. They had decided early in the pregnancy they wanted something different. They wanted a name that was unique, yet something not very uncommon or weird. She found many names but nothing they could both agree on.

One day while she was reading, the names came to her. Michelangelo, for a boy and Monalisa for a girl. She loved the names, and she couldn't wait to tell Nicolas.

When Nicolas got home that night he was exhausted. He took a shower and they sat down to eat the chicken salad she had prepared for him, while she ate her chicken-less salad. When they were finished eating, Mia went to Nicolas and sat on his lap. He wrapped his arm around her and leaned back in his chair. "Nicolas, I have a surprise!"

He smiled and said, "Tell me baby, what's the surprise."

She said, "Ok, close your eyes, and open your hands." He did as she asked. She dropped something into each of his hands. He couldn't identify what she had placed in his hands and curiously asked "Can I open my eyes now?"

"Yes, yes, now!" she replied. She was now standing at his side, smiling, waiting for him to see what the surprise was. When he opened his eyes he saw two neatly folded pieces of paper, one blue and one pink. Mia said, "I hope you love them, like I do."

Nicolas began with the blue paper. He opened it slowly. Mia grasped her hands nervously and looked at Nicolas for his reaction when he read the names. Written on the blue paper was the name Michelangelo. He smiled, nodded his head slowly and said, "Michelangelo, yeah, I like it a lot and in Spanish it would be Miguel Angel, yeah, very cool." Then he added, "Hey, and maybe he'll become an artist" and winked at Mia. He placed the blue paper on the table and began to open the pink paper.

Mia watched his expression as he read the name. He raised his eyebrows and said, "Hmmm, Monalisa? Hmmm, that's unique, but very pretty. And, if it is a girl, I know she'll be beautiful like the name, because she'll look just like her mama."

He looked at Mia as she stared out into the distance, "Mia, I love them both!" he said in a reassuring tone. She smiled slowly and turned to kiss him firmly on the lips. She took the pieces of paper from him and placed them in the small silver box on the side table. Mia loved saving memorable things and Nicolas knew it was why she placed them in the box.

"Michelangelo and Monalisa it is!" Nicolas said.   She smiled the happiest smile as he spoke.   Seeing Mia happy was what mattered most to Nicolas.

CHAPTER II

At the beginning of her second trimester, during a visit to her doctor, Mia's obstetrician recommended she have an ultrasound to determine the exact stage of growth for the baby. Mia appeared to be further along, based on the weight she had gained and size of her belly.

She scheduled the ultrasound for Monday so Nicolas could be present. Mondays were usually slower days at the restaurant and she knew he could get away easier on that day than any other.

Monday came and Nicolas picked Mia up at 1:00. They drove to the medical center in the southern part of town. Mia was unusually quiet during their drive and held onto Nicolas' hand tightly.

When they arrived, Nicolas parked and they went up to the third floor to the ultrasound area. They waited in the reception area for about 30 minutes. Mia nervously flipped through the pages of the magazines on the table next to where she sat. She stopped momentarily to look at the photos in the magazine, but could not concentrate on anything she read. She was anxious and as she turned to ask Nicolas what could be the reason for the long wait, an elderly woman wearing reading glasses, which sat close to the tip of her nose, walked out slowly, looked at Mia and said "Mia Diaz." Mia nodded and stood up. The woman asked her to follow her. Mia did as she asked and Nicolas followed Mia down a long hallway, which led to a room with 3 dressing stalls covered by pink and blue curtains.

Mia was given a pink gown with white flowers and told to strip from the waist down. The nurse motioned toward the stalls where she could change, then pointed toward a closed door and told them they could sit in the smaller waiting area for more privacy.

Mia was full from the water she had been told to drink before her visit and was anxious for the procedure to be completed. Mia squirmed in her seat like an impatient child and continued nervously flipping through the pages of the magazines. Nicolas rubbed her leg to calm her.

Mia lifted her head when she heard footsteps echoing in the empty hallway, which became louder as they neared the waiting area. When Mia heard the footsteps, she grabbed Nicolas' hand and asked, "Think she's coming?" Nicolas smiled at her, lifted his eyebrows and slowly nodded his head. Mia smiled back nervously.

The same woman entered the room and asked them to follow her. She led them to the room where the ultrasound would be performed. The nurse, in the room, asked Mia to sit up on the table, then pointed toward a small stool at Mia's side and told Nicolas it was where he could sit. She let them know the technician would be in shortly and left.

Nicolas helped Mia onto the bed and covered her legs with a small blanket that had been placed near the pillow.

Nicolas sat on the small seat with wheels and rolled himself closer to the bed. Mia turned to him and looked deeply into his eyes, while searching for his hand. She slipped her petite hand into his for comfort when she found it. He held her hand tightly and they waited quietly for the ultrasound technician to enter the room.

Mia and Nicolas were both very nervous. This was their first ultrasound and they didn't know what to expect. Mia had researched online, and would show Nicolas photos of ultrasounds, but now that they were in the actual ultrasound room it all seemed so foreign and intimidating.

The ultrasound tech entered and asked Mia to lie back on the table and to get comfortable. She explained what could be expected during the procedure. Mia was curious and asked a few questions. She was also a bit frightened. She looked at Nicolas and he winked at her and squeezed her trembling hand for reassurance. Nicolas placed his hand on the top of her head and rubbed her head softly. He wanted to help calm her in whatever way he could. He looked at Mia as she stared at the ceiling while biting down on her bottom lip.

The technician warned Mia she would be placing a cool gel on her stomach. Mia nodded her head in acknowledgement and smiled while looking toward the ceiling. The technician squirted the slimy gel from a bottle onto her belly and began to slowly move the ultrasound wand in a circular motion.

The ultrasound screen began to show shadows. Mia and Nicolas watched in amazement. Some shadows were lighter and others were black. They heard an echoing sound and Mia asked what the noise was.

The technician explained, "That is your baby's heartbeat." And, just as she finished the sentence, the technician's eyes opened widely. She tried to regain her composure and change her expression when she looked at Mia.

Mia asked, "Is everything ok?" immediately looking directly at Nicolas as his expression changed to one of concern, because he too had seen the look of surprise on the ultrasound technician's face.

The technician said, "Give me a minute, I have to find Dr Santos to come in and verify what I'm seeing." Mia's eyes filled with tears and she looked at Nicolas. Nicolas stood up, then bent down, placing his elbows on the bed. He kissed her forehead and said, "Don't worry Mia, everything will be ok." He pushed away the strand of hair that had fallen over her face when she propped herself upward.

Nicolas watched the clock and nearly five minutes passed before the technician entered the room with Dr. Santos following behind. Dr. Santos grabbed a pair of plastic gloves and as he put them on he said, "Mr. and Mrs. Diaz, lets see what's going on here."

The technician began to move the wand slowly over Mia's stomach area. The Dr. smiled slightly as he saw the movement through the ultrasound and asked, "Do you hear that sound?" Mia said, "yes that's my baby's heartbeat, right?" Dr. Santos said, "do you hear what seems to be the echo behind it?" Mia and Nicolas both nodded and looked at each other. Dr. Santos said, "It is a second heartbeat, and I'd like to be the first to congratulate you on your twin babies."

Mia jumped suddenly and threw her arms around Nicolas and said "Nico, baby, we're having twins!" She began to cry as he filled her face with kisses.

Dr. Santos then continued, "They appear to be identical twins. Do you see the sack around them? They are both in the same amniotic sack, which means they are identical. They will either both be boys, or both will be girls. Right now because they are huddled so closely together and because of their positioning, it is difficult to tell their sex."

Mia looked at Nicolas with a concerned look and said, "But Nico, now we're going to have to find two more names." She shook her head slowly with a slight look of defeat on her face. Nicolas laughed and said, "Now, that should be the easy part." Dr. Santos nodded in agreement and both he and the technician laughed at Nicolas' response.

The next few days Mia spent most of her time looking online for baby furniture. She wanted something that could be used for either boys or girls. They had decided early on that they didn't want to know the sex of the baby. But as she looked more at the different themes for bedrooms, she became curious about the sex of the twins. She decided she would talk to Nicolas about it that night during dinner.

Mia had already decided on the decorations and the color scheme for the bedroom. Little chubby bears were what the theme would be. Tan, brown and cream would be the color scheme until the babies came, then she'd add pink tones if they were girls or blue if they were boys.

It seemed everyday got harder for Mia. She was constantly tired. She usually went to the shop for a few hours, then went home and spent a lot of time in bed reading, doodling new designs or watching TV. When Nicolas was off work, he took her out to places he knew she loved. Mia was so happy, and of course, it made Nicolas happy. The babies were everything to her and were all she talked about.

The week had been extremely busy at both restaurants. Nicolas' old friend, Antonio, managed Nico's II and Nicolas ran Nico's in South Beach because it was closer to the home he and Mia had purchased a few months earlier.

Sunday, the day Nicolas usually spent at home, started off lazy. It was raining outside, the sky was dark and they slept in later than usual. Nicolas got up before Mia woke up, and made breakfast consisting of toasted bread with tomato for Mia and eggs and sausage for himself.

Mia woke to the smell of the toasted bread. She got up from bed and went into the kitchen. "Good morning. I slept so well and I feel so good, I think I'll clean the kitchen before lunch, then we'll relax the rest of the day."

Nicolas laughed and said, "Now, don't over do it."

"I won't. I feel great today, maybe I've gotten over the worst part of my pregnancy" she said and turned her music on and gathered the dishes from the table. As she reached for Nicolas' plate, she kissed him. He stood up and took her in his arms and hugged her closely. They laughed as they both looked down at her big belly that separated them. "I love you Mia" he said. Mia said, "And I love you!" He kissed the top of her head like he always did, then she turned toward the sink.

For a second their eyes fixed on each other. It was that look which always brought them closer. The look they once realized united their souls.

Nicolas said, "I'm going to try to get some work done in the garage. We only have 2 months to get the room together." He winked at her and walked out of the kitchen.

Mia scraped and organized the dishes as the sink filled with water.

She began to hum, but it was not the song coming from the speakers, it was the song she always hummed when she was deep in thought. She gazed trancelike, out toward the back yard, while she slowly washed the morning dishes.

The small waves in the fountain moved slowly as a gust of wind blew in. She watched the delicate splashes of water as the raindrops gently fell from the sky. The glass chimes sang in the cool autumn breeze.

The melody she hummed took her back to her childhood, as it so often did.

Off in the corner of the yard Mia caught a glimpse of a small blue bird on a tree branch. As the wind picked up, the bird flew toward the fountain that once belonged to her parents. The bird had landed on the fingertip of the beautiful lady who delicately sat in the center. Her legs crossed underneath her, her long flowing hair fell over her breasts, as strands seemed to trail off as the wind blew. Her hand outstretched, femininely, as if she were cautiously awaiting the arrival of the bird.

Mia watched the bird, and saw it move when another blue bird landed at its side. They huddled closely on the small space of the woman's finger. Mia thought they were huddled so closely to shelter each other from the wind that blew colder than usual. She wondered if the birds were migrating further south for the winter. Mia concentrated on the stillness of the birds, and watched their feathers flutter with the breeze. Then she slowly shifted her gaze upward, realizing the woman in the center of the fountain was staring directly at her.

A wave of uncertainty flashed through her mind. She felt herself spinning. She grabbed for the counter edge to stabilize herself but her legs could no longer hold her and she felt herself falling…falling...falling.

In the garage, Nicolas had just finished applying the final coat of varnish to the old dressing table that Mia found at a garage sale. As he placed the cap on the can of varnish, he remembered the day she bought the table. Nicolas smiled as he thought of the excited expression Mia had when she arrived at the restaurant. Following him as he worked, describing just what it looked like and asking, "Please,

please, please can we pick it up today?" He laughed to himself, thinking how such little things made her so happy.

He began to clean his work area as he listened to her hum. Suddenly there was silence and in that instant he instinctively knew something was wrong but waited for the next note in her tune. What he heard next was a thump and the sound of shattering glass, which broke the silence. Nicolas ran quickly to the kitchen yelling Mia's name. He froze, as he walked through the doorway seeing her body as she lay motionless on the kitchen floor, surrounded by red broken glass.

More silence... he felt paralyzed and could not move during the few seconds that passed. Seconds, which felt like an eternity, made him feel helpless.

He shouted her name. "Mia!" Silence... He felt a sense of desperation fill him and the only sound he heard was his heart thumping in his chest. "Mia" Nicolas yelled louder... silence... he ran... he picked up the phone and called 911. A woman's voice on the other end seemed so distant, yet it echoed loudly in his ear.

He was at Mia's side, touching her face. He felt her breath, but could get no response. He felt his heart beating deep inside himself. It pounded in his ears as the dispatcher's voice echoed through his brain. He lay the phone down and began to yell her name. "Mia! Mia! Miaaaaaa!!!!!" He grabbed her shoulders and shook her gently, so he could wake her. He was desperate for a response, any response.

She did not move. He wanted to shake her gently back to consciousness, but the dispatcher told him not to move her. They reassured him the ambulance would be there shortly. The seconds ticked by slowly, as he watched her lying motionless on the cold kitchen floor. Mia was not responding.

In his overwhelming feeling of insanity, he comforted her. He leaned over her and talked to her gently, telling her everything would be ok. He felt helpless until he heard, in the far off distance, the sound of sirens. As he listened to the sirens approach, he sensed his life would never again, be the same…

CHAPTER III

Five years prior…

The day was hot and humid in Miami. There hadn't been much relief from the heat for at least two weeks.

Nicolas walked out of the sidewalk café feeling the breeze work its way toward the city from the warm ocean waters. Although it was only 3:00, his day had been long. He needed to get away.

He walked out into the humid air, which felt so heavy for a late September day. It always took him a few minutes to adjust to the air after being in the air conditioned restaurant. For a moment, he stood with his hands on his hips, at the entrance to the restaurant, and looked around.

He decided to go home for a few hours and return later for the evening rush. He walked toward the street where he had parked his car that morning. He stopped at the corner looking at a group of people who had just come off a tour bus, while the traffic inched slowly by. He stood hesitantly, wondering if the busload of people would make their way to the restaurant where he would be needed. He pushed his shoulders back in a way that relieved his stress then slowly tilted his head to crack his stiff neck and continued to walk.

The heavy air and heat seemed to wrap itself around his body. The day seemed hotter than most. Suddenly, a strong burst of air came in from the ocean. He welcomed the breeze, which had momentarily given him relief from the unbearable heat that covered the city.

He looked around and saw the crowds of people walking down the street. It was Friday and the streets were filled with tourists. It seemed to be busier than usual and he wondered why, but was too tired to elaborate on the possible reasons for the large crowd.

The light changed for the pedestrians to cross the street. As Nicolas started to walk, he was caught off guard by a group of teenage boys on skateboards who skated rapidly at his sides. As they shot around him he yelled "Hey, hey, hey" then immediately stopped in his tracks, trying to catch his balance as they almost knocked him over.

The boys turned back laughing as they passed Nicolas. The last one, who shot by, yelled "Sorry, bro!" Nicolas recognized the kids, who were regulars in South Beach. He shook his head and said in a sarcastic tone "Yeah, right, bro" and laughed as he continued walking down the sidewalk, shaking his head.

He walked slowly down the street, mechanically following the tourists who walked in front of him.

The locals who placed tables out on the street selling homemade jewelry and who sold souvenirs for the passing tourists were in their usual spots.

He walked near the old Haitian woman who sold small paintings of the beach and ocean, which she made with colored sand. He nodded his head toward the woman and she smiled at him, saying, "a painting for you to take back to remember your visit?' He wondered why she never remembered him. She saw him every day and every day he tossed a coin in the cup she had placed before her. He wondered if it was due to memory lapse or just something she said to everyone. He hoped for the latter.

The street was filled with cars driving slowly. A mix of tourists looking for places to park, and the local kids in their cars looking for tourists to meet, made traffic unbearable. He crossed the street hurriedly as soon as the light changed. He slid his hand in his pocket and pulled out his keys. He had two sets--one set for the restaurant and the other for his truck. He immediately looked down to get the truck keys and walked toward his truck.

Nicolas drove an older white Range Rover, which he bought when he first moved to Miami five years earlier. He called it Faith, short for Old Faithful. It was a used 2005 model and had seen its better days, but it never failed him.

Nicolas fumbled with the keys and placed the key in the keyhole. As he turned the key to unlock the door, he instinctively looked back and that is when he saw her.

"Damn!" He whispered in disbelief. His mouth hung slightly open as he watched her. Her long black hair blew in the wind as she walked. "Damn!" he said again and continued staring at her in such an obvious manner. His eyes were fixed on her and he whispered, "Wow, she is gorgeous."

She grasped her hair at the top of her head as she walked, keeping it away from her face because the breeze wouldn't let up. She looked up at the building addresses and then at the street sign and then down at the paper she held in her hand.

"Is she lost?" he wondered.

Nicolas stood there wondering what she was doing. He watched her walk. The lower part of her body, was accentuated by the tight black skirt she wore. Her white blouse fit her loosely. The wind pushed it against her body, outlining the shape of her breasts and flat stomach The high heeled shoes she wore made her already toned legs look incredibly sexy.

He continued to stare, with a half smile frozen on his face. With his key still in the door, he watched her. His body faced the car but his head turned to follow her. Slowly, he began to turn his body, pulling the key from the lock. He moved slowly in a circle and watched her.

Her long ebony hair glowed in the sun, as the warm wind blew it in her face. She stumbled as she walked, looking for whatever it was she was looking for. "She looks worried," he thought.

Smiling, he continued watching her. "She is a bit clumsy, but damn she is so beautiful." Entranced, he watched her as she crossed the street.

He crossed his arms and leaned back against his truck with a smile on his face and watched her walk. He could not take his eyes off her.

As she crossed in front of him he called out, "Are you lost?"

She turned to see who was there. She laughed and said, "It's that obvious, huh?" He said, "You could say that," and they laughed. She nervously said, "Yes, I am looking for 402 8th Street." He laughed and said, "402 8th Street is a few blocks west. You are on the 800 block of 8th street. If you'd like I can show you how to get there."

She laughed and said, "Figures I'd get it wrong when I'm running late. I tried to leave early because I know I always get lost down here, and even leaving early, I am so late." She extended her hand outward with her palm facing upwards, tilted her head and said, "Figures, huh?"

Nicolas smiled and said, "If you'd like, I can drive there, and you can follow."

Looking at him apprehensively, then at her watch, she instantly agreed. She was late and she had no idea how to get to the address where her client was waiting to meet with her.

She carried a small briefcase, which hung from her shoulder on a wide strap, and a satchel hung crosswise over her body accentuating her breasts. She also carried two books and a notebook. "Do you need help?" he asked.

Her hair was on her face again and Nicolas instinctively tried to remove it from her face and as his hand neared her face, he asked, "May I?" then nervously looked toward her books. He gently slid the hair from her face before she could answer and with a sigh of relief, she said, "Would you?" and before he could reply, she pushed her books forward, dropped them in his arms and said "Thank you."

She nervously began explaining how she had forgotten her GPS on her table when she left to work that morning and didn't have time to go back to her apartment.

Nicolas listened and watched her push back the hair that had fallen onto her face again. He smelled her as she moved. She smelled like berries, a fragrance he didn't recognize. She smelled fresh and he liked it.

She continued to talk nervously, motioning with her hands, as they walked to her car. Nicolas was quiet. He watched her every move and listened to her ramble on. As they walked, he noticed a dark ruby ring on her finger. A ring unlike any he had ever seen before.

Thinking she was married because she wore the ring on her wedding ring finger, he disappointedly asked her name. She replied, "Mia."

"Mia, nice to meet you, I'm Nicolas."

She smiled and pushed her face to him and kissed him first on one cheek, then on the other. "Nice to meet you too, Nicolas."

Nicolas thought it strange that she kissed him on both cheeks. In Miami most people kissed only on one cheek. The only women who kissed him on both cheeks were usually women from Spain.

Mia nervously continued talking about her appointment, he smiled politely and listened as she spoke. He listened carefully and thought she had the most fascinating voice. Her tone was innocent, yet soft and sensual. Her accent was one he didn't recognize and for the life of him, he couldn't place its origin.

"Where on earth are you going with all these books?" he asked, wanting to know more about her. "I am in the process of doing an interview for a project I'm working on," Mia replied.

As they continued to walk he got up the courage and said nervously, "Nice ring. Whoever designed it must have taken a lot of time and put a lot of thought into the design."

She lifted her dainty hand and looked at it. He watched her. Her beautiful eyes seemed to sparkle as she looked at the ring on her finger. She tightened her lips slightly and smiled. He sensed from the smile and the look in her eyes, that she must be in love. He watched her and noticed the look on her face vanished and what he now saw was a slight glimmer of sadness. Mia stared out into the distance, not concentrating on the ring on her finger, as she appeared to be lost in a memory.

"Thank you," she replied as she pushed her hand forward and looked at it. Then she placed it on her chest and said,

"It was my grandmother's ring when she was young."

He smiled, and let out a quick, obvious sigh of relief. Embarrassed, hoping she hadn't noticed his reaction, he chuckled nervously.

"No I am not married!" she said. "I wear it on that finger because it's the only finger it fits, but most guys think it's a wedding ring." A slight laugh escaped her, as she realized the assumption of her being married was made quite frequently, because of the where she wore the ring.

"Excuse my reaction," he replied. She smiled and turned away, swinging her hair in the wind then said, "Don't worry about it."

Mia looked at her watch and gasped, "Oh my gosh, I am so late. I'm going to make a horrible first impression." Then she continued to explain to him how she was almost 15 minutes late getting to her appointment.

He said, "Let's get going," and handed her his business card before turning. "Call me," he yelled as he ran down the street toward his truck, "I'd love to take you out for coffee or dinner or a movie…. anything!"

She waved without saying a word, put the card in her book and got into her car and started it up. Mia watched him as he ran to his truck.

He got in and drove slowly past her as she waited in her blue 2-door Mini Cooper. He motioned for her to follow. They drove away, each with a smile on their face.

"Oh my God, he is so cute!" she thought as she drove and twisted her hair around her finger. Mia always twisted her hair when she was nervous or deep in thought. It was a habit she had since she was a little girl.

"Wow, she's gorgeous!" he said as he drove away, watching her through the rear-view mirror, following behind to the address she had given him.

He drove quickly, once she caught up to him. He wanted to make an impression on her by helping her get to her appointment as fast as possible. He glanced in the rear-view mirror often, making sure she was close behind.

He pulled into a parking space in front of 402 8th Street. She parked behind him. Rushing, she got out of the car and walked past Nicolas thanking him for his help. He replied, "My pleasure!" "Call me, will you?" She smiled shyly, nodded her head and said, "I will!"

CHAPTER IV

Nicolas, handsome, near 6 feet tall, looked younger than his 32 years. He was slender with a defined muscular body. He had piercing brown eyes and dark brown shoulder length hair, which fell into perfect curls and which he usually wore pulled back. Nicolas was the type of man who definitely stood out in a crowd. He was used to women coming on to him. Nicolas hadn't dated anyone seriously since high school. But, he had many girls who he dated off and on throughout the years.

He had never gotten serious with any one of them after his high school love was killed in a tragic accident so many years ago in Spain.

So many of the girls he met were immature and not what he wanted. Most of them still wanted to hang out in clubs and that to Nicolas was something he no longer desired.

When he first moved to Miami and began hitting the clubs with his friends, they told him that many of the girls in Miami were looking for men with money. He realized this was somewhat true when he had very little and now that he had become more financially stable, he noticed the way more of them seemed to be interested in him.

He was cautious with women, not knowing what their real intentions were, always remembering the words of his friends, "They want men with money!" Also, knowing he was not ready to settle down, he took none of them seriously.   What Nicolas did not realize was just how handsome he was and it was not his financial status, which attracted them, but his good looks and carefree personality.

Nicolas drove home.   He was surprised Mia had affected him this way.   He couldn't remember the last time any one had, especially not this quickly.

Two weeks went by.   Every time his phone rang, he held his breath hoping it was Mia.   She never called.

After about a week and a half, his excitement began to diminish.   When the phone rang he didn't reach for it as quickly as he had the first few days after meeting Mia.   He didn't think she was going to call.

He thought of her often as he worked in the busy café every day.   He fantasized of touching her, of looking into her eyes as he ran his fingers through her silky hair.   He replayed her actions of the day he met her, over and over again, in his mind.

"Why hadn't she called," he kept asking himself.   "She must not have liked me, huh?" he asked himself often.   He finally came to the conclusion that either she didn't like him or she must have a boyfriend.   But still, each time the phone rang, he reached for it hopefully, and when he realized each phone call was not hers, it showed on his face.   By now, he figured she would never call.

He was disappointed.   He really wanted to get to know her.   He thought what he observed in her body language that day, is she also was interested in him.   Could he have been wrong? He thought. Just maybe he could have been. Then he'd reanalyze their meeting and would reaffirm what he believed was her interest in him as well. This made him only think of her more, even though by now, almost two weeks later, she hadn't called.

Mia, who worked for a law firm in downtown Miami, was busy interviewing witnesses for a difficult case she was working on. She had been working nonstop on the case and the date had been set for trial at the end of the month. She thought of him often, but had misplaced his business card. All she remembered was his name, Nicolas.

As the trial wound down, Mia was able to concentrate on other things. She took her daily walks on the beach. Today, because the weather was so beautiful, she decided to go to the beach and study as she listened to the waves, which had a way of calming her.

When she got to the beach, she intentionally parked on the street where she met Nicolas, hoping she would see him. She walked past the place she met him, the place she remembered he had parked his truck. She did not see it. She wondered if she would ever see him again, yet hoped she would.

She regretted not exchanging business cards with him when he gave her his card. She scolded herself for talking only about her appointment, which distracted her from giving her card to him and from learning something…anything, about him. She realized she knew nothing, at all, of him.

She looked through her purse, briefcase, car, and through the pages of the books she carried that day. She looked everywhere to see if she could find his card, but couldn't find it anywhere.

After about an hour of studying, Mia realized she couldn't remember a thing she had read. She wasn't concentrating on what she was reading, she was thinking of Nicolas. She gathered her books and placed them neatly at the end of the lounge chair where she sat and stared out toward the water.

She watched two children as they played in the sand. This left her in a bit of a trance.

She applied sunscreen to her face as she watched a couple walking by the edge of the water. The guy's hair was longer and made her think of Nicolas. The couple laughed and touched each other teasingly. Mia sighed and smiled then instinctively grabbed her book to distract herself from looking at the couple. She opened it to where she had placed the bookmark and began to read where she had left off. Still, unable to concentrate, she glanced toward the couple until they were out of sight.

She lay on her stomach trying to concentrate on what she read. Suddenly, there was a shriek bark behind her. Mia jumped and turned toward the barking dog. When she turned, she saw him.

"Nicolas? Could it be? Is it him?" She wondered and second guessed herself, was it him? "No," she thought. She sat up and watched him walking on the path near the beach. "Yes, it is Nicolas," she thought.

She stood up, high on tiptoe, trying to get a glimpse of where he was going. He stopped at the corner where a crowd waited for the light to change, so they could cross the street. Mia wondered if he was alone.

She clumsily picked up her books and shoulder bag, and began to run in the direction she had seen Nicolas.

As she ran through the sand, the barking dog, who had startled her, ran toward her and she tripped. Her books scattered in front of her as she fell to the sand. She jumped up quickly, knowing she couldn't lose sight of Nicolas.

She laughed from embarrassment, and brushed the sand from her legs, quickly. The dog's owner helped her gather her belongings and apologized profusely as he handed her the things she had dropped. Mia took her things from the gentleman and thanked him.

She patted the dog on the head and said, "thank you." A slight giggle escaped her when she realized she had thanked the dog. With a confused look on his face, the dog's owner apologized again. He did not know the reason she had thanked his dog.

Mia was thinking, "If the dog had not barked, she would not have turned and would have not seen Nicolas." She felt like hugging the dog. She was so happy. She quickly placed everything she had in her shoulder bag, looking around to see where he was.

Anxiously, she walked in the direction where she had seen him, hoping he would still be near.

She crossed the street quickly looking up and down the street filled with people. She stopped momentarily and brushed her legs and arms of the remaining sand before she entered the hotel across the street from where she had seen Nicolas standing. She began looking through the lobby. Nicolas was nowhere in sight.

She looked at her watch and wondered whether he was there on a lunch date. She hoped he wasn't there with a girlfriend.

Many scenarios ran through her mind as she contemplated whether or not to wait. She walked down the street looking casually into the cafés that lined the street. A sense of disappointment overcame her, as she thought, he was so close, yet so far. She chuckled to herself, remembering what seemed to be the dog alerting her to Nicolas and then her desperate quest to find him. Mia walked slowly down Ocean Drive in the direction of her car, hoping she would see him again.

While walking back to her car, she decided to get a café con leche at one of the sidewalk cafés. She walked into a small restaurant on the corner and chose a table near the entrance hoping to see Nicolas if he happened to walk by.

A waiter, no older than 18, approached her table. She looked up and he smiled and asked, "May I help you?" She replied, "A water and a café con leche, please."

Waiting for the waiter to bring her order, she nervously flipped though pages of her writings and drawings in a journal she always carried. Her eyes shifted from her book toward the people who passed the café. She was nervous about seeing Nicolas again. She couldn't concentrate on what she read. Each time the door to the café opened, she looked up.

The waiter returned quickly and placed her café con leche and water on the table. She thanked him. She added a packet of the brown sugar and stirred the coffee slowly with the small spoon that had rested on the saucer. She stared out the window, as she slowly stirred her coffee.

She looked through the crowd of people who walked past the restaurant hoping to see him again. Mia swirled the spoon in the cup, making invisible designs in the foam at top of the coffee and wondered what she would do if she saw him walk by. Would she run out and yell his name? What if he was with someone? Mia was lost in thoughts of seeing Nicolas again when she heard, "Excuse me, Mia?"

Looking up, slowly, he was there. Mia blinked in disbelief, then smiled as her eyes casually inspected the beautiful man who stood before her. Nicolas was dressed in black pants, a neatly pressed white shirt and a black tie. His hair was pulled back. It was him. It was Nicolas.

Nicolas stared down at her with a smile, which made her melt.

Mia opened her eyes widely and excitedly said, "Nicolas!" Then, immediately put her head down as she realized her own reaction.

Holding her breath and pursing her lips, Mia looked at him and nervously they both laughed. He leaned toward her as she stood up. He took her hand, and kissed her on both cheeks. "Wow, what a surprise!" he said.

Fidgeting with her napkin, she said, "Please sit down." I'm having a coffee and studying. "Would you like to join me for a coffee?" He said, "I'd love to," and walked toward the counter to place his order.

She watched him as he walked toward the counter and subconsciously licked the corner of her upper lip with the tip of her tongue.

His white shirt accentuated the strength of his body. And, she admitted to herself that he was the most beautiful man she had ever laid eyes on. She watched him at the counter and saw him as he joked with the waitress while she prepared the espresso he ordered. Mia smiled.

He looked back toward her and smiled, as he waited. Mia also smiled, then nervously looked away. She didn't want him to see the desire she knew was written all over her face.

He approached her table, and pulled out the chair, turned it around and straddled it, then leaned forward on the back legs of the chair. As he leaned forward he asked, "What are you reading?"

"I'm doing research on different types of fabric and designs." She explained. Then, went on to tell him she was interested in designing clothing and was studying how different designers had gotten their start.

Nicolas told Mia he had forgotten something in the café and had to return for it, and that is when he saw her sitting there.

He told her he worked in the restaurant. She was surprised and thought she had chosen this restaurant out of all the restaurants on the street, only because of fate. It was the hand of fate that brought them together initially and today, she knew, it had reunited them.

Mia often thought about fate. She had done this since she was little. It all started when she tried to understand why her parents had been taken from her. Later on in life, she realized this was her way of accepting tragedy. And because of her grandmother's way of looking at life and how things always happen for a reason, Mia learned to cope, placing blame on fate.

Today, she again thought of fate, and unlike the justification of tragedy in her life, she was realizing that fate too was responsible for her meeting Nicolas. She thought of where it had taken her a few short weeks before and bringing her back to what could only be something meant to be. Nicolas.

"I've thought about you for the last couple of weeks, you know?" Nicolas said nervously. She smiled as she looked at him and said, "I've thought about you too, Nicolas." "I waited for your call," he continued.

"I lost your card," she replied, "and I looked everywhere for it, and I couldn't find it."

Nicolas watched Mia stir her coffee nervously and realized this meeting was meant to be. Synchronicity was what brought them together, again. He stared at her. She smiled and looked away not wanting to tell him about seeing him from the beach. She'd wait for another time to tell him her silly story.

They drank their coffee and talked. Nicolas told her about the busy day they had at the restaurant. When they finished their coffee, Nicolas asked her if she'd like to go for a walk on the beach. She said yes.

It was close to 6:00; they still had about two hours of sunlight. Nicolas paid her tab and they walked out onto the street crowded with people. First, they walked to her car to leave her books and so she could grab a sweater, just in case it got cold, as she was wearing only shorts and a light t-shirt.

They walked toward the beach slowly Nicolas looked at Mia and noticed how her t-shirt hugged her perfect body. The cleavage between her round firm breasts peeked over the scooped neckline. Nicolas placed her sweater on her shoulders so she would not get cold because of the cool breeze that came in from the ocean.

He loosened his tie and let it hang, and opened the top

button of his shirt and breathed deeply, as if he had just been set free from the tie that restricted him from breathing. She smiled and said, "Now you look comfortable." He laughed. He took off his shoes and rolled up his pants a couple of times. He carried his shoes in one hand and let the other hang freely. What he wanted was to touch Mia. He hadn't stopped thinking of touching her since the day he met her.

As they walked along the shore, the water got closer as the tide rose. The waves began to crash at their feet. It was cool. Mia said she loved the feeling of the water as it touched her skin.

They walked along the soft sand and talked about the little birds scurrying along the beach in search of food. Suddenly, a large wave came in and nearly knocked Mia down. Nicolas immediately grabbed her by the waist and as he did, his tie fell into the water. He pulled her close to keep her from falling as he tried bending down to pick the tie up. Mia saw the tie as the wave took it further from the shore. She pulled away and they both ran toward the water to rescue the tie from the vastness of the ocean. They laughed as they ran after the tie. Then, suddenly another wave came rushing in, bringing the tie toward them and wrapping it around Mia's leg.

She laughed and screamed playfully, "I caught a tie, I caught a tie," while she freed it from her leg. She waved it over her head and laughed. The tie had soaked up the water, which splashed around her, wetting Nicolas' face and it ran down her arm wetting her t-shirt.

Nicolas wiped the water from his face and stood there and watched her. She looked at him and dropped the tie to her side. He was smiling. She realized just how silly she had been acting and put her head down and put her hands over her face and giggled. He walked toward her and pushed her hands aside, lifted her face and looked into her eyes. He didn't say anything, but the side of his mouth turned up. She stared at him and he moved closer, pushing the hair from her face. He then unexpectedly bent down and kissed her gently on her lips.

Mia was not expecting Nicolas to do this, and hesitantly returned the kiss. She pulled away and then looked up and into his eyes. What she saw made her happy, for what she saw was something genuine. She felt the depths of his soul spilled from his eyes. She had never seen anyone look at her the way he did. She wondered how someone's eyes could show so much emotion.

Feelings stirred in her, she wanted to cry. It scared her, but it also made her feel safe. "Why?" she wondered. How was it possible that he could make her feel this? She didn't know him very well. Actually, she didn't know him at all. But what she felt, was something she always desired, and never thought she would find.

Mia turned. She did not want Nicolas to see she was so vulnerable. She turned, to hide the expression on her face and literally to change her thoughts. She was afraid he would see what she felt for him at that moment. Because, what she felt was something so strong between them and did not want him to see it had weakened her.

She picked up a seashell to change the mood and said, "Look Nicolas, isn't this beautiful?" She held her hand out and opened it and in the palm of her hand was a small white seashell. He placed his hand beneath hers and touched the shell gently, smiled and said, "It is beautiful. But, not as beautiful as you are Mia." Mia smiled and looked up and into his eyes.

She stood on her tiptoes and wrapped her arms around his neck. She pulled him down toward her and gently kissed his lips. He placed his hand on the back of her neck and pulled her into him, kissing her deeply. As they kissed, he felt the smile on her mouth. He opened his eyes to see her smiling with her eyes closed.

Just then, another wave came rushing in, almost pushing them over. Mia jumped and said "It's getting cold. Let's go higher on the sand. I'm freezing." She hugged herself and ran higher on the sand. Nicolas grabbed the tie, which was now covered in sand and rinsed it in the water then turned and followed her up the small hill of sand. He then helped her put her sweater on so she would stay warm.

They slowly walked on the beach, forgetting the time. They didn't talk much, but felt a certain peace being there together. So much was going through each of their minds. Mia felt safe near Nicolas. It was something she had not felt for so many years. When they realized how far they had walked Nicolas asked if she wanted to sit down for awhile. Mia nodded and they found an area on the sand not far from the lifeguard station.

They sat on the beach, talking, as the sky grew darker. The cool ocean air moved closer to shore. She caught a chill and moved closer to Nicolas. He put his arm around her and pulled her into him as he turned his face toward her pushing it into her hair, deeply inhaling the fresh smell of Mia.

She looked up into his eyes, then quickly looked down nervously. He took her by the chin and lifted her face to look into her eyes. "I like you Mia, and I'd like to get to know you better. I hope you give me that chance." She looked at him seriously, then smiled and pushed away the hair that had fallen onto his face. She touched his cheek softly and said, "I think I'd like that too, Nicolas."

The wind pushed in from the ocean, only growing colder. Nicolas leaned to the side resting his elbow in the sand. They moved in closer, Mia inched herself toward Nicolas to warm herself. He tried to shield her from the wind and just as Mia turned to get even closer, he turned toward her. Instinctively they found shelter in the other's warmth and they huddled together keeping out the wind.

Their eyes met and he pulled her close and kissed her. She pushed her mouth into his, as she had longed to feel his lips envelope hers. He guided his tongue slowly into her mouth, searching for her tongue, he pulled her closer, as they fell slowly back onto the sand, hungry for the other's kiss. He touched her face, pulling her in, closer to his. She ran her hands through his hair, entwining her fingers through the silky strands. As the kissing slowed, he pushed his fingers through her hair, and sighed. He looked at her, and in her eyes saw the reflection of the lights in the distance. She looked at him, with a frightened look. He did not know why but he pulled her closer, feeling the need to protect her

She was so attracted to him, but she was afraid. The only love she ever knew between two people had ended in such sadness.

She was unsure of what true love really felt like. And, although she wanted it more than anything, there was one thing she never wanted to feel again. And, that was the loss of somcone she loved. It had always been her deepest fear.

The only thing Mia remembered about love was loss. The people she loved more than anything were all taken so suddenly. She was so afraid to find love, for the fear of losing the person she loved.

She outlined his face with her fingertips and remembered the fairy tale her grandmother told her when she was younger. It was a sad and tragic love story she had made up. The story always seemed so real when her grandmother told her of a love so beautiful until it ended in tragedy.

The emotion her grandmother put into the story seemed so real, and because of this, it left a heavy impression on Mia and what she believed true love to be. True love to Mia was sad yet something beautiful and only happened once in a person's life. Once, only once, Mia thought, because she knew there would be a time when the person you truly loved would be taken from you. Leaving you forever empty or searching for what you had once shared with the love of your life.

Mia knew she wanted Nicolas in her life but was afraid to lose him, and she also did not want to be hurt. He held her closer seeing the look in her eyes, because he too, knew from that very moment, that he would never let her go. He wanted her to be his and he would do anything to achieve it. But, what was the look of fear he saw on her face? He wondered.

The wind began to blow harder and the waves were not far from reaching them again. He stood up and took her by the hand. "Let's walk over to a café for a bite to eat and have a cup of coffee to warm up?" Nicolas suggested. She agreed.

He didn't want to return to the restaurant where he worked. He knew if they went there, the other employees would approach him as well as the customers who knew him. He wanted time alone with her.

They walked over to the row of restaurants. People, dressed for a night out, had begun to gather on the street for the night scene. He took her by the hand, looking for a quiet place where they could be together.

There was loud music coming from a dance club. Outside the club was a line of people waiting to get in. He led her by the hand through the tightly crowded South Beach walkway.

They walked a block past the restaurant where Nicolas worked and saw a small Italian restaurant, which was dimly lit. They looked through the window and saw the coziness of the restaurant and decided to go inside.

They walked in and Nicolas asked for a table near the back. The hostess guided them to a table in the corner at the back of the room. They sat next to each other and ordered coffee so they could warm up.

Nicolas asked Mia about her family while they waited. Mia looked away when he asked and then told him she was an only child. She didn't want to tell him about her mother and father yet. She usually didn't tell people about her family until she felt she knew them well enough. In order to avoid him asking more, Mia quickly directed the same question back at Nicolas.

He told her about his family, an older brother and sister. He told her he had moved to Miami from Barcelona, Spain, when he was 24 and had been in the states for eight years.

Mia told him she was born in the United States, but her grandparents were from a place called Murcia, Spain.

When Mia mentioned Murcia, Spain, Nicolas said, "Wow, Murcia? That's where my family lived for many years until my parents moved to Barcelona and then my grandparents came to live with us for a few years. They eventually moved back to Murcia and lived there 'til they died."

"Wow!" he continued excitedly, "I can't believe it! Who would have known I would meet the only girl I've ever met outside the region of Murcia, who is from Murcia, here in Miami! What a small, small world." Nicolas nodded his head slowly as he wondered if it was the reason they were so attracted to each other. He chuckled to himself, and brushed off the silly thought.

Mia laughed and shook him from his thoughts. She didn't realize the significance, because she didn't know much about the different regions of Spain, unlike Nicolas, who lived there most of his life.

The waitress returned with their coffee and recognized Nicolas from the restaurant and began to talk to him in Spanish. Nicolas spoke to her in the Spanish accent, which brought back so many memories for Mia. Her memories were vague, but had been sparked by his accent.

Mia's parents and grandparents spoke Spanish but not with the strong Spanish accent Nicolas had. Their accent was not as distinct as Nicolas'. She thought it may be because he lived in Barcelona and her family was from southern Spain, or maybe it was because they had been in the United States longer and had lost their accents over time.

Mia listened to Nicolas talk, but not to what he was saying. She concentrated more on his accent. She knew she had heard a similar accent somewhere and tried to remember, as she drifted off into memories of her own childhood.

She tried to recall when and where she had heard it. Then remembered a friend of her grandmother's who would visit at night. She never met or saw the man, only heard their conversations through her open bedroom window.   Now that Mia was older, she often wondered who this man was, and now she wondered why his accent was so similar to Nicolas' accent.

It was so long ago, when she played in her grandmother's garden. She was lost in the shadowed memories she could not remember fully, when Nicolas said her name. She looked up and he asked, "What do you want on your half of the pizza?" Without thinking, she said, "Mushrooms and tomatoes." Nicolas said, "I'll have the same," and he continued to talk with the waitress as she scribbled on the ticket book.

Mia again tried to remember the man in the garden with her grandmother. She recalled hearing them talk through the open window as she lay on her bed every night until she fell asleep.   Mia hadn't thought about this for many years.

Mia mixed her coffee slowly as she thought about her childhood. She didn't realize Nicolas and the waitress had finished talking. Mia, in her trance like state, continued stirring the coffee.

Nicolas began to explain the waitress was from Northern Spain and they knew each other from working on the beach. Mia then felt him kiss her on the side of her head. She looked up at him and smiled. He looked at her so intensely and pulled her face toward him.   He kissed her lips and she pushed her body close to his.

They drank their coffee slowly as they waited for the waitress to return. They talked about the quaint restaurant, which had been open since Nicolas moved to Miami. He told Mia it was one of the first places he had eaten when he arrived.

Nicolas had ordered the large pizza of tomatoes and mushrooms, and an order of bread made with olives. When the waitress arrived with the food, Mia opened her eyes, and said, "You must be very hungry." Nicolas laughed and said, "I'm so hungry I could eat you…and teasingly nibbled at her neck."

She squirmed and he pulled her closer as she tried to get away. They laughed and talked as they ate their pizza.

When they were done, they slowly walked toward Mia's car, holding each other at the waist. She told him how much she loved the moon over the ocean waters. He pulled her closer, kissing her lightly on her forehead and didn't say anything…then he closed his eyes and slightly looked upward and said, "um…" hesitated, then continued, "You are like a star on a moonless night." Nicolas winked his eye then waited for her reaction and wondered what she thought of his spontaneous poetry.

She looked at him curiously and laughed, and asked sarcastically, "A star?" He looked at her and laughed and said, "Yeah, on a moonless night." She pushed him teasingly and said, "That's what you were cooking up in that mind of yours?" She pushed him again and he grabbed onto her arm pulling her toward him where she fell into his arms. He held her closely and kissed her gently.

"Well, I tried to win you over with my poetry," he said laughingly. Mia laughed and hugged him tighter and said, "I think you're going to have to work a little harder!" They continued laughing.

They walked slowly and talked. Nicolas told her he was so glad she stopped by the restaurant. She said, "Oh my gosh, I had no idea you worked there!" Then continued in a whisper, "I guess it was meant to be, huh?"

"Yeah, just like the day you walked into my life," he replied.

Mia said, "Yeah, that was a good day, I am so glad I got lost." Nicolas replied, "Yeah, you got lost that day, so I could find you." She smiled and said, "In my getting lost, we found each other."

Nicolas stared at her, and knew what he felt was something he had never come close to feeling before. He wondered why this was happening. He was imagining her in his future. Nicolas had never done this with any of the girls he had dated previously. He wondered why with only a few hours together with Mia, he was imagining them together in the future.

He walked her to her car. As she unlocked it, he asked, "When will I see you again?" She hesitated, then smiled at him and asked, "When do you want to see me?" Nicolas didn't respond. Instead he winked, then took her face into his hands and pulled her face toward him. He kissed her lips softly, and sighed deeply. He felt the smile form on her lips as they kissed.

He waited until she was in her car, with her seat belt strapped on. She rolled her window down and asked "I'll see you soon?"

"Yes, very soon," he replied. She put her index finger to her puckered lips and kissed it, then gently placed the tip of her finger on his lips and smiled.

She then pulled from her purse a business card and placed it in his shirt pocket and confidently said, "I know you won't lose it."

Nicolas took the card from his pocket and placed it near his nose. He smelled her on the card. She rolled up her window, waved and left. She watched him through her rear view window as she drove away.

He placed the card back in his shirt pocket and he stood there with his hands on his hips. He watched until her car disappeared into traffic. And, when he could no longer see her, he walked slowly back to the restaurant.

As he walked, he took in the evening air, watching the dimly lit clouds roll over the sky and muttered "I must be dreaming. She can't be real. She's perfect. And, what I'm feeling is something I've definitely never felt before. I don't even know her, but I want her." He ran his hand through his hair, shook his head, and laughed in disbelief.

He reached the restaurant and leaned on the brick column at the entrance. He slid his hands into his pocket and pulled out her card and read: "Mia Martinez." He put it close to his mouth and as he slowly tapped it against his lips, he smelled her. What were these feelings he was feeling? He wanted to touch her. He wanted her near. He did not want to let her go.

He went into the restaurant, grabbed his laptop, and told everyone good night then walked to his car.

Mia slowly drove home and when she realized she was smiling, she giggled. Thinking, "Wow, how could this be? Is this what love feels like? No, it can't be. I'm infatuated? Is it lust? Maybe! Or, am I horny?" She laughed and thought, "No, I'm in love… no I can't be in love, it's too soon. Oh but I want him next to me." She giggled to herself, and began to move to the music playing on the radio, and tapped the steering wheel to the beat of the music. She smiled as she sang loudly to the music blasting from her stereo. She thought, "If this is what love feels like, I want it always."

That night as Nicolas lay in his bed, and Mia on her sofa, it was hard for them both to think of anything else, but each other, as they looked out their windows, at the moon, knowing that earlier, the moon had lit their way. It had lit the way into the other's heart. Mia thought of Nicolas' silly poem, chuckled, then hugged her pillow tightly and fell asleep with a smile on her face.

CHAPTER V

Mia woke up to the pouring rain pounding fiercely against her bedroom window. She lay in bed thinking of Nicolas and smiled. Then noticed the time and realized she was already running late and the rain would surely slow her down more.

She grabbed the pink chenille robe with big yellow flowers that hung behind the bathroom door. The robe was her favorite. She had it since she was a teenager and most of the flowers had started to fade. It was what she always used when she was cold or when it rained.

She went to the kitchen and put on a pot of coffee to brew while she showered. She walked toward the bathroom and switched the radio on as she went through the living room. She adjusted the speakers so she could hear the music in the bathroom then got into the shower.

She had woken up so happy, but when she heard the rain, it made her sad. Mia didn't like gloomy days. They reminded her of the day she lost her parents. The day her parents died, it rained nonstop and although she was only 5 years old, she never forgot the dark skies overhead when the police officers arrived at her grandmother's door.

She remembered so vividly, the police officer explaining to her grandmother that the cause of the accident was the heavy rain. What she vowed on that day was she would forever hate the rain. So when it rained, and more so when the sky was so dark, her memories, of the worst day of her life, came rushing back.

Mia knew the only way out of the sad feeling was to try to think of other things. She got into the shower and sang and moved to the song that played on the radio. She got out and dried herself quickly. She towel dried her hair then scrunched it. She didn't have time today to straighten it and knew she had to leave earlier than usual to avoid the traffic the rain always seemed to slow down.

She reached for her favorite vanilla lotion and began to run it over her body slowly as she thought of Nicolas. She watched herself in the mirror as she rubbed the lotion on her breasts and down her stomach as she moved to the music, moving her hands around to her butt. She then moved forward to the area between her legs, then put more lotion in her hand and rubbed the area slowly as she closed her eyes.

Just then, the radio DJ began to talk and it shook Mia out of her trance. She looked at the clock and began to spread the lotion quickly over her legs. She was late.

She quickly slipped into her robe and went to her closet to get dressed. She chose a red blouse and a black skirt. She put her black pumps on and went to the bathroom. She put her hair up, leaving a few strands to outline her face and some hung along her neck. She grabbed her frosted pink lipstick and swiped it over her lips, then quickly applied mascara to her already long eyelashes and left the bathroom, turning the light off on her way out.

She picked up her black purse and computer bag and prepared her coffee in her mug and left her house, pulling the door shut behind her.

Driving through traffic to reach her office was always slow. When it rained it took twice as long. After 45 minutes she arrived.

She couldn't stop thinking of Nicolas, his beautiful hair, his dark brown eyes, and lips. His fingers. His scent. She longed for him. She wondered when they would see each other again and did not want to wait.

She parked her car, and ran into the office, umbrella in one hand covering her briefcase, which she had swung forward, and held her books in the other, trying to keep from getting wet as the rain pounded against her legs. As she ran toward the door, she wished she had purchased the cute red rain boots she saw last week.

On her way into her office, she stopped to pick up her messages and said hello to the receptionist. The receptionist looked at her with a sly smile and said "Good morning to you, Mia." Mia smiled and wondered what she was up to. She figured she was in love again. Her receptionist seemed to have a new love interest every week and expected to hear about it shortly.

Mia read her messages as she walked into her office. When she looked up she saw a beautiful crystal vase filled with long stem red roses. She smiled and put her things down on her desk and took the card attached to the flowers and read:

"Mia, I can't stop thinking about you. Nicolas."

She bit down on her bottom lip and held the card close and sighed. Feeling like a schoolgirl, she looked up to see if anyone had seen her reaction. There was no one around. She put her face close to the rosebuds and inhaled deeply as a smile appeared on her face.

Mia put her things away and began to work. It was hard to concentrate with the roses on her desk and with Nicolas on her mind.

Mia's secretary, Tania, walked in a while later and said, "They're beautiful. Who is he?" Mia laughed and said, "Someone special."

Tania laughed and said, "Sounds interesting, you need to tell me all about him!" Mia laughed and shook her head as Tania left her office.

Tania was always trying to set Mia up with someone in the office, and was especially curious about who had sent the flowers.

Nicolas woke that morning thinking of Mia. He lay in bed, looking up at the ceiling. He got her business card from where he left it on his nightstand near his bed. He looked at it and was thinking of an excuse to see her again. Then he thought of something.

He jumped from bed, and got online to search for a florist. He called a florist and asked for a dozen roses to be sent to the address on her business card. He quickly drank a cup of coffee he had warmed up from the day before and left for work.

He expected a busy day at the restaurant. There was an art show on Lincoln Road, which always meant a busy day. He picked up his friend, Antonio, like he did every morning and headed toward South Beach.

Antonio was a friend Nicolas met when he first moved to Miami. They worked together at a small Spanish deli, the first place Nicolas worked when he arrived. Antonio lived nearby and started working with Nicolas when the restaurant opened.

Antonio, an American born Cuban, tall and slender, with short brown hair, was always happy. He got into the car and said, "What happened to you last night? You disappeared with that babe you were talking to."

"That was Mia," Nicolas said, and he began to tell Antonio about her.

"Mia? That's the girl you met a few weeks ago, the one that was lost, right?" Nicolas nodded and continued telling him about Mia.

Antonio listened and then said, "Bro, you weren't kidding when you said she was hot." Nicolas laughed and looked ahead as he drove through the quiet side streets of Miami. Antonio looked at Nicolas, laughed and said "Hey, what's that I see in your eyes when you talk about her? You're crazy bro, you just met her."

Nicolas laughed and Antonio teasingly said "I'm serious, you have to slow down, wait a minute brotha, wait a minute, hold up, you can't fall in love. There are too many girls on the beach for you to fall in love." Nicolas laughed. "We have too much territory to cover before we fall in love brotha." "We're young!" Nicolas, with a smirk on his face, nodded slowly in agreement, as Antonio rambled on.

Nicolas parked his car and they got out. Antonio, hyper as always, walked backwards as he shadow boxed, talking to Nicolas about Mia, and about the life on the beach, and asking Nicolas how he could leave all that prime real estate and said, "You know brotha, location, location, location," a common real estate phrase, "and Miami is where the beautiful women are."

Antonio loved to joke around, he was always happy. Nicolas knew his friend didn't mean it. Yet, he knew his friend very well and he knew Antonio loved all women – short, tall, thin, full-figured, and often used the statement "if I had a type, then she would be mine."

Antonio knew that the girl, Nicolas met, had to be something special. Nicolas liked the Miami life just as much as he did. Antonio laughingly said, "The women flock to you brotha, like bees to a honey tree and you know I like that, because I get all the ones you don't want, and you know that means a lot of ladies for me right?" Nicolas laughed. Antonio continued, "Tell me man, what's so special about this one?" Nicolas turned and smiled coyly.

Nicolas shook his head and shrugged his shoulders and said, "Now, Ton, they're ALL yours brotha, and that's the ONLY thing you have to worry about!" Antonio rubbed his hands together quickly and smacked his lips…and said "Damn, now all the babes are mine." They both laughed and continued walking.

Nicolas was outgoing, yet a bit shy, when it came to women, especially toward the ones who came on to him. He never liked the girls who were so eager to fall in love. They seemed so needy.   And, most of the girls at the dance clubs annoyed him.

He had always been attracted to the girls who were not dying to be the center of attention, the ones who did whatever it took to get a guy's attention. He liked the quiet ones, the ones who hung out on the sidelines, the ones who didn't drink much. Those were the kind of girls he thought were more easygoing.

Of course, he liked a pretty face and body. Hey, what guy didn't? What attracted him more were women who had more than looks, he was attracted to brains, as he always told Antonio.   He wanted someone with dreams and who stimulated his curiosity. Nicolas liked someone who was ambitious and knew what she wanted. All in all, he desired someone with drive similar to his own and who would inspire him. Nicolas believed inspiring one another to do and be more, made a relationship stronger. Antonio always laughed at that statement. Antonio always said, "I like them all!"

Nicolas also liked women who were curious, it was a trait, which could appear to be almost childlike. He was amused by it and thought it was refreshing.

During lunch break, Nicolas decided to call Mia. She was in her office eating a salad when her phone rang. "Hello," she said, then heard him say, "Hi Mia, It's me Nicolas. I called to see if the flowers arrived." She sat back in her chair, smiling, as she recognized his voice. "Yes, they're beautiful. Thank you Nicolas," she softly said.

"You're welcome," he said nervously, not knowing what to say next. Then blurted out "Another thing, would you like to have dinner with me on Friday night? You could come over and I could cook dinner, how does it sound?" He felt so nervous talking to her, just like a kid calling his first crush.

"Friday?" she asked. "Saturday, I have an early morning interview and was going to prepare for it on Friday night."

He said, "Bring your materials, I'd love to help you prepare." Mia hesitated, then she agreed.

"My address is 402 NE 20th St, Apt 1204," Nicolas blurted out with a sigh of relief.

"I'll be there at 6:00," she said.
He said, "I look forward to seeing you."

"Same here," she replied.

The week passed slowly. He worked hard… thinking of

her… wanting to hear her voice… wanting to feel her touch. He wanted the week to go by so bad. He was anxious. He wanted to talk to her but he didn't call, not to seem overly anxious or pushy. He wanted this to last, he wanted her and he was not going to ruin it in any way.

Usually the days would have seemed to fly by due to how busy they were, but Monday, Tuesday, Wednesday, went by so slowly. Thursday seemed like it would never end. Friday morning he woke to the sound of the rain, he looked at his clock: 4:30 a.m. His first reaction was "It's too early to be awake," then realized what day it was, and smiled. He lay in bed listening to the rain as it pounded on the windows. He loved the sound of rain. It reminded him of summers in the country with his grandparents. He loved it because it was not a regular thing in the region of Spain, where he came from. It was dry where he grew up, unlike Miami where when it rained, it usually poured.

Friday… she walked around with a smile on her face, and a sparkle in her eyes. She had to work late and it was almost 5:30. She knew she had to be at his place at 6:00, and called to let him know she would be late.

She went home and showered quickly. She applied the perfumed lotion over her body, concentrating between her legs and breasts. She stood in the mirror and looked at herself. Her breasts were full. The tan line outlined them just slightly above her nipples. She smoothed the lotion over her body knowing it would soon be his hands running the same path her hands knew so well.

She wanted him to touch her.

She dried her hair, and put it up in an untidy bun. She nervously changed outfits four or five times, finally deciding on a short skirt and a black, fitted scoop neck blouse, which had small white flowers painted delicately throughout. She applied her favorite raspberry oil to her body and stood in front of the mirror and smiled. She was ready.

She picked up her books and computer and walked out of the house.

At the corner stoplight she saw the lady who sold flowers on weekends. She chose the assortment with small daffodils with a sweet fragrance. She knew they'd be perfect. She paid the lady, placed the flowers on the seat and drove off.

She drove to his apartment, which was about a half hour away. The traffic was still heavy with the remnants of a rainy Friday afternoon. When she got to the gate, she let the security guard know her name. They called him, "Mia is at the gate." Nicolas said, "Let her in," and she was allowed to enter.

Mia parked near the valet area and got out of her car. She handed the driver her keys and he gave her a ticket. She placed it in the usual side pocket of her bag so she wouldn't lose it.

She walked into the building. It was familiar to her and, as she walked thru the front door, she remembered a childhood friend lived there when she was younger. She walked into the elevator and looked into the mirrored back and checked her hair and clothes. She lifted her eyebrows and smiled. The elevator door opened on the 12th floor and she walked down the long hall looking for his condo. The door was open when she arrived. She tapped on the door and Nicolas walked out of the kitchen, wiping his hands on the towel that hung from his belt. He bent down and kissed her on the lips then, took the books and computer she carried and laid them on a table near the sofa.

Mia offered him the flowers. He took them, smelled them and said, "They're perfect, just what this place needed," winking at Mia.

She followed him into the kitchen, where he headed quickly saying, "I have to stir the sauce or it'll burn." He placed the flowers near the sink then handed her a glass of wine as he stirred the white sauce. Mia stood there and watched him cook, slowly sipping her glass of wine.

Mia asked, "Where can I find a vase for the flowers?"

"In the cabinet over the sink," he replied.

Mia found the vase and filled it with water then arranged the flowers neatly.

"What are you cooking, it smells delicious?" Mia asked.

Nicolas said, "I'm making a shrimp and pasta dish."

"Wow, sounds so good and it smells delicious. And, boy am I starving," she said with a giggle.

"Well, perfect timing, dinner is ready. Sit down and I'll serve you," he said.

Mia walked into the dining area carrying the vase of flowers and set it in the middle of the table. The table was set perfectly with crystal dinner plates, blue salad plates, silverware, and glasses for water. She smiled, thinking, "He sure has it together."

She sat down at the table and watched him as he worked with ease in the kitchen. He brought out a platter of pasta, topped with shrimp and placed in the center of the table. He took her plate, and served a large portion. Then served himself a larger portion.

Nicolas reached for her hand and held it. With his other hand he lifted his glass. Mia lifted her glass, while he said, "To more todays and many more tomorrows with you, Mia." She smiled, and they tapped their glasses together, saying "Salud!"

They ate slowly and talked about work. He told her about the restaurant business and how he got started working there. She listened attentively as she ate her pasta. When dinner was done, he went into the kitchen and took a bowl of homemade lemon sorbet from the freezer and served two dishes. They talked and laughed as they enjoyed their sorbet. When they finished their dessert, he stood up and gathered the plates and took them to the kitchen.

Mia began to help gather things, and he told her he would do the dishes, so she could prepare for tomorrow. He took her by the hand and walked into the living room to a soft comfortable sofa, and sat with her for a moment, "Get comfortable, I know when I study I have to be comfortable." He reached over and kissed her, before leaving her to her work. She put her glasses on and began to study.

Nicolas went into the kitchen and put the dishes in the dishwasher and prepared a pot of coffee. While he waited for the coffee to brew, he walked into the living room and stood at the doorway drying his hands. He watched her. She was deep into her studying and didn't realize he was there.

When the coffee was ready, he fixed two small cups and returned to the living room. He placed the tray with coffee cups, a small pitcher of coffee and small sugar bowl filled with brown sugar on the table. He asked her if she wanted one spoonful of sugar or two. She asked for two. He added it to her cup, stirred it, and handed it to her.

He sat in the corner of the sofa and she leaned against him and continued writing. Mia worked as he watched her. He watched the movement of her hands as she wrote. "Everything about her is beautiful," he thought.

Nicolas smelled her essence as she moved her head. He felt the smoothness of her hair as it fell onto his arm when she pushed it away from her face. He watched her, admiring her movements as she worked, not realizing so much time had gone by. He knew he would never tire of looking at her and for an instant, felt as if she had cast a spell on him.

When she finished, she placed her books neatly on the table, took her cup of coffee and leaned against him, where he was nestled in the corner of the sofa. He played with her hair as she began telling him of the designs she had planned for her line of dresses.

She felt comfortable sitting so close to him, leaning against his body and sharing her dreams with him. Mia then looked at her watch and saw it was midnight, she told him she had better head home. Nicolas helped gather her things and walked her to her car.

They kissed, holding each other closely, not wanting to let the other go. She kissed the tip of her finger and placed it on his lips as she turned to walk away. He grabbed her hand and pressed it close to his lips kissing the palm of her hand firmly. Mia lingered as her body warmed from his open mouth on her hand. She wished she could stay but knew she couldn't and pulled away from him and got into her car. She sat in the car, opened the window and placed both hands on the wheel, as if trying to gain strength from all that was happening inside her body. She wanted him badly.

She nervously looked at Nicolas and said, "Thanks for dinner, it was delicious."

Nicolas thanked her for coming, then instinctively bent forward and placed his body through the window and kissed her deeply. Mia held onto Nicolas tightly, grasping his hair as they kissed passionately. He stopped and sighed. He wanted her, and wished she didn't have to leave. "Is it okay if I call you tomorrow?" he asked. She smiled and nodded. He winked at her. Mia rolled up the window and drove off. He watched her until she turned the corner outside the building entrance.

Mia arrived home and quickly washed her face and brushed her teeth. She put on a tank top and got into her bed. She lay there and began to run her hands over her stomach, thinking of Nicolas and their evening together. She fell asleep with him in her thoughts.

Saturday, after her scheduled appointments, Mia called Nicolas to thank him for the delicious dinner. He didn't answer his phone, so she left him the message, "Nicolas, it's me, Mia, I called to thank you for the delicious meal, and making me smile last night. Call me! Besos."

Nicolas had a full house. The beach was crazy with tourists and he had not heard his phone, since he usually turned it down while working. He had it on vibrate and didn't hear or feel her call. When he took a break he sat to eat a chicken sandwich. He pulled out his phone to call her as he said he would and saw he had a missed call from her. He called his messages, and sat back in his seat, legs kicked out from under him, he heard her voice and smiled.

He clicked the number 1 to hear her message again and again, and caught himself smiling. Antonio standing at the front of the restaurant saw him smiling, as well, and walked over and jokingly said, "Brotha, can you tell me what that smile is all about?"

Nicolas laughed and said. "Mia, Mia, Mia." Nicolas stood up and pushed his chair under the table and picked up his dishes. Antonio shook his head and said, "Yeah, yeah, I know she's yours, she's yours, she's yours." Antonio said this because Mia means, she is mine in Spanish. Nicolas laughed and said "yeah, man, I'm making her mine." Antonio turned and said "You better, because brotha, looks like you have it bad." They both laughed.

When Nicolas got off work, he sat in his truck, wondering if he should call her, it was getting late. He decided not to and drove home, thinking of her.

Nicolas got home and threw his keys and computer on the table. He showered and put on a pair of boxer shorts and then went to the living room and turned on a movie. He walked into the kitchen and rummaged through the cupboard for something to eat and found a bag of microwave popcorn and placed it in the microwave. While he waited for it to finish popping, he looked at his phone contemplating whether he should call Mia or not.

When the popcorn was done popping he put it into a big plastic bowl and sprinkled his favorite cheese topping over it and went into the living room, where the movie had already started. He sat back into the corner of the sectional sofa and watched the television set, looking through the movie. He couldn't concentrate. He could only think of Mia being next to him like she had been the night before.

He looked at his watch, 12:00 a.m., then looked at his phone and picked it up. He instinctively dialed her number. It rang three times, and he was about to hang up, when he heard her sleepy voice. "Hello," she whispered. He remained silent for a second, as feelings of desire for her rushed to the pit of his stomach along with regret for waking her. He wanted her. He needed her. He remained quiet.

"Hello" she repeated. "Mia, hi, its me, Nicolas." He felt his body awaken, as he heard her breathe deeply then whisper his name.

"I'm sorry to bother so late, but I got your message late and have been thinking of you."

"Nicolas... don't worry, I'm glad you called!" And with a smile on her face, she asked, "Do you know I fell asleep thinking of you?"

He smiled at the sound of her sweet sleepy voice and said, "I heard your message, thanks for calling."

"You're welcome, Nicolas." She whispered hugging her pillow closer to her body.

He loved the way she said his name. She asked him what he was doing, he told her about the movie he was watching. "Which one?" she asked. He told her the name. "And what is it about?" she asked. Nicolas started telling her about the movie and then noticed her deep steady breathing. He knew she had fallen asleep.

"Mia?" he said.

She didn't answer.

He lay back on his pillow, and pressed the phone to his ear to listen to her breathe. He wanted her near. He wanted to feel her warm breath on his body. He held the phone close, and listened until he was also asleep.

Nicolas woke up to the ring of his phone the next morning. It was Mia. "Nicolas, it's me, Mia, I'm soooo sorry for falling asleep."

Nicolas said, "Don't worry, I listened for awhile, until you started snoring, and I couldn't listen much longer so I hung up."

She let out a slight scream and said, "Noooooo, you heard me snore? I don't snore! Or do I snore? Ohhhh no, I am soooo embarrassed!!!!" Nicolas laughed and she squealed from embarrassment. Nicolas smiled as he listened to her reaction and after a few seconds, told her he was kidding. Mia continued to laugh.

She apologized again, for falling asleep on him. He chuckled and said he should be the one apologizing for waking her. He thanked her for calling, since he had to get up early to open the restaurant that day. It was Antonio's day off.

She told him, "Call me later."

Then an idea flashed through his mind and he asked, "Why don't you meet me at the restaurant this evening, we can have dinner after it closes?" She excitedly agreed to meet him there at 10:00.

Mia had the day off, so she spent most of the day cleaning house. She also went through her clothes for something special to wear on her first date with Nicolas. She wasn't sure what to wear, whether a sundress or jeans. She finally picked out a pair of faded skinny blue jeans and a black top that hugged her body. She pulled out a pair of wedge black sandals and placed them near the side of her bed. She rubbed her raspberry oil between her breasts, behind her ears, and at the top of her legs, then got dressed. Mia stood in front of her full-length mirror to make sure everything was perfect. It was. She was ready.

She arrived at the restaurant a few minutes before 10:00. When she entered, the lights were dim and every table had a lit candle placed on it. The restaurant appeared empty, with no one in sight. She heard the soft Spanish guitar music as it spilled from the speakers. The music surrounded her, it entranced her and she extended her arms and turned in a slow circle to the sound of the music, then suddenly stopped as she heard footsteps and someone humming coming toward her.

Nicolas turned the corner, dressed in blue jeans and an untucked blue denim shirt. "He is gorgeous," she thought. He smiled and Mia dropped her head slightly to the side as her eyes opened widely, looking up to him. He placed his hand on her chin and lifted her face to him. He kissed her on her mouth so softly.

"The place looks beautiful," she told Nicolas.

"Thanks, I let everyone off early tonight."

Mia responded, "Won't the owners be upset?"

He said, "I am the owner, this is my place, Mia! Nico's-- the name comes from Nico, you know? Short for Nicolas," he said laughingly.

Mia opened her eyes widely and placed her hand on her mouth and said, "Oh my gosh, I didn't put it together." She laughed. "Crazy me!"

He smiled and said, "Yeah, Nico is what my family called me since I was a kid."

"Tonight, we're going to eat whatever you'd like, Mia," he said. Mia lifted her eyebrow and pursed her lips together then asked "Yum, whatever I want?" He nodded his head slowly.

Mia looked at him and asked, "Hamburgers?" Smiling, he said "Hamburgers it is! How about sweet potato fries with those hamburgers?" Mia said, "sweet potato fries it is," and followed him into the kitchen.

He grabbed an apron from a hanger on the wall and put it on. Then he took another one and placed it over Mia's head, and wrapped it around her body, intentionally hugging her closely as he tied the strings behind her. She grinned and stared into his eyes, as she let him slowly dress her in the apron.

She saw the chef's hat and grabbed it and placed it on her head, looking at him in a teasing way. He laughed and blew her a kiss then said, "Guapa." She knew it meant beautiful. She blushed.

They prepared the hamburgers while he explained how he got into the restaurant business. Nicolas began by telling her his first job was a prep cook for a small restaurant, when he arrived in Miami. He said he enjoyed cooking because he loved to eat. He also said, with the inheritance his grandparents left him, he opened Nico's. He said he was named after his grandfather and couldn't think of a more appropriate name for the restaurant.

Mia leaned against the prep table as she watched him cook while he talked. He was so comfortable in the kitchen. He was playful with the spatula as he flipped the burgers, then quickly turned around, and flipped the buns. She laughed at his silliness.

While the burgers were grilling, a song came over the speakers. It was a Spanish love song that Nico knew from his teenage years living in Spain. He began humming the tune, turned and said, "May I have this dance, beautiful?" She curtsied in a playful way and said, "Yes you may, Sir Nico."

He took her in his arms and spun her around as he sang "la la la la la lana." Mia hung on tightly as she was not prepared for the spin. She looked at him curiously, wondering where the words had come from, since they were not a part of the lyrics. Nicolas continued to spin her around the kitchen as he sang. "Now, that's what I wanted!" he said as he pulled her in. She held on tightly until he slowed down. They finished their dance holding each other closely in the kitchen as the food cooked. "The food is burning," he said… and laughed as he turned to grab the buns from the grill. "Cheese?" he asked.

"Yes, please. Cheddar!" she replied. She stood next to him as he cooked, running her hand along his strong back.

He served the hamburgers on the two plates he had prepared with lettuce, tomatoes, onion and pickles. He took the sweet potato fries from the deep fry basket and placed them on a separate plate and carried them into the dining area. Mia followed him to the table he had prepared toward the back of the dining room, which was beautifully set. He had placed a single red dinner candle on the table, unlike the other tables which had small votive candles in the center.

Mia carried the bottle of wine Nicolas had set out and placed it on the table.

They sat down and began to eat. Nicolas said, "Now it's your turn, tell me about your work." Mia began to explain how she started working for the law firm after a law course she took in school where she met the attorney, who offered her a job.

She told Nico it was only temporary and what she wanted was one day to open a clothing shop with the clothes she designed. She told Nico she had already begun researching what she needed to do to get the line she designed on the market. She told him her passion had always been clothing and what she had designed was beach and city wear with a Mediterranean flare.

He smiled as he watched her talk. She felt so comfortable sharing her dreams with him. When they were done, they washed the dishes together. While she was washing the glasses, she playfully threw the bubbles toward him. He laughed and acted as if he was going to clean himself, and threw the dishtowel around her waist and pulled her toward him.

She wrapped her arms around his neck and tiptoed to meet his mouth with hers. She threw her head back as he pushed his mouth over hers. He held her head in the palm of his hand pushing his fingers into her hair.

Nicolas began to slowly kiss his way down her neck. Mia moaned as she pushed into him. He pushed his hand under her shirt touching her soft skin. He then lifted her and sat her on the stainless steel table. She opened her legs to let him stand between them.

He kissed his way down her chest as he pushed his way under her shirt, lifting her bra and cupping her breast. She moaned. Her shirt was tight and would not go lower to expose her breast, so he began to suck and gently bite her nipple over the soft cotton. He felt it harden in his mouth.

She felt the bulge in his pants, hard, pushing against her. Making her wild. She moved her hips in a circular motion as he pushed into her. She felt him through the thickness of their jeans. She moved faster, grinding forcefully, unable to stop.

He held her close, kissing her neck as she threw her head backward. He lifted her off the table and felt her body tremble. He held her closely as they remained frozen in the kitchen. Mia felt so safe in his arms.

As he held her, her fingers began to trace his back, and she started to hum. She hummed a song he had never heard before. He kissed her and she smiled.

Mia excused herself and went to the bathroom while Nicolas cleaned up the kitchen. Mia entered the kitchen still humming and approached him slowly, hugging him from behind. He turned to kiss her.

They closed up and left the restaurant and walked to their cars. He leaned against the car and held her in his arms. They were quiet with thoughts of the love they were feeling racing through their minds. He kissed her forehead and she looked up and smiled, but what he saw was sadness in her eyes. She put her head down then looked up slowly and said, "I have to get home."

"Sure," Nico said, wondering what was wrong. Had he done something to make her sad? He didn't ask. Mia got into the car and rolled down the window and said, "Call me, Nico."

He smiled when he realized it was the first time she called him Nico. She kissed her finger and placed it on his lips and held it there. He said, "I'll call you, Mia." She drove away, and he watched until she was out of sight, then got into his truck and drove home.

Nicolas lay in bed thinking about the restaurant and how she made him wild. He pictured her body as she moved so eagerly to feel him, and how she lost control. He was hard again, just thinking of how she felt in his arms and imagined her as she pushed her crotch into his hard cock. Feeling him, through their jeans. Wanting him, him wanting her. He began to stroke himself and replayed how she moved her body over and over again, until he exploded. He knew he needed her. He also knew, he could never let her go.

CHAPTER VI

The days passed, and Nicolas was busy with tourist season. Mia was also busy with the caseload she was working on. She stopped at the café a couple of times during the week to have lunch with Nicolas.

One day, Nicolas received an invitation to a dinner given by a community organization he belonged to. When he and Mia were having lunch one afternoon, he mentioned the fundraiser dinner.

"Mia, there is a community organization I belong to, they're having a Christmas auction for at-risk kids. They are having their annual dinner and auction next Friday night, would you like to go?"

She looked at him with wide eyes and said, "I'd love to go!"

"Great," he said, and went into the office and brought out the invitation. He handed it to her and said, "The specifics are on the invitation. You can keep it. I've already written it in my calendar." She looked at the black invitation with gold embossed lettering and opened it briefly seeing the vintage photo of Vizcaya Museum, where it would take place.

She wondered what she would wear, then smiled at Nicolas. He watched her as she opened it. This was not his first time attending one of these events and wondered if it was Mia's first. He was involved in different organizations, volunteering and helping with troubled kids. He told her, "I'll pick you up at 6:30 and, by the time we drive down to the museum, we should arrive near 8:00." She nodded and said, "I'll be ready."

They finished their lunch, and he walked her to her car. He sat in her passenger seat while she placed her seat belt on. He watched her, concentrating on everything she did. He knew he would never get tired of looking at her. She looked at him, pushed her lips into a pout, squinted and said "What'cha lookin' at kid?" He grabbed her face and turned it toward him, and placed his full lips over hers. She pulled him close, and they kissed passionately.

When they stopped, they realized an elderly man and woman were standing on the sidewalk watching them. Mia quickly sat up straight and Nicolas waved at the couple and said, "I'd better go, or they'll call the cops on us for indecent behavior in the parking lot." She laughed and said, "Yes, if they haven't already." She started the car and before he got out, they turned to each other and kissed quickly. Nicolas got out and Mia drove off.

Nicolas began walking back to the restaurant and saw the older couple staring at him. He waved again. The man nodded his head and the woman looked at him, shook her head, and turned way with a disappointed look on her face. He laughed to himself and continued toward the restaurant.

Friday came, and Mia left work at noon. She wanted to buy a special dress for the event. She drove to the Mall in Aventura, walked through hurriedly. She found a new dress shop near the far south entrance. She tried a blue taffeta dress on with black lace at the hem and around the neckline. "Too gaudy," she thought. She didn't like it.

Then she turned and saw a black velvet dress. Mia loved velvet. It had the scoop neckline she loved, because it accentuated her breasts. The dress hugged her body perfectly and the back hem of the dress hung longer than the front.

She looked in the mirror and took a flamenco dancer stance as she lifted her arms and started laughing. The dress was perfect. Dressy and sexy, she thought. She then saw a pair of black shoes with ankle ribbon ties that would go well with the dress she tried on. They were perfect. She paid and rushed home. She needed time to get ready and be perfect for her first formal date with Nicolas.

Nicolas went home early. He put on the tuxedo which he had had cleaned and ready for the occasion and left to pick her up. When he arrived, she opened the door. Nicolas took a step back and looked at her from head to toe, slowly shook his head and uttered, "Beautiful!"

Mia turned in a circle, slowly so he could see her outfit. He smiled as he watched her. He noticed her beautiful legs, as the dress was shorter in front. Her hair was pulled back loosely and a few strands fell over her shoulders. He shook his head again and said, "Wow Mia, you are stunning!"

Mia looked at Nicolas in his black tuxedo, with his hair neatly pulled back. "He's so handsome," she thought, as he stood in the doorway admiring her.

"Hello, beautiful," he said. "Hey, handsome," Mia replied. He took her hand and pulled her toward him and kissed her. She fell into his arms. But, when she realized his shirt would wrinkle, she pulled herself from his embrace, turned to get her bag and said, "Let's go!"

Nicolas closed and locked the door behind them. They walked down the hallway holding hands. The doorman greeted them with a smile and nodded his head as he said, "Looking good!" Mia picked up her step, walking even more confidently and said "thank you," swinging her small purse at her side.

They drove down I-95, which was the fastest way to the museum. When they arrived at the museum, the valet driver took their car. They walked onto the gardens lined with trees highlighted by dim lighting. A small crowd had already gathered in the garden, where a harp player played a beautiful song. She had never attended anything like this. A waiter approached them with champagne and they each took a glass.

The people in attendance were dressed beautifully, Mia thought. The men in black tuxedos and the women wore beautiful dresses in every color and fabric imaginable.

Nicolas greeted people he knew as he walked in and introduced Mia as his girlfriend. She recognized people she had seen in the Miami magazines. There were beautiful people everywhere, Mia thought.

The crowd was then directed to a large room in the center of the museum where a tall Christmas tree stood in the center of the room. The decorations were white and from every branch, crystal icicles dangled. The small lights, which were wrapped around the tree, twinkled brightly.

The lights, from the candles on the tables and Christmas lights throughout, reflected onto the ornaments and the mirrors along the wall. The room sparkled making Mia feel she was in the midst of an ocean of stars.

As they approached the tree, she saw tiny birds in birdhouses on the branches. They were so lifelike. She was in awe. The tree skirt was white velvet with glitter and looked like snow under the sun. It sparkled brilliantly.

The packages under the tree were wrapped in different hues of silver paper with white ribbons on each. She told Nicolas how much she loved the tree. He smiled and nodded in agreement as he looked around the room.

Toward the back of the room, the walls were filled with artwork painted by the talented at-risk youth. Mia was amazed by the beautiful work done by the kids. She looked toward the end of the room where the artwork was displayed and saw 10 teenagers. Eight boys, no older than 16 dressed in tuxedoes, leaned against the wall. One boy pulled at his tie and another fidgeted with the button on his tuxedo jacket.

There were also two girls, dressed in evening dresses, who looked very uncomfortable in their high heel shoes. Mia noticed they both leaned against the table, twisting their ankles and fidgeting, because they were uncomfortable, she thought. She smiled because she knew exactly how it felt. Nicolas saw her looking at them, and said, "Yes, they are the talented artists, and I want you to meet them."

Nicolas took her by the hand and led her to where the teenagers were standing. The kids' faces lit up as they saw Nicolas approach them. The kid with the big smile and deep dimples you couldn't miss, immediately walked toward Nicolas and put out his hand. Nicolas shook his hand, and the kid asked, "What's up Nico?" Nicolas replied, "Dominic, how are you? The pieces are awesome." Dominic confidently replied, "Just another day's work," then nudged the kid next to him. He smiled confidently and stood taller with pride, while nervously tightening his tie, as he looked at Nicolas for approval.

The other kids approached Nicolas, the boys shook his hand and Nicolas kissed the girls on the cheek. Then he introduced Mia. They all kissed Mia on the cheek and told her how glad they were to meet her. When Dominic kissed her on the cheek, he turned to Nico and winked, giving him thumbs up. Nicolas laughed.

The night was filled with meeting people. There were people from all walks of life. Mia loved meeting new people. She had never experienced an event quite like this. Everything was beautiful. It reminded her of her visions of what a fairy tale ball must have felt like. She chuckled quietly at her child-like thought.

After dinner and before the auction, Nicolas took Mia out through a side door and headed toward a courtyard with a gazebo. There were people in the garden, some walked together thru the beautifully decorated paths, and there was a group of elderly men who laughed loudly at the jokes one told.

Nicolas held Mia close as they stood in the moonlight, looking toward the beautiful museum at one side and the open waters at the other.   Mia was amazed by the beautiful structure. She was amazed at how the delicate lights illuminated the gardens and were mirrored on the calm bay water.   Mia thanked Nicolas for inviting her. Nicolas told her, "You're the only one I want to be with," and he pulled her close.   She smiled and began to hum the song she so often hummed as he held her from behind. When she began to hum, she felt as if someone was watching her and a chill ran through her body.   She quickly turned toward Nicolas and pushed in close as they swayed to the music she hummed.

Throughout the night, Nicolas asked Mia which painting she liked most.   She said she liked one painted by one of the girls. It was a painting of a little girl in a white nightgown, playing under the moonlight and in the distance was a farmhouse with lights on, thru the small windows.   She told Nico it reminded her of herself as a little girl.

She told him she remembered going out to the garden at night, in her white nightgown. And said her grandmother allowed her to play outside while she sat on the swing watching her.

She also told Nicolas she remembered her grandmother always put on her prettiest dresses at night and she would apply her red lipstick and always sprayed on her perfume to sit outside and watch Mia play.

Mia also told Nicolas, that some nights a strange man would come to the house. She remembered the man would come every night for many days, and then, would disappear for many as well. But her grandmother never changed her routine and was always perfectly dressed and ready in anticipation of his arrival, even when he wouldn't visit for days at a time. Mia wondered, as she explained to Nicolas, why her grandmother never knew the exact night he would arrive and yet, was always put together perfectly for him. Mia wondered if it was because she loved him and knew he would always return.

Mia said, when the strange man arrived, she was always ordered to her room and to bed. She was never allowed to meet the man.

When the auction began, there was a frenzy of people bidding. When the painting of the little girl in the nightgown was placed on the auction block, no one bid. Nicolas looked around the room then confidently placed his bid of $5,000.00. No one bid. He was sure he would win the painting for Mia. And just as the auctioneer was about to hit the gavel for finalization of the bid, a man in the back of the room raised his hand and bid $50,000.00. The crowd gasped and everyone looked toward the back of the room. The girl who painted the painting squealed with excitement and began jumping. The other kids started high fiving and took turns hugging her.

Mia looked toward the back where the bid came from. The area was dark and the shadows fell over the gentleman's face. All Mia could see was the silhouette of a man in a topcoat with a hat. The only thing that stood out was a shiny silver ring he wore. It was as if her sight was immediately directed toward the ring and only the ring, which was enveloped by the shadows of the silhouetted tall slender man.

She pushed herself toward Nicolas, as if looking for shelter from a deep, almost evil feeling she felt within. When Nicolas looked back to see the winner of the painting, he saw no one. He laughed and said, "The winner has left the building." Mia, looked at him strangely. He thought her look was one of disappointment. And, what he didn't realize, was the look on her face, was a look of fear.

Nicolas didn't think much about losing the bid, as this happened all the time. The only thing he felt at the moment was disappointment from not having won the bid for Mia. He wanted to win the bid so he could give the painting to Mia as a birthday gift. Yet, on the other hand, he was glad the bid was so high, as there had never been anything over $10,000 for any of the kids' artwork and he knew the kids could use the money.

When the auction ended, the crowd was directed toward another room where music played. Mia shivered as they entered the room. She held her body close to Nicolas and looked around the room. She was uneasy and couldn't understand why. Nicolas placed Mia's shawl on her shoulders, thinking she was cold. Then as the orchestra began to play an upbeat song, he asked her to dance. Mia accepted.

Mia felt someone watching her the entire time they danced. And, as they circled the dance floor she was quiet, and looked into the crowd trying to figure out why this feeling was so strong.

She remembered the shiny ring on the winning bidder's hand and she searched the room for the ring and the man who wore it. Was he someone she knew? She looked into the crowd of blank unfamiliar faces and saw no one she recognized.

"Who am I searching for?" she wondered. The blank almost hollow faces in the crowd gave no clues. When Nicolas suggested they leave, a sense of relief filled her and she accepted anxiously. They told the kids good-bye and wished them luck. Nico congratulated them on the high bids and told them to use the money wisely.

The kids thanked Nicolas for coming. Dominic went up to Nicolas and shook his hand and hugged him and said, "See you around, Nico!" Nicolas told Dominic, "Hey, why don't you all stop by the restaurant next weekend? It's on me! I'll send a car to pick you up at the rec center and bring you over." Dominic said, "We'll be there!" and looked at the other kids, who nodded their heads in agreement, excited to be invited to the South Beach restaurant.

While Mia and Nicolas waited for the valet driver to bring the car, Mia turned toward the museum. Her eyes were directed instinctively to the dimly lit balcony in the center of the building.

It was there where she saw him. Looking down on them, was the silhouette of the man who had won the bid. There was no definition in his face because of the shadows covering him. She knew he was staring at her and knew it was where the stares had come from all evening.

He stood on the balcony. Standing straight, with his hands gripping the wrought iron railing, he looked down upon them. She could see his eyes and then he smiled. Mia saw his teeth, which appeared to glow in the darkness that enveloped him.

His silhouette, accentuated by the lights of the decorated museum behind him and the ring he wore shone brightly in the dark night, reflecting the light of the full moon.

Mia quickly said, "Nico, it's him, up there. Look! On the balcony."

"Who?" Nico asked.

"The man who won the bid," Mia replied. Nico turned and looked up toward the balcony and saw no one. "There isn't anyone up there, baby," he told her. Mia looked again and the man in the shadows was no longer there. The balcony was empty.

She turned to Nicolas and said, "Hold me close." Nicolas did as she asked. They felt the cool air as it passed between them, almost as if it had gone through them. Nicolas also shivered.

He had no idea Mia was seeking shelter from a horrible feeling she felt within.

Mia, as she so often did when she was happy, sad or scared, began to hum the song she loved. The song, her grandmother sang to her as a little girl. It was the only thing that truly gave her a sense of security.

She hummed, and let the words escape her lips in a whisper. Nicolas looked at her and said, "That's a beautiful song Mia, what is it?"
"It's a song my grandma sang to me since I was born, the song that makes me happy and makes me feel safe," she replied.

He kissed her while thinking just how much he loved hearing her hum the song.

They walked toward Nicolas' truck and he opened the door for her. He got in and said, "We'll be at your place in 30 minutes." Mia leaned toward Nico and said, "I enjoyed myself so much Nico, thank you." He turned, leaned toward her and kissed her and said "I'm glad you did, you looked stunning." She smiled… and said "You, Nico, were the most handsome man there."

When they got to Mia's he got out of the car and opened the door and helped her out. He walked her to her door and kissed her. She pulled him close and said, "Don't leave me, I need you." He said, "Sure, I'll stay… but, are you sure?" "Yes!" she said. He parked his car while she waited by the door.

They went into the condo and closed and Mia locked the door behind them.

Mia sat on the chair in the living room and quickly took her shoes off, then went into her room and changed into her nightgown.

Nicolas took the remote for the television and turned it on. There was an old series playing. He sat and began watching it while he took his shoes, shirt and pants off. He was so glad to be out of that tuxedo. He lay back on the sofa and began to doze off, when he heard Mia coming toward him.

She took his hand and he sat up. She led him to the bedroom and he followed. She showed him where the bathroom was and told him she had new toothbrushes in the cabinet. He took a toothbrush from the cabinet and began to brush his teeth.

While he brushed his teeth, Mia sat on the floor of her closet looking though a box. The box held pictures of her grandmother, her parents and of Mia, when she was little. The box held all her most cherished belongings. She pulled out the picture of her grandmother and kissed it, then placed it in her pillowcase. She knew her grandmother always calmed her fears when she was growing up. And after what she felt at the event that evening, she needed her grandmother close.

When Nicolas was done brushing his teeth he came out of the bathroom. Mia, came out of her closet holding her pillow tightly and placed it on her bed. She looked at him with a smile on her face and thought, "He is so beautiful." Mia went into the bathroom and washed her face and brushed her teeth. When she walked out of bathroom she saw Nicolas lying on the bed.

He turned to her and told her, "You are so gorgeous." She laughed and said, "Even without my make up?" "Equally gorgeous," he replied. She jumped on the bed, landing on her knees and pushed her pillow with her grandmother's photo carefully to her side of the bed. Nicolas sat up on the bed, then turned onto his side, propping his head up on his arm.

He looked at her as she sat on her knees. His look was so intense she thought. No one had ever made her feel so special just by the way he looked at her.

She leaned forward placing her hands on the bed and pushed her face toward his. He held his gaze as she neared him. She rubbed her nose against his and could see his eyes frozen on hers. A playful look filled her eyes and suddenly she stuck her tongue out and slowly licked the tip of his nose. He grabbed her and playfully threw her on her back. He straddled her and began kissing her neck. She laughed and pushed her hands through his hair and pulled him down, close to her. She kissed him, sucking his lower lip into her mouth. She wanted him and wanted to make him wild.

Mia also wanted to wait, because she wanted the first time they made love to be special.

He slowly kissed along her neck. She moaned. He lifted her nightie up and began to kiss her stomach. She breathed in deeply. He slid his lips up toward her breasts, cupping one and pushing his mouth over her nipple and sucked it in slowly. He pulled up and then blew over the wetness from his mouth. She arched her back and said, "Love me."

Although Mia wanted to wait, she so desperately wanted him now. She looked into his eyes and told him. He began to push her panties lower and she grabbed his hand. He stopped and kissed her forcefully.

Mia looked deep into his eyes and took his hand, guiding him to continue lowering her panties. She lifted her hips to make it easy for him. Their gaze was frozen, as they moved.

He kissed her stomach as he separated her legs slowly then pushed his face between them. She grasped his hair in her hands and pushed into his face. He then pushed himself up and ran his tongue slowly upward, along her body, until he reached her neck. She pulled his face to hers and kissed him passionately, pushing her tongue into his mouth as she felt him against her.

He was so hard and as he began to grind on her leg, it felt so big. Mia moaned and guided him. She gasped from the pain as he thrust into her. She cried out, "Nico!"…as every nerve in her body tightened, letting out a slight scream, she pulled Nicholas closer. He pushed harder into her as he felt her muscles grip his shaft, then moved faster and exploded inside her.

They held each other, as their sweat melded together. She ran the tips of her fingers along his back as he lay above her. He then rolled over and pulled her to him. Mia snuggled closer to get as close to him as possible. She hummed softly and rested her head on Nico's chest while running her finger tips along his stomach. Nicolas caressed her hair and listened to her hum. Mia stared out the window at the dark sky and although she knew something or someone was out there, she was safe in Nico's arms.

The silence of the night reminded her of the quiet nights in the country when she was a little girl. The stillness of the country home she was raised in with her grandmother gave her peace, yet the nights which were too quiet always made her uneasy because she felt someone was always out there, looking in.

Just as she felt now, in the stillness of the night, she knew there was someone out there looking in, and although Mia lived on the fifth floor, she couldn't shake the feeling that someone was watching. The only thing that made her feel better tonight was knowing Nicolas would be with her until the morning light.

Mia's thoughts suddenly shifted to the man at the auction. She wondered who he was. She wondered why he seemed so familiar. She pushed herself into Nicolas even more. He wrapped his arm around her and with his other hand, he turned the light off. Mia positioned herself at his side and they looked up toward the ceiling where there were miniature glow-in-the-dark stars on her ceiling. He said, "Love the stars." She giggled and said, "I do too." Within just a few moments, he felt Mia's breathing steady and heard her whisper, "Hold me tight and please don't ever let me go. Never let me go." He pulled her close to his chest and dug his face into her hair, pulled her closer and whispered, "Not ever."

A low hum escaped her mouth as she sighed deeply. Nicolas kissed the top of her head and they fell asleep as they lay.

They woke up in the same position. Mia woke first and when she opened her eyes, she realized they had not moved. She turned slowly and kissed his chest. She knew at that moment she would never be without Nicolas again. She kissed his chest again and then straddled him.

He opened his eyes to the most beautiful sight he had ever woken to. She kissed his lips. He held her face and kissed her. She pulled slightly away from him and looked into his eyes. At that moment, he knew he wanted her always, and would do anything to make Mia his. While looking into her eyes, she whispered, "Nico, I am falling in love. Nico kissed her lightly and said, "Mia, I've already beaten you to it."

They kissed deeply and held each other.

CHAPTER VII

The days went rolling by. Nicolas worked hard at the restaurant. He was thinking of opening another restaurant in North Miami Beach. The South Beach location had grown steadily over the last year, and Nicolas wanted to branch out.

Mia worked on her designs and also was busy with work. They saw each other every chance they could.

December 4th, Nicolas' birthday was a few days away. Nicolas had told her about his birthday when they first met and they realized they were both Sagittarius. Mia's birthday was December 20th. They had decided they would celebrate them together on the 12th, the day between their birthdays.

Although Mia knew they had agreed to celebrate both their birthdays on the 12th, she decided to prepare a surprise dinner for him. She decided she would pretend she didn't remember his birthday. She would sneak into his house, decorate it, and prepare dinner for him.

Mia was glad they had exchanged keys to their places the day after the Christmas auction event and while he was at work, she could go into his apartment without him even knowing.

The day before his birthday, Nicolas asked if she'd like to go to dinner on the beach the following day. She agreed.

He said he'd have to swing by his condo and get ready and then he'd pick her up at 8:00.

Mia thought about how she would get it done. Mia calculated he'd leave the restaurant at 6:00 and get home about 7:00. She had to get there by 4:00 to decorate and cook dinner. She had already gone shopping for his birthday present and the groceries she would need.

She would make his favorite dinner, lamb, baked potato, and baked tomatoes, the food he said he ate on special days when he was a little boy in Spain. She had bought him an orange flavored cake from the Spanish restaurant downtown, which was decorated beautifully with candied orange slices on top.

Mia decorated the living room in blue and black streamers and balloons. She strung a "Happy Birthday" banner across the living room wall. Everything was ready, now she had to get herself ready.

She showered and dressed in a black strapless dress and black high heel sandals. She put her hair up with a hair clip and applied the mascara to her long lashes and red lip gloss to her lips. She was ready.

Nicolas called when he left the restaurant. He told her he'd pick her up in an hour after he went home and showered. She laughed when she hung up. She was so excited and knew he was definitely going to be surprised.

Dinner was in the oven. The table was set and the music was paused on their favorite song. She sat on the sofa and turned off the lights.   She heard the key in the door.   The door opened slowly and a cold breeze entered the room. The door remained open.   Mia held her breath.   She froze. She sensed, whoever was at the door was not Nicolas. She held her breath and looked at the figure push the door open.

It was Nicolas.   She placed her hand on he mouth to silence her surprise. Why had she felt it was someone else?

Nicolas walked in with four bags of groceries in his arms and placed them on the floor, then pushed the door closed behind him.   When he switched the light on, he saw her as she stood up and said, "Surprise!" He laughed and opened his arms, and she ran to him.   She threw her arms around his neck and started kissing his face quickly.   She was on her tiptoes, kissing his lips and between kisses saying, "Happy Birthday Nico…Happy Birthday Baby!"

Nicolas held her closely. And fell onto the sofa with her in his arms.   She straddled him and kept kissing his face.

"Were you surprised baby?" she asked.

Nico laughed, and said, "You know I was. I thought you were an intruder who caught me with my arms full, with no chance of defending myself."

"You're silly!" she said and laughed.

Nico grabbed her face with his hands and pulled her toward him. "Thank you Mia, you don't know how much this means to me. I honestly thought you had forgotten."

"Me? Forget? Never!" Mia replied.

He traced the side of her face down to her jaw and kissed her tenderly. He looked deeply into her eyes, as if he were looking into her. He knew how lucky he was to have her, the most beautiful woman, inside and out.

He pulled her close. She rested her head on his shoulder and asked if he was tired. "I was, until I saw you," he said.

Nico's hands traced the line of her back and moved toward her hips. She sat up and cupped his face with her hands. She continued to kiss him. He held the roundness of her bottom in his hands and pulled her toward him as he pushed his hips toward her. He slid his hands up her legs as she ran her hands over his pants. He pushed his finger along her panties, pushing into her slit feeling how wet she already was. He slid his finger in through the side and started caressing her. She moaned and continued kissing him, only more sensual and not as playful.

He felt her inhale deeply, sucking his breath into her. She pushed into him, moaning. Moaning deeply, she said "Nico, baby, make love to me." Nico pulled her closer, pushing his tongue into her mouth while feeling her tongue push into his. Nico then stood up and picked Mia up and carried her into his bedroom with her legs wrapped around him. He placed her on his bed gently looking down at her intensely.

He stood over her and took his shirt off. He unbuckled his belt, unbuttoned his pants and removed them. She looked up at him, staring into his eyes intensely, with a slight smile and with hunger in her eyes. Mia slowly licked her lips as she touched her slit. He watched her. He bent down and kissed her slowly. Mia kept her eyes open, looking into his, as they kissed. He slowly took Mia's dress off as he kissed her neck. Looking into her eyes, he began to slowly remove her panties. She lifted her hips as he slid them down, because she too, wanted them off.

He kissed her breasts. Sucking her nipples into his mouth, as he pulled up, he'd release them and blow air onto them, driving Mia crazy. Her body moved, she was ready for him. He removed his shorts, and placed himself above her. His strong arms supported him as he leaned down and kissed her mouth deeply.

He kissed his way to her neck then slowly kissed his way down her stomach. He parted her legs and began to push his mouth into her mound. He felt her thrust into him while pushing her hands through his hair, grasping and slightly pulling it, as she arched her back and moaned loudly.

"Nico, you're driving me crazy," Mia whispered. Nicolas breathed deeply and did not respond, yet continued. He kissed his way up her stomach, licking his way up to her chest, arriving at her mouth and kissing her deeply.

She opened her legs and wrapped them around his waist. She pushed into him, feeling him so very hard. She rotated her hips, feeling the tip of his cock slide along the slit. She pushed into his hardness and moaned "Baby, fuck me, I'm yours." Nicolas put his hand near her wetness and rubbed the tip of his cock over her clit, teasing her. She moaned softly.

He slid his shaft slowly, finding the entrance and pushed into her slowly. She inhaled deeply, feeling the pain as he entered and pushed into her... slowly and pulling out slowly... until she pushed into him, bucking her hips. She held him tightly and pushed her fingernails into his back and said "Nico, I love you." He pulled her closely as he felt her climax. She clung to him tightly during her orgasm. Nicolas pushed deeper and faster and as he exploded Mia felt the warmth of his body enter her.

She held him tightly, as he fell limp in her arms. His face rested on her chest. He kissed her chest softly as she ran her fingertips through his hair. Mia knew at that instant their souls had united.

His body covered hers. Their breathing fast. He pulled her into him. She pushed her face closer to his. And as he ran his fingers through her hair, she traced the sides of his body with her fingertips, touching him gently. He kissed her ever so lightly on her lips. And as she opened her mouth to breathe in, he whispered into her mouth... "I Love you Mia." Nicolas felt her mouth smile as he enveloped it with his. He realized he had never loved anyone more than he loved her at this moment.

They held each other closely in silence. Touching each other softly. Nicolas then turned to Mia and said, "What's that smell? It smells delicious?" She looked at him with a playful smile and said "It must be your neighbor cooking. Aren't we supposed to go out to dinner?" He said "Yes, let me take a shower." She said, "I need to rinse off too, and then I'll put your groceries away."

He kissed her and stood up and walked into the shower. She watched him while pinning her hair up and followed him into the shower. She washed her body quickly without wetting her hair then stepped out and dried herself, and handed him a towel. She slipped into her dress and went into the kitchen to set out their dinner.

Mia took the lamb, potatoes, and tomatoes out of the oven and placed them on plates. She lit the candles and poured wine into the glasses. She walked into Nicolas' bedroom where he was getting ready. She watched him as he stood in front of the mirror buttoning his shirt.

When he was dressed and ready, Mia told him to close his eyes. She took his hand and guided him to the dining room and said, "You can open your eyes now!" He did as she asked and saw the meal she had prepared on the table. Also, in the middle of the table was a package wrapped in dark blue colored paper with a black velvet ribbon.

"Mmmmm it smells delicious," Nicolas said.

"I hope it's as good as your mom use to make," she replied. Nicolas smiled and said, "It looks delicious, lets eat. I'm starving!"

Mia laughed and sat down. They ate their dinner, and talked about their day.

During dinner, Nicolas kept telling Mia just how perfect the meal was. He ate three pieces of lamb, two potatoes and two tomatoes. When he was done, he sat back in the chair and told her he was full. She said, "You can't be full, you have to eat your birthday cake!"

"Yum, birthday cake," he said as she walked toward the kitchen and pulled the cake out of the refrigerator. She placed 32 multi-colored candles on the cake and lit them.

With the cake in her hands, she walked slowly toward the dining area singing "Happy Birthday to you, Happy Birthday to you, Happy Birthday Nicolas, Happy Birthday to you."

Nicolas sat there and watched her as the candles painted a warm glow on her face. He loved looking at her expressions, and seeing the joy that spilled from her. He knew she loved him and smiled as he watched her, reveling in her every move.

She placed the cake on the table and he grabbed her head from the base and pulled her close and opened his mouth to kiss hers. She pulled away and said, "Wait, wait, wait, blow out the candles baby, or we'll be eating wax!"

Nicolas got ready to blow the candles out, she said, "Wait! You have to make a wish, the most important wish of your life!" Nicolas closed his eyes and thought for a moment. Then wished, "I wish Mia will be mine forever." He looked at her and winked, then blew out the candles. Mia clapped when he finished and reached for the knife.

She began cutting the cake while humming her song. When she was cutting the cake Nicolas stuck his fingers in the frosting and put it on her nose. He stood up and kissed her nose, then stuck his fingers in again and put them toward her mouth. She kissed him with a mouth full of frosting. They laughed. She sat on his lap as they shared a slice of cake.

Just then, Mia remembered his gift and said, "Nico, I have something for you, close your eyes and put out your hands." She placed his gift in his hands. He looked her directly in the eyes, and said, "You shouldn't have." She put on her pouty smile then blew him a kiss.

The box in his hands was the wrapped package that had been on the table. He opened it slowly, watching her grow more impatient with his slow moves. He smiled at her impatience and unwrapped it even slower. When he opened the box, he looked toward her and her hands were grasped near her chest. She had given him a watch with a silver face and black band and on the back the inscription - Mia Loves Nico.

"Wow, Mia, I love it. Thank you." He put it on and said "How does it look?" She smiled and gestured a thumbs up for approval.

After dinner they cleaned up the dishes together, laughing and talking about birthdays they remembered growing up.

Nico asked Mia if she would spend the night. She said yes.

They went into the bedroom and Mia took one of Nicolas' old shirts from the closet and put it on to sleep in. Nico was in his boxer shorts. They lay on the bed. Nico watching the news and Mia lay on her stomach reading a book she had on her iPad.

While they were in bed, Nico said "Mia, will you go away with me for Christmas?" She was quiet for a moment, then she said, "Hmmm, I'm not sure if I can," and kept looking down, and then looked up through the side of her eyes and saw the worried look on his face. She started to smile and a slight laugh escaped her lips as she placed her chin into the palms of her hands with her arms propped on the bed.

"And where is it you want to take me away to?" she asked.

"Far away from Miami, but since you have plans, I'll ask someone else," and he looked down seriously, then slowly lifting his head he saw the confused look on her face. He said, "Don't be silly, you're the only one I want to run away with."

"And, of course, you are the only one I'd let take me away." Mia pushed her iPad out of the way and made her way into his arms. He pulled her close and hugged her tightly then reached for her iPad, placed it on the table and turned the light off. In the darkness, Mia asked "So, where are we going?" Nicolas laughed and said, "Now that's my surprise!" They laughed.

He looked down at her and saw her eyes in the darkness. He kissed the top of her head, pushing his lips into her hair. Mia ran her fingers over his chest and stomach as she hummed. Mia fell asleep first. Nico held her and listened to her steady breathing.

"I will always protect her, and make her the happiest woman in the world," he thought. He wanted to keep her with him always. He did not want to let her go and decided he would ask her to marry him. He couldn't live away from her again.

Nicolas held Mia closely. This was the best birthday he had ever had and as he reminisced of the things she had done, his eyes filled with tears that ran down his face to her beautiful hair. He closed his eyes and listened to her breathing. He pulled her closer and after a short while was also asleep.

CHAPTER VIII

Two weeks until Christmas.

Nicolas, busy with the holiday crowd at the restaurant, started planning their trip. He would take her to Colorado for Christmas, where his family had a cabin. He thought it would be the perfect place to spend their first Christmas together. He wanted to make it special, something they would both remember always and would someday share with their kids. He wanted to start a tradition with her.

One day, he decided to go to Mia's office. He picked up a couple of Spanish sandwiches of serrano ham, manchego cheese, and tomato spread from the restaurant that reminded him so much of his hometown in Spain. He called and told her not to make plans for lunch because he was taking lunch to her office.

When he got to her office, he went in and closed the door. She had cleared off her desk. He placed the sandwiches on the desk and pulled out the sodas he brought. They sat across from each other. Nico, said, " Mia, your birthday is next week, and you know we're taking off for Christmas. Do you think you could take a couple more days off so we can spend your birthday away too?" Mia looked down and then up again with a smirk on her face and said, "I'll have to give my notice to my boss, but I don't think it'll be a problem." Mia smiled, clapped her hands and said, "We are going to have so much fun!"

He laughed at her and thought to himself how he loved her childlike ways. It was one of the things he loved most about her. She continued, "I have to use up my vacation days before the end of the year and this will be perfect. But, where are we going?" she asked. He winked and told her to start shopping for clothes for cold weather. "Cold weather?" she asked. "Yes, we're going north," Nicolas said. Mia squealed and jumped up and kissed him.

Mia started talking rapidly about what she needed to prepare for the trip. "I'll have to pick up a jacket and some boots. Oh, I have my warm boots that'll keep my toes warm. Oh! And, I need some warm pajamas. "Or"… she asked as she rolled her eyes… "will you keep me warm?" Nico sat back and watched her, he laughed and said, "I want to see you in warm flannel pajamas," then hesitated, "but just until I take them off that hot body of yours." She laughed then opened her eyes widely and gasped. Nicolas looked at her curiously and she said "I forgot! My grandma and I share the same birthday, and we've always spent it together. I won't be here, I hope she won't mind, ah, I know she won't mind."

The days before the trip Mia looked for a jacket, and some sweaters. She had enough with her jeans and her boots. She went into the lingerie store and found a pink flannel nightshirt. She put it on and imagined Nico taking it off her, like he said he would. She smiled and walked toward the counter to pay.

December 18. Nicolas picked Mia up at her apartment and they drove to the airport. When they got to the airport he parked and handed her the boarding pass. She opened the envelope and said "Wow, destination … Aspen, Colorado. I can't wait, I've never been there before" she said. "It is going to be beautiful. The snow, and brrrr the cold weather. Nico, you have to keep me warm or I'll turn into an icicle… and I won't thaw out 'til summer." Nicolas laughed.

They arrived in Aspen close to midnight. He rented a black Range Rover and they drove to a hotel near the airport. When they arrived at their room, there was a fire in the fireplace and on the table was a bottle of wine, and a tray beautifully decorated with cheese and fruit. They sat down in front of the fire and ate. They hadn't eaten anything since noon and were both starving.

Mia took her sweater off and said, "I think I need a shower, I feel awful after the trip." Nicolas nodded in agreement and said, "I need one too." They both showered and got into bed naked. Nicolas turned out the lights and held Mia.

"This is the beginning of our vacation, tomorrow we will begin celebrating the holiday." He said. They held each other and talked about the beautiful hotel and watched the fire, until they were asleep.

He woke up early and ordered coffee, croissants and fruit for breakfast while she was in the shower. After they were delivered, Mia walked out of the shower in her bathrobe, and hair in a towel. He looked at her and watched her move across the room. She was beautiful. He concentrated on her neck, where the same strands of hair, which always seemed to escape the towel, lay. She

watched him as he walked toward her. She wanted him.
He stood in front of her and looked into her eyes and
grabbed her closely and kissed her, saying "Good morning,
beautiful." "Morning baby," she replied.

Their breakfast arrived and they sat and ate their fruit and
drank their coffee.   Nicolas put some butter on a croissant
and ate it with his second cup of coffee. When they were
done, he went through the room making sure they weren't
forgetting anything.   Then he gathered the luggage and
took it down to the lobby and waited for the truck.

Mia finished getting ready, and got her last bag and purse
together, then did a quick sweep of the room making sure
she had everything.

He wanted to warm the truck and told her to be down in
half hour.   He drove the truck to the hotel entrance and
went in for her.   Mia was ready in her coat and boots.
She held onto his arm as they walked toward the truck, so
she would not slip on the icy ground.

They drove through the mountains until they arrived at a
small town. He stopped to get gas and coffee Mia stayed
in the truck waiting for him, she couldn't get warm, even
with the heater on high.

They drove another half hour and he stopped on the side of
the road. He looked toward her and told her to hold out
her hand. She looked at him curiously. He asked her to
close her eyes. She did as he said. He placed something
cold in her hands then told her to open her eyes. She did,

and in her hands lay a key. It was an old key. She looked
at him curiously, wondering what the key would unlock.

He told her to close her eyes once again, and not open
them until he told her to do so. He drove another five
minutes and stopped. He turned off the engine and
remained quiet.

"Can I open them now?" she asked.

"No," he replied.

Mia obeyed.
He got out and walked around to her side. He opened the
door and told her to take his hand, but, had to continue
keeping her eyes closed. She giggled and said, "ok."
They walked slowly. Mia counted 12 steps before they
stopped. He said, "It's ok, you can open them now."

Mia slowly opened her eyes. They were standing in front
of a small cabin surrounded by the newly fallen snow,
which glistened with the rays of the sun. She turned to
him and said, "Wow Nico, this is beautiful, it's just like a
Christmas card!" She hugged him and kissed his face.

Nicolas told Mia the key was to open the door to the cabin.
She placed it in the lock and turned it. The door opened
up to a small living room with a fireplace at the end of the
room. To the right was a Christmas tree leaning against
the wall. It was not decorated. There were bags of
decorations, groceries, and wood near the fireplace.

"How did you manage this?" Mia asked.

He winked at her and turned to get the bags from the truck. Mia followed him and got her purse and small bags. They went in and Nicolas started a fire in the fireplace. She began emptying the bags of groceries. There were 3 bottles of wine, and her favorite crème liqueur. There were chocolates and two cans of stuffed green olives, one with anchovies and the other with blue cheese. There was a box of crackers and two loaves of fresh baguette bread and also a bag of potato chips. When Mia opened the refrigerator door, she saw fruit, cheese, prosciutto, fresh vegetables, and steaks. She wondered how he had accomplished all of this. She wondered if he had done it while she was sleeping and would ask him later.

He took the suitcases into the room and placed them by the door. Mia said she would unpack after she finished with the groceries. He walked out and as he walked by her, he smacked her on her butt gently, squeezing a cheek into his hand, and then pulled her close while he kissed her on the forehead. She kept moving busily, accommodating everything in the refrigerator.

Nicolas began setting up the tree. Mia took the decorations from the bags. There were silver and glass ornaments. At the bottom of the bag was a box wrapped in black velvet with a thin red bow tied around it. She asked what it was. He said it was her Christmas present and she had to wait until Christmas to open it. Mia picked it up, shook it gently, winked at Nico and placed it near the tree. Mia then went into the kitchen to prepare hot chocolate. It was something she remembered always having, while decorating the Christmas trees, throughout the years.

That afternoon they decorated the tree together. They shared their childhood memories of decorating their Christmas trees as they grew up. They also talked about their favorite childhood ornaments. Mia told Nicolas of a ballerina ornament her father bought for her on a business trip. The ballerina wore a blue gown and blue slippers with silver ribbons. Nicolas said his favorite thing on the Christmas tree was the star at the top, which had been handed down to his family by his great grandparents.

He told her of the Christmases his family spent in this cabin after they came from Spain. The cabin belonged to a family friend and later to his grandfather and every year the family would come and spend Christmas there. The little cabin was filled with love every Christmas, with everyone sleeping on the floor waiting for Santa to arrive. He also told her New Year's Day and Three Kings Day were celebrated in Spain.

She watched him as he told his story of the beautiful memories he had growing up. He noticed the sad look in her eyes as he talked. She said she wanted to have Christmases like that with him someday. He promised every Christmas they spent together, would be one she would never forget.

She told him of the beautiful Christmases she spent with her mother and father until she was 5. "I can't remember much," she said, "but I do remember decorating the tree with my mother and father." She told him she remembered making Christmas cookies with her mother. She also told him after her parents died, the Christmases spent with her grandmother were very special. They would bake wonderful pastries, and decorate the tree together.

She said she still had all the ornaments, which belonged to her parents. She told him of the wonderful meals her grandmother prepared over the holidays and always the same wonderful meal of Cornish hens and stuffing for Christmas. She explained to him this was not a traditional meal but one learned from the woman who cooked for her grandmother when she moved to the United States.

She told Nicolas when she was older, her grandmother told her she had continued to do the things Mia's mother and father had done for her before they died so she would never forget the memories and traditions of her parents.

When the tree was done, they lay on the plush white rug near the fireplace and admired the fire. It was so beautiful and so relaxing. She told him the ornaments he had selected were so romantic. He said he chose them because he wanted to see her reflection in every ball and it was why he chose the glass. When she looked into his eyes, she knew he loved her. She had never felt this before. What she saw in his eyes made her realize she could never live without him.

She reached for him, she needed to be in his arms. She said, "Hold me Nico... hold me close." Mia pushed her head into his chest as tears escaped her eyes. Tears of joy. Tears of fear. She loved him so much, but was so afraid to lose him.

He lifted her face and looked into her eyes. The tears formed in pools and slowly escaped the corners of her eyes, trailing down her cheeks to her neck. And, before they reached her neck, he kissed the tear so it would fall no further. He knew what she was thinking and said, "I am yours," and sighed, as a whisper of "forever" escaped his mouth. She kissed him lightly on the lips and fell into his arms again and softly repeated "forever."

They fell asleep in front of the fireplace. When she woke up, she was wrapped in his arms. She looked out the window and saw the snow slowly falling. It was so peaceful. They were in a world all their own, away from the sounds of the city, just the two of them. She pulled the soft blanket over their bodies and moved even closer to Nicolas and stared at the fire, as it dwindled.

Before the fire died, she quietly slipped out from under the blanket and went to the fireplace to place a log in the fire then wrapped herself in a white fluffy throw that was on the sofa and went into the kitchen. The kitchen was small but the corner was framed on both sides by windows. She looked out as she hugged herself. The snow was beautiful. The sun would be setting in about an hour, and the sky was already turning a dark orange. She hoped Nico would wake up to see the sunset, but did not want to bother him.

She started to prepare something to eat, knowing he would be hungry when he woke up. She made a spread of tomatoes and spices, and toasted bread and melted mozzarella cheese over it. "Voilà!" she whispered to herself, and took the bowl to the table. She set the table with the china she found in the cupboard and took out a bottle of wine.

He lay motionless on the floor and listened to the sound of her footsteps, and to her softly humming her favorite song. He opened his eyes slightly, watching her arrange the table. She looked over to him, as she realized she was being watched. She giggled, and ran to him, "You're terrible, you've been awake and didn't let me know."

"I woke thinking I was dreaming as I watched you move around the room, and until you ran to me, I thought I was lost in a dream, and I didn't want to wake up. Now, I know I am living the dream, and I never want to wake up, I want us to be together always." He pulled her down and kissed her hungrily.

She laughed and grabbed his hand, pulling him to stand up. "Baby, come and look at the sun, its about to set." She wrapped the throw more tightly around herself. He stood behind her and she opened the blanket so he could stand inside it with her. He held her as they looked out toward the west. The sky was a dark orange, with hues of red and gold. They quietly stood holding each other and watched the last hint of light, as the sun crept slowly behind the mountains surrounding them.

"Are you hungry?" she asked. He said, "I am so hungry, I could eat a cow." She began to make a mooing cow sound, and he wrapped his arms around her from behind, and began to nibble on her neck, she began to scream, broke away from him and ran into the kitchen, dropping the blanket on the floor.

He ran after her, and caught her in the corner where the cabinets met and they began to kiss passionately. He wanted her and she wanted him. He kissed her neck slowly, running his lips on her soft neck, smelling her, needing her. She moaned and pulled him closer. He began to unbutton her blouse, as he gently kissed his way to her breasts. "Make love to me, please," she said. "I want you here, and, I want you now!"

He lifted her and she wrapped her legs around his waist. He felt the moistness through the silky fabric of her panties as he pushed his hand between her legs. His body, so strong and he was hard. She rubbed herself close to him. He pushed her panties to the side and she felt him enter her. Her body trembled as he pushed into her harder. She felt him explode and pulled him closer as his body weaken.

Nicolas held her in his arms. He smelled her hair as he rubbed his face in the silkiness. He watched the falling snow outside the window and held her close. He felt her breathe. She was still.

She looked up at him. "Nico, what are you looking at?" He said, "I'm watching the snow fall.   It is so peaceful here and, I feel complete with you in my arms." He looked down at her. Her eyes had filled with tears. He tilted her head upward and kissed her lips.

"Hungry?" Nico asked. Mia smiled and said "Starving!"

"Ok, I'll take out the steaks and get the grill started. You can make a salad and put the potatoes in the oven," Nico said. "It's a deal!" Mia replied. They went to the sink together and washed their hands.

While the steaks were cooking and Mia was preparing the salad, Nico asked her to tell him more about her family. Mia smiled and looked down. Mia took a piece of toasted bread and placed the tomatoes on it and gave it to Nico to eat as he cooked the steaks. Then she began:
"Ok, when my father and his twin sister were 5 years old, my grandmother brought them to the United States. They came from a city called Murcia." Nicolas nodded his head and said, "Yes, I know it."

Mia continued, "My grandfather died the month before and my grandmother wanted to start a new life with her children. They moved to a ranch south of Miami and lived there until my father and aunt were about 18 and ready to go to college, it's when they moved into the city.

"My mother lived with her parents in Cartagena, Spain and at 18 years old came to Miami that summer as an exchange student. She was taking a photography course at the university when she met my father."

"After they met and started talking, they realized they were from the same region, and incidentally my grandparents in Spain knew my grandmother. They later asked my grandmother Ana for a special favor, which was to watch over my mother from time to time. My grandmother agreed and invited my mother over frequently for dinner. She and my dad became good friends."

"They later fell in love and married the following year. I was born two years later. We all lived in the city with my grandmother, who took care of me, while my parents worked and went to school."

"When I was 5, my grandmother and I were at the farm for a week. My parents and aunt were driving out to the farm to meet my grandmother and me so we could spend the weekend together. On the way, we think my father fell asleep at the wheel and drove into a canal. It was also raining that night and initially the policeman said it was the rain, but the accident report did not mention any brake marks because of the rain. It was as if he drove directly into the canal and it's why we believe he had fallen asleep. It was an area where there was very little traffic and there was no one to help them. The three of them died that night."

"My grandmother and I were left alone. We moved back to the farm permanently. My grandmother still lives there. She comes into the city every week to spend a day or two with me. I really want you to meet her, Nico." He smiled and nodded in agreement.

Mia continued. "My grandparents in Spain still live on a farm near Cartagena, and I go to see them once a year."

Nicolas grabbed her hand and squeezed it. He kissed her on the top of her head as he got up to check the steaks. Then he heard Mia say, "Now tell me about your family."

"Well, about 8 years ago, my grandfather and grandmother decided to move to the United States, specifically Aspen.

For many years my grandfather had a restaurant in Spain where tourists frequented. He had a regular patron who was from Aspen. They became good friends over the years. His name was Mr. Jose Martinez, whose family had once been from Valencia. He was alone. He had no kids and his wife had died. He was a lonely man and my grandparents basically took him in and they became very close. He owned a home in Valencia as well as a ranch in Aspen."

"When Mr. Martinez visited Valencia he spent almost every day with our family. He became part of our family. I even started calling him Tio Jose. We would come to visit him in Aspen every summer and during Christmas as well. He was good to our family. When he died, he left the house in Valencia to me and left the cabin to my grandparents. The summer after he died, my grandparents decided to move to Aspen for a year. I came with them to study and my parents stayed in Valencia running the restaurant. Since then they moved back, but come out during the summers to the cabin."

"I told you, I also have a brother and sister who still live in Spain. My mom and dad remain there because of the grandkids and I would love our next trip to be to Spain so you can meet them and my grandfather. My grandmother died a year ago. He's not doing very well since she died."

Mia said, "I'd love to visit Spain! But my grandmother gets very nervous when I go there. It's almost as if she is afraid for me to go. I don't know why, I have never asked. That is usually why I only stay a week when I see my mother's parents. I love it there, it is part of my heritage, and I would love to visit with you some day."

"It's a date!" Nicolas said. "We'll plan a trip there in a few months. How does that sound?" "Awesome!" Mia said.

Mia remembered the food in the oven and jumped from her chair and ran to the stove. The potatoes were done. Nicolas placed the steaks on plates and set them on the table. Mia served the potatoes on a plate and brought out the salad from the refrigerator.

They ate and reminisced about things they did when they were young. Nicolas told her about playing on the beach, which was walking distance from their home. Mia said they never went to the beach much growing up and had begun to go more the last year, when she moved into the city. She said her grandmother loved the peace and quiet of the farm. She loved gardening and took pride in her flower garden. Mia also told him of her visits to Spain, she told him of one of the secluded coves near Cartagena where her grandparents took her during her visits there.

After dinner, Nicolas pulled out the orange sherbet. He served them both a dish and they went into the living room to eat it near the fireplace.

Nicolas turned on the tree. It warmed the room. It was beautiful. The room had windows from the floor to the ceiling on two adjoining walls, similar to the ones in the kitchen. The tree was in the corner, and its reflection on the windows lit up the house.

Mia asked Nicolas if they could go outside to see what it looked like from the outside in. They put on their boots and jackets and went outside and stood in each other's arms admiring their first beautiful Christmas tree.

The night was cold, but they stood and watched the tree and the sky. Mia noticed the shadows of the trees in the darkness. She shivered and said, "Let's go inside." She took Nicolas by the hand and walked toward the house.

Mia shivered as she took off her jacket and boots and walked toward the fireplace. The fire was perfect. They sat in front of the fireplace, while they ate their sherbet.

When they were done, they put the dishes in the dishwasher and returned to the living room. They lay on the couch and listened to music. She snuggled against his chest as he played with her hair. They didn't talk, yet each thought about what they had talked about earlier.

They were together, and nothing could feel more perfect. Mia felt Nicolas begin to breathe heavily and knew he was asleep. She looked up at him and his eyes were closed. She went to the bedroom and pulled the thick, white down comforter from the bed and placed it over him. Then she went into the bedroom and put on her baby doll nightgown, put two logs on the fire and got under the comforter with him, snuggled closely and fell asleep.

CHAPTER IX

Nicolas woke up and realized they were still on the couch wrapped in the warm comforter.   He kissed Mia on her forehead. She was so comfortable wrapped in his arms. She moved when he kissed her and slightly opened her eyes.   She looked up at him and said, "Good Morning,." He said, "Happy Birthday, my love!"   She pulled the covers over her head and said, "It's my birthday!" and laughed.

Nicolas got up and said, "Wait here, I have something for you."   He went into the room and came out with a big box, wrapped in dark red wrapping paper with a wide black ribbon.

"Happy Birthday Mia, I hope you like it."   Mia was surprised by the huge box and wondered how he had arranged to get it there.

He placed it at her side and said, "Open it." Mia said, "It's so beautiful, I don't want to ruin the beautiful wrapping." Mia grabbed her phone and took a photo, saying, "I have to show it to Gram." Nicolas laughed. She untied the ribbon, and placed it gently at her side.   She then began to slowly unwrap the box.   She lifted the box top off and inside was a dress the color of the wrapping paper, with a tie the color of the ribbon.   It was beautiful.   She lifted the dress and said "Nico, it's the most beautiful dress I have ever seen."   He smiled, and said, "I'm glad you like it. You will be absolutely stunning tonight for dinner."

She got up from the sofa and straddled Nicolas. "Thank you my love," she said. He winked at her and pulled her close as they kissed.

Nicolas asked, "How would you like to have breakfast at the little diner in town?" "Sure," Mia replied, "Let's shower." They went into the shower and shampooed each other's hair, scrubbed each other's backs, and slid their bodies up against each other. In the shower while she was rubbing her hands over his back, lathering it up, she wrapped her hands around him and felt he was hard. She began to stroke him using the soap suds for lubricant. He turned and tried to reach down and touch her, but she pushed his hand away. "No, it's my turn." She stroked him until he exploded in her hand. He leaned down and kissed her deeply, and looked into her eyes. She loved the way he looked at her. His eyes were so intense. She saw so much love in his eyes, and the strongest desire she had ever seen before.

She washed his body. Then he turned her around and lathered her body. He kissed her neck as he lathered her breasts and pinched her nipples. She moaned. Then he pulled her close to his body and his hand went down between her legs. He rubbed her until her body weakened in his arms. They stood under the water letting it hit their bodies. Then she laughed and said, "The water, is getting cold. Let's get out of here." They rinsed off and grabbed the towels and dried themselves off quickly.

Nicolas pulled the robes off the door hanger and held hers so she could slip her arms in. She was shivering and wrapped it tightly and went to the sink to brush her teeth.

He followed her. They brushed their teeth in front of the mirror, making faces and laughing.

When they were ready, they drove into town. They stopped at a small diner and ordered breakfast. Nicolas ordered the eggs, sausage and hash browns. Mia ordered fresh fruit, a banana nut muffin and a piece of sausage. They ate and talked and laughed as they watched a small child, who was with his mother, mimic everything the waitress said.

When they were done with their breakfast, they paid and went outside. The day was beautiful. The mountains were snow covered and the sun was warm. They walked through the small town center and went into the small boutiques that lined the street. People were friendly. Mia and Nicolas spent the morning wandering through the town. He was familiar with the town because he had been there often. She was so curious. He loved watching her. She was so beautiful and so vibrant. She had so much life in her and made him happy.

Around lunchtime, Mia said, "I'm hungry." Nicolas said, "Let's stop in here, I remember they have great nachos." Mia says, "Nacho's, yum!" They went inside and ordered the large nacho platter and 2 sodas. They ate and listened to the loud music that shook the speakers against the wood panels which covered the walls of the restaurant. When they were done, they began to walk back to the truck, when she saw a candy shop.

She grabbed his hand, and pulled him, and said, "Please, can we go in?" He grinned and followed her. Like a small child, she marveled at all the wonderful sweet things in the shop. She pulled out her wallet and asked, "May I have the biggest, reddest candied apple, please?" The attendant looked at her, smiled and took the biggest candy apple from the shelf and handed it to her. Mia paid and thanked the lady at the counter.

They walked outside and Mia carefully took the clear wrapping off the candied apple, not wanting any of the candied covering to stick to the wrapping. She told Nicolas that in order to have good luck, they had to bite into the apple at the same time and when they bit into the apple they had to make a wish, and this had to be done until the apple was finished. Nicolas looked at Mia curiously.

They sat on a bench. Then each took hold of the stick, and with the other hand held on to the other's hand. Together, they bit into the apple and took a chunk off. She pushed her face toward his looking at him deeply in the eyes and they awkwardly kissed as they chewed the sticky candied apple.

When they were done chewing their first bite, Nicolas asked, "Where did you hear of this good luck story?" Mia said, "I didn't, I made it up." Nicolas laughed and said, "That's the best good luck charm I've heard of." She placed the candied apple between them again and reminded him a wish must be made for every bite. He nodded his head and did as she said.

They again, took another bite and continued to do so until there was no more to share. When they were done,

Nicolas said, "This will always be our good luck charm, red candied apples." Mia said, "But only if we share them," and smiled. Nicolas smiled, thinking he loved her spontaneity.

Nicolas sat back on the bench and looked at her. "Mia, do you know how much I love you?" Mia smiled and replied in a questioning tone "Probably as much as I love you?" Then winked and giggled. She sat back and snuggled near him as he wrapped his arm around her. They sat there for a while, people watching.

When the wind began to blow stronger, they decided to head back to the cabin. They got up and walked quickly to the truck and slowly drove to the cabin admiring the beautiful snow covered scenery that surrounded them.

When they got to the cabin, he asked if she wanted to watch a movie or sleep the siesta. She said, "Let's cuddle and watch a movie." He put on a comedy. They watched it for a while but soon they were both asleep.

They woke up close to 6:00. Nicolas told her they had reservations for dinner at 9:00. Mia got up and said she was getting into the shower. Nicolas said he had to make a phone call to the restaurant to check on how things were going.

Mia showered and then applied her make up, while Nicolas showered. Then, she went into the bedroom and took her dress from the closet and placed it on the bed neatly. She ran her fingers down the soft fabric, admiring it. She slipped it on, hoping it would fit and to her surprise, it fit her body perfectly. It was made of a deep red velvet fabric, which clung to her body. The wide, black ribbon wrapped around her body, just beneath her breasts, accentuating them. The neckline was rounded and rested on the edge of her shoulders. She put on her black shoes and adjusted the strap around her slender ankles. They were perfect with her new dress. She stood in front of the mirror and smiled.

Nicholas walked in from the bathroom and stood behind Mia and watched her. He moved closer to her and hugged her. He placed his hand on her stomach and watched her through the mirror. "Thank you Nico, I love it, it's beautiful," she said. Nicolas replied "I knew it was perfect for you when I saw it. You are absolutely stunning, my love."

Nicolas dressed in black pants and a white shirt, which he had placed on the bed. He walked back into the master closet tying his black tie then took his suit jacket off the hanger and put it on. He looked at himself in the mirror then turned and grabbed Mia's coat. He walked into the bedroom and asked if she was ready. She nodded her head, and he held her coat out so she could slip her arms through the sleeves.

They were quiet, and held hands as they drove to the restaurant. When they pulled up, three valet drivers approached the vehicle. One to help Mia and one at Nicolas' side if he needed assistance, and the third took the keys and drove the truck to the parking garage.

Mia was in awe. The trees outside the restaurant were covered with small twinkling lights. The snow glistened from the lights on the tree. It was breathtaking.

Inside, the restaurant was decorated beautifully. There were Christmas trees decorated with red ornaments and red bows. The trees lined the hallway, which led to the dining area that had been reserved only for them.

There were tree branches covered in glitter, which were hung throughout the restaurant. Mia thought they were in the midst of a million twinkling stars as they walked down the hallway. They were led to a small dining room, where four beautifully decorated trees, stood in each corner of the room. The Christmas balls hanging from the tree were the color of her dress.

They sat down at the table. "Nico, this is beautiful." He said, "It's a special place, for a special day, and all for you Mia, the most special lady in all of my life." He leaned over and kissed her. The waiter brought them water, and asked what they would like to eat. Nicolas ordered salmon with asparagus and the garlic mashed potatoes. Mia asked for the same. They were brought salads and bread and wine was served.

They ate their meal and talked. When dinner was done, they were served poached pears in a white wine sauce garnished with a dollop of fresh whipped cream. Mia loved her dessert.

When they finished their dessert, the waiter came for their plates. The table was cleared except for their wine and water glasses. Nicolas ordered two espressos. When they brought the coffee, Nicolas placed his hand in his pocket. He pulled out a box covered in the same paper and ribbon he had wrapped the dress in.

He placed the box in front of Mia. Mia looked at him curiously. She smiled as she tilted her head. "Please open it," Nicolas said. She took the box and carefully removed the ribbon and then the wrapping paper. Inside was a black velvet box. Nicolas took the box from Mia. As he began to open it, he looked deeply into her eyes and said "Mia, will you be my wife? Mia smiled as he continued. "Mia, will you be mine forever?"

He had opened the small box and in the middle was a beautiful diamond engagement ring. The band was dainty like Mia's fingers and the stone sparkled with all the lights in the room. He took it from the box and placed it on her finger and kissed her lips.

Mia's eyes filled with tears and she reached for Nicolas. She held his face in her hands and stared into his beautiful eyes. Then she gently kissed him on the lips and said, "There is nothing more that I want than to be your wife, and yes Nicolas yes, I want to be together forever."

He pulled her close and kissed her deeply. "Mia, I love you more than I've loved anyone in my life." I will always love and protect you. And I promise to always make you smile." Mia smiled and said "Nico, I love you baby, I always have, since the very first moment I saw you on that street and I have many times felt, I loved you in another lifetime."

That night they went home and got into bed naked and held each other. They didn't talk, but the wonderful life they would spend together was on both their minds. They fell asleep to the sound of the wind blowing outside. It was calming and almost poetic and was the perfect ending to a beautiful day.

They spent Christmas alone at the cabin. They exchanged gifts and prepared a special meal of Cornish hens, stuffing, mashed potatoes, gravy and salad.   Mia prepared the meal with Nicolas' help. They followed the recipes Mia's grandmother had given her, which she had always prepared for their traditional Christmas meal since they moved to the United States.

Neither had ever been happier.   They felt so complete together.

They flew home on New Year's Eve.

When they arrived in Miami, Nicolas drove toward the beach. It was 10:30 p.m. and he wanted to start the next year with her in his arms, under the stars, watching fireworks.

He stopped at the grocery store and told her he'd be right out. He went in and bought cheese, fruit, bread, and a bottle of wine. They drove toward the beach and parked in a lot nearby then walked to a secluded spot on the beach. He had a blanket in his truck, which he took for them to sit on.

The fireworks in the sky lit the ocean up. It was beautiful.
But what was even more beautiful was, they were together
under the lights, and it was the start of a new year together.

Nicolas told her of a saying his parents taught him.   They
said, what you are doing on the first day of the year is what
you will continue to have throughout the year.   Nicolas
knew the only thing he couldn't live without was Mia.

When he finished telling her the story, Mia smiled,
because if the tradition was true, then Nicolas would be a
part of her life for the entire year… and every year after.
She knew this was how they would spend every first day
of the year, for the rest of their lives together.

They both knew this was only the beginning of their love
story.

CHAPTER X

The wedding was scheduled for April 1st.

Nicolas said he would take care of scheduling the place for the ceremony and for the reception. Mia would deal with the wedding details.

Nicolas had a friend who owned an older Mediterranean style home on the bay front. He thought it would be perfect for the wedding. It was private, and had a view of the bay and the city.   When he took Mia to see the residence, she also thought it was perfect for their special day. They walked out toward the dock and looked back at the house and had no doubt it was where the wedding should take place.

Mia decided on wine colored velvet dresses for her bridesmaids and a black tuxedo for the best man with wine colored accents. She was busy with the wedding planner, picking flowers and the decorations for the tented area, as well as deciding how the house would be decorated.

They went to a tasting with the caterers and decided on Spanish style tapas to start with and a choice of seafood paella or prime rib with small baked potatoes and grilled vegetables.

Mia and Nicolas chose the cake. It was a tiered alternating white and chocolate cake, filled with Bavarian cream and decorated with large ivory roses made of butter cream frosting.

It was beautiful and so delicious. The cake top they chose was a couple standing, holding hands, as they faced each other. She looked up into his eyes and he looked down. They thought it resembled them.

Mia had not chosen her dress yet and only had two months until the wedding. One morning, Mia called her grandmother and asked if she'd join her to look for wedding dresses. Her grandmother started crying on the phone and said, "Yes, my niña, I would love to. We can have lunch at our favorite place, and go dress hunting."

"Sounds wonderful Gram," Mia replied. "I'll pick you up tonight after work, we'll have dinner at Nico's with Nicolas, and you can spend the night so we can get an early start."

"I'll be ready, I love you and please be safe on the road, my niña." Ana said.

"I will Gram… see you soon." Mia replied.

Mia called Nicolas and told him of her plans. He asked if she wanted him to drive her there. Mia knew he was very busy and told him she'd be ok. She left from work and got to the farm close to 7:30. Her grandmother was ready with a small suitcase, which she had placed near the door.

Mia thought her grandmother was so beautiful. She was wearing a red dress with small white flowers, which fit her upper body snuggly. She wore a thin belt at her waist, the skirt flared out hanging just below her knees.

Mia admired her grandmother's sense of style. She reminded Mia of the sexy women in movies from the 50s and 60s, movies they often watched together. Her thick dark hair, graying on her temples, was pulled back and held together with a silver comb she had always worn. Two small strands of hair fell on the sides of her face framing it. She always wore a hint of red lipstick and also applied mascara to her long eyelashes, which made her big brown eyes look even bigger. She was a beautiful woman and when she smiled, a deep dimple appeared on her left cheek.

Mia smiled when she saw her and ran up to her and kissed her on both cheeks, as she always did. She hugged her tightly and said "Hi Gram… you look beautiful." "Thank you. So do you my Mia," she replied.

Her grandmother always called her My Mia, which was basically a bilingual oxymoron, as Mia always explained it, because "my" and "mia" meant the same in English and in Spanish.

Mia grabbed the suitcase and put it in the back seat of her car and they drove toward Miami. They talked and laughed. Mia told her all about the plans for the wedding. Her grandmother easily imagined everything as Mia described it all in such detail. She squeezed Mia's hand in hers and listened.

Ana was so happy Mia had found true love. She knew it was true when she first saw them look at each other. It reminded her of a love she had experienced, the love that would remain in her heart always. She smiled as she reminisced of a time so long ago, while looking out toward the open lands and listened to Mia.

When they arrived in Miami, they stopped at Mia's condo to drop off the suitcase and to freshen up. They drove over to the restaurant where Nicolas waited for them. The restaurant was unusually quiet. This allowed Nicolas to sit and have dinner without any interruptions.

They shared a thin crust pizza with tomatoes and mushrooms. They talked as they enjoyed their pizza. Antonio had also pulled up a chair and was talking to Ana, making her laugh. Mia and Nicolas watched them, quietly. Antonio always won over women, and Ana sat there looking quite intrigued by his stories.

The following morning, Ana and Mia were up early. Ana made coffee, cut up some fruit and made toast for breakfast. Nico ate quickly as he was rushing to open the restaurant that morning.

Ana and Mia left for the bridal shops. They went into three different stores on Miracle Mile in the Coral Gables area and found nothing. When they got to the fourth, it was a very small shop. Mia looked at her grandmother and asked, "I wonder if this is any good?" Ana shrugged her shoulders and said, "Let's give it a try. Sometimes the one you think will be the least appealing is where you find the magic."

When they walked in, there was a receptionist sitting at the front desk. The receptionist didn't make eye contact with

Mia or Ana.   Mia let her know they were there to see wedding dresses.   The receptionist was nervous.   She called over the intercom and a tall woman came out of the back room.   She looked nervous as well.   She asked Mia and her grandmother to follow her to the bridal room.

They followed her through a darkened corridor.   There were no pictures on the walls.   Mia looked at her grandmother and grabbed her hand as they walked down the long hall.

At the end of the corridor there were double doors made of metal.   As they got closer, the doors opened slowly, as if someone had been waiting for them.   There was a stage toward the back with four models wearing wedding dresses.   The models were breathtaking.   Two were identical twins with long braided black hair.   Another had red short hair and the fourth with hair the color of honey.

They were dressed in bridal dresses by designers from around the world.   Mia looked at her grandmother, and smiled.   Her grandmother winked at her and whispered, "They're beautiful."   They were all Spanish style wedding dresses made of lace, the attendant explained.   They were very sexy dresses, not the traditional Spanish wedding dresses which Ana remembered being more conservative.   She laughed to herself, thinking the wedding dresses were definitely from another era, but then again she hadn't gone wedding dress shopping for many years.

She reminisced of looking for her own wedding dress in Spain.   But what she remembered more was the sadness the day she found it. Mia began to talk and stirred Ana from the trance of her memories.

The dresses were beautiful. Mia loved them all. She told the woman, who had taken her in, she wanted to try each one on. The woman motioned to the models lifting her hand with four fingers up, referring to all 4 dresses needed, and they left the stage.

Within a few minutes, each model returned, dressed in matching black dresses. They carried the wedding dress design they had each worn. They stood at the attendant's side and she asked Mia to follow her to the dressing room. Mia did as she said, and Ana followed.

The four models stood outside the dressing area. The attendant gave Mia the first dress and let her know if she needed help, she would be there.

Mia put the dress on. It fit her body perfectly. It was cream colored. The neckline plunged low revealing her cleavage and the fullness of her breasts. It had cap sleeves and the small crystals throughout, had been hand sewn, the attendant explained. The crystals covered the bodice and trailed down along the a-line shape of the dress. The train was simple with a veiled layer over the Spanish lace. Mia placed the shoes on which were near the chair. They fit perfectly. She walked out of the dressing room. Her grandmother was astonished, and put her hand to her mouth as the gasp escaped from her slightly open mouth.

Mia stood in front of a 3-way mirror and looked at herself. She lifted the train and turned slowly.

She was so beautiful. The dress looked like it had been made especially for her. Mia looked at her grandmother with tears in her eyes then turned back toward the 3-way mirror. Mia said, "Gram, it's perfect. I don't need to try anything else on. This was made for me."

The attendant looked at the models and nodded her head. All, but the model, who carried the dress Mia chose, left the room in a single orderly line.

Mia looked at the attendant and said, "I'll take this one." She smiled at her grandma and said, "Everything is perfect. I have been so lucky to find everything I dreamt of. Nicolas is going to love it!"

"Mia, but you can't tell him about it. It's bad luck." "I know Gram," she replied. "I won't."

The attendant put the gown in a cream colored. velvet garment bag and handed it to Mia. Mia took her credit card from her wallet and handed it to the attendant. The attendant looked at Mia and said, "It has already been taken care of." Mia looked at her grandmother and Ana lifted her eyebrows in surprise. Mia winked and smiled, thinking Ana had arranged payment when she was in the dressing room. What Mia didn't know is, she hadn't.

Mia and her grandmother went to the condo and put the dress in the closet like the attendant told her to hang it as soon as she could and to make sure it was hung loosely, with no other clothing items near it, so it would not lose its shape.

Mia sat at the kitchen table and sighed. "It's done, Gram, everything is finished. The only thing left is the wedding."

Ana said, "It is going to be perfect, I know it my niña." Mia made a pot of coffee and they sat and watched an old movie, eating Mia's favorite cookies Ana had baked and packed to bring to Mia.

CHAPTER XI

March 31ˢᵗ…

Mia was in the bedroom of the guesthouse and Nicolas would spend the night in one of the bedrooms in the main house.

The master bedroom, where they would spend their first night as husband and wife, was on the second floor of the main house. The three story house had an attic at the top. The second floor had a balcony, which wrapped around the home. The third level had a terrace, which opened up toward the bay. The house was decorated beautifully. And, on the grounds, a tarp sheltered an area from the sun.

Mia looked out over the moonlit water as she brushed her hair.

The still boats on the water and the lights of the city seemed more like a painting. Miniature white lights lit up the grounds beautifully. Mia thought they looked like twinkling stars lighting up the night. The twinkling lights reminded her of the night Nicolas proposed. She loved the house that Nicolas had chosen. The home was built in the mid-1960s. The design was Spanish Mediterranean, similar to homes built in the 1940s. It was painted in a dark cream color and was accented with black wrought iron throughout. The windows were arched. Big strong columns supported the balcony overlooking the water. The house was beautiful.

Also, on the grounds was a gazebo made of crystal. The gazebo stood between the main house and the guesthouse. There was a stone walkway connecting the main house to the gazebo and the guesthouse, then led out toward the water, where a yacht was docked.

The arched windows and gazebo were also lit up with thousands of tiny lights. The house glowed under the exceptionally dark skies. Mia thought it looked like a scene from the Spanish fairy tale her grandmother often told her at bedtime.

Nicolas told Mia the gazebo was a small replica of a building called El Palacio de Cristal, which was located in Madrid, Spain. He went on to translate it to The Crystal Palace. Mia chuckled and told him she understood. Embarrassed, he laughed.

He told her the man who built the home, had lost the love of his life. They were to have been married in the Crystal Palace in Madrid. He told her, the man built the home and the small Crystal Palace in memory of the woman he loved. The man never married, and after many years of living in the home alone, he disappeared. No one knew what had become of him.

After his disappearance, the home was deeded to a family who knew the man. The family had been given a special deed, or guardianship of the home, stating the home could be lived in by the family or donated for special events. There was also a clause in the deed stating the gentleman, who had disappeared and who had not returned for the last 10 years, would remain the primary owner.

The family said they had befriended him during the time he was building the home. It was this family who Nicolas met when he opened his restaurant. He never quite understood the ownership legalities of the home. What he did know was it was used for many fund raising events he participated in.

No one lived in the home since the gentleman's disappearance. The family lived in a large home nearby and took full responsibility for the upkeep of the property. When Nicolas began to search for a place to have the wedding, the family offered the home to them, while they were having dinner at Nico's restaurant, one evening.

When Nicolas told Mia the story of the man who built the home, it saddened her. There had been so many love torn stories surrounding her. Like always, she feared more than anything, finding her love and someday losing him.

Tonight she forced herself not to think of the sad love stories in her life. Tonight was the beginning of a life she knew would make her the happiest woman on earth. And together with Nicolas, their life would be one of happiness and love, because she knew he loved her as much as she loved him. And together, with their children, they would accomplish their dreams.

Mia thought of the gazebo where they would be married. She knew it had been built because of a love so deep, and tomorrow night, they would be united under the full moonlit night, in this crystal palace, which signified love for the person who built it. Tomorrow, Mia thought, this beautiful crystal palace would be the place they would start their love life, together.

Mia knew their love was strong, and was convinced only happy events would follow since their wedding would be the first to take place there. She believed it, and knew it would be. She smiled as she thought of all the beautiful events which would take place after their wedding.

The guesthouse was quiet, Mia was alone She played soft music, and served herself a glass of water and added two slices of lemon to her glass. She wanted to get a good night's sleep. She washed her face and applied cream to her face, neck and eyes. She had to be perfect tomorrow.

She sat on a chair and looked outside. The water on the bay was calm. There were no boats at this time.

Mia sipped her glass of lemon water and became entranced by the still waters. The reflection of the guesthouse seemed to hover over the water in its stillness.

She concentrated on the reflection of the main house mirrored clearly on the calm waters. The lit windows glowed brightly in the darkness of the water. Then a small light toward the top of the house caught her attention and she quickly turned toward the house.

She wondered why all the lights were on and what the light in the attic was for. She thought it may be to light up the house for appearance, since they were going to be married there the following day.

Mia finished her water and went into the bathroom to brush her teeth. She looked at herself in the mirror and smiled and thought, "This is my very last night as a single woman." And, although the thought made her nervous, she knew from the moment she fell in love with Nicolas, she wanted to be his wife.

She went into the bedroom and took her phone from the dresser and called Nico. It rang three times and then she heard his voice.

"Hello," he said. He sounded out of breath Mia thought.

"What are you doing baby?" she asked.

"Nothing," he said, "Just doing a few sit ups. I have to be strong tomorrow." Mia laughed and asked, "Strong?" "Yeah" he said, "I have to carry you over the threshold, right?"

Mia laughed. She thought he was joking and said, "You're kidding right?" Nicolas, still out of breath, laughed and said, "Baby, I have to be my best for you."

Mia shook her head and said, "Baby, don't stress. You're already the best. The best man for me, I could not have found a better man. Never forget that, ok?"

Nico said, "Mia, you know I love you right?"

Mia pursed her lips and nodded confidently.

"With all my heart and soul, right?" he continued.

Mia said, "Yes, my love, with everything, I know you love me. And you too, know that I love you, right?"

"Yeah baby, with everything," he replied.

"Mia," he said. Then hesitated, "Sometimes, I wonder how someone could love someone so much. Sometimes, I love you so much it hurts. Like tonight, I can't stop thinking of you. I want to be with you so bad, in this beautiful house, just you and me. I hate being away from you, even though you are only a few steps away from me, it's killing me that I can't go to you."

Mia said, "I know baby... I know how hard it hurts. But Nico, please let's promise each other something tonight."

"What's that Mia?" he asked.

"To always be there for each other, to do everything in our power to keep our love alive," she replied.

Nicolas said, "Mia, don't worry, that's going to be the least of our worries, because it will be the easiest thing to do."

Mia said, "Seriously. Promise me."

Nico said, "I promise beautiful, I promise!"

"Ok, baby, lets get some sleep. I'm exhausted and I know you are too. I'll miss you in my arms tonight," Nicolas said.

"Me too," Mia said. "Sleep tight baby. I love you." Nicolas replied, "I love you too. Sweet dreams my love. Muaaa. Muaaa."

Mia blew him kisses over the phone, then hung up and went to the window and closed the curtains. She left the door open so the cool breeze from the bay would enter.

Mia got into bed. Her mind wandered. She began to go through the things that needed to be done then rolled over to get her phone from the nightstand where she had everything noted. She double checked her list, turned off the phone and placed it back on the table.

The city was quiet, as though it were sleeping. Although Mia knew Miami never slept.

She closed her eyes and within minutes she was asleep.

CHAPTER XII

Mia woke up early, before the sun came up. She was nervous and anxious. The wedding wouldn't start until 7:00 pm. How would she keep calm until then, she wondered. She got up from bed and filled a cup with water and put it into the microwave in the small kitchenette next to the bedroom.

She dipped a bag of tila tea in the hot water and swished it around. Tila tea was commonly used in Spain for relaxation. Her grandmother always had it on hand and Mia recalled the first time she had it. It was after her parents died. Her grandmother prepared the tea before bedtime so she would sleep well. Sleeping became a problem for her for months after she lost her parents, and tila became a nightly ritual.

Mia added two small spoons full of sugar and stirred till the sugar dissolved. She walked out to the small patio where there were lounge chairs with big fluffy pillows and sat on one facing the house. She looked toward the house and all lights were out except for the one in the attic. She wondered who would be in the attic at this time.

Mia felt uneasy and went into the bedroom, closed the door behind her and pulled the drapes closed. She went to the side of the room and stood by the window slightly opening the curtain and looked toward the house. The light in the attic was still the only light on in the house. She reached over and turned the light out, then again peeked out toward the house, looking directly at the attic window and saw the silhouette of a person in the illuminated window. Someone was in the attic! She pushed herself away from the window, hoping whoever was there, had not seen her.

She stood still and pulled the curtain slightly away from the wall and stared up at the house, wondering who would be awake this early. Suddenly, the light in the attic went out. Mia continued peeking out at the house, wondering if whoever had been in the attic, was now going down to another part of the house. The house remained dark.

Mia began to worry. She hated being alone when she felt like this. She began to hum her song and lay down on the bed, covering herself with a light blanket, as she thought of the silhouette in the attic window. The tea she drank made Mia drowsy and soon she was asleep.

Mia woke later to the sound of the crews getting the wedding area ready.

She took a quick shower, and called her grandmother who had slept in the main house. "Gram, where is Nico?"

"He is out with the crews making sure they get everything right," Ana replied.

Mia asked, "So, if I go to the main house, he might see me?"

Ana replied, "Uh hum! Mia, I am making breakfast, I'll have someone take you a tray and then I'll be over when I am done here."Mia agreed.

Not long after she hung up, she heard a tap at the window. She saw a young man she didn't know, standing there with a tray filled with her breakfast. She opened the door, he entered and placed the tray on the small table near the door. Mia thanked him and he left.

Mia took the bowl of fruit out to the patio and sat and ate her breakfast while watching the boats cruise by. "I love this view," she thought, "it's so peaceful and quiet, even though we're in the middle of the city. I would sure love to live here and come out here every morning."

Mia heard footsteps and turned to see her grandmother turn the corner and enter the patio. Her grandmother had a cup of coffee in her hand. Mia stood up and kissed her and said "Buenos dias, Gram."

"Good Morning my niña," she replied and sat next to Mia on the sofa where she was sitting.

"So, tell me, how are you feeing today? It's your special day," Ana asked.

"I'm nervous Gram, so very nervous. I want to go upstairs to the room and make sure I have everything ready. I think we need to send Nicolas out on an errand so I can sneak up to the room."

Ana laughed and said, "I'll arrange it, give me an hour, but until then, is there anything I can bring down for you?"

"No, I brought everything I need, I'm just feeling anxious and have cabin fever, just knowing I can't go up there and I have to remain hidden here."

Ana listened to Mia talk nervously about all she needed to do before the wedding. Ana watched her, remembering the day Mia's parents were married and how nervous her father was. Mia's nervous rambling, reminded her so much of him. She did not want Mia to know what she was thinking. She knew she would spoil her happy mood if she mentioned it. What Ana was feeling today was a deep sadness knowing Mia's parents couldn't be here to share this special day with their beautiful daughter. Ana knew they would be so proud of her and happy for the man she had chosen to be her husband.

Ana's eyes filled with tears. Mia noticed and said, "Gram, what's wrong?"

Ana replied, "It's just your special day, and I'm so proud of you my Mia."

Mia kissed her and nervously giggled as she choked up a small cry and said, "I can't cry today!" She fanned her face with her hand quickly, "I won't have swollen eyes in my wedding pictures."

Ana sat up straight, and said, "Yes, the wedding pictures." She wiped her eyes of the tears and kissed Mia on the cheek and said, "I'll call you as soon as it's safe to go up."

"Deal!" Mia said, "Thanks, Gram," and placed her open hand toward her grandmother so she could high-five her.

Ana returned the gesture, high-fiving her then grasping her hand and kissing it. Ana laughed as she walked away realizing that raising Mia had brought so much life to her world, after losing her son.

About half hour later, the phone rang and it was Ana. "It's safe now, you can go up. Nicolas is in the shower."

Mia grabbed the things she would need and ran up two flights of the outdoor staircase to the master bedroom suite.

The bedroom was rounded. The balcony outside the bedroom was also rounded, completing the shape of the bedroom. The king sized bed made of heavy wrought iron was covered with a dark silver bedspread that fell freely onto the floor.

A canopy of light silver airy chiffon hung to the floor at all four corners. The bed was at the far end of the room. It was positioned this way so whoever slept in the bed, could look out onto the open waters through the tall glass windows without leaving the bed.

The tall windows were covered with long cream colored transparent curtains. They fell onto the floor in the same fashion the bedspread covered the area around the bed.

The cool wind from the bay blew in and moved the curtains in a whimsical way.

Ana was waiting for Mia in the room when she arrived.

She grabbed the long curtains and secured them on the hooks at the edge of each window. They were draped perfectly. Mia admired the romantic setting as she looked out onto the gardens and over the bay.

It was 11:00 a.m. Mia wanted to arrange her things, and told her grandmother she would start getting ready at 5:00. She also said she wanted to take a long bath, condition her hair, and just relax.

"I'm going down to the kitchen area to see if everything is ok and also to check on the caterers. They should be here at 3:00 to start setting up. Don't you worry about a thing. Everything is going to be perfect, Mia."

"I know, I have no doubt Gram," Mia replied.

Mia turned on the TV as her grandmother left the room. The television sometimes calmed her. She changed the channel to a series based on a 1950s ad agency she often watched. She went into the bathroom and applied a cucumber mask to her face, then sat on the large chair at the side of the bed and watched her movie.

Mia flipped through the photos on her iPad and listened to her show in the background, while the mask on her face dried. She looked at the photos of herself with Nicolas. The photos were from the time they first met. The photos were of days on the beach to nights out on the town. She stopped at one they took of themselves near the Christmas tree at the auction.

Mia spread her fingers over the screen and amplified the photo, and looked at the crowd. She remembered the strange gentleman. She flipped through other photos of that evening and then came upon one where she noticed the faint image of the gentleman. He was standing at the top of the stairs behind them in the photo.

Chills ran down her spine and she turned off the iPad and pushed it away. She relaxed deeper into the big chair and watched her show until it ended, then went into the bathroom and started the bath water. While the tub filled, she stood in front of the mirror and carefully peeled the mask from her face. She always tried to remove it in the perfect shape of her face and today it came off perfectly. She placed it on the sink and would later show Nicolas since this was the first time in many tries she successfully pulled it off in one piece.

Mia poured lemon bubble bath into the water and watched the bubbles form, leaving a pillowy layer at the top of the water. The tub was big and had a Jacuzzi, which she knew would relax her. She took her clothes off and got into the water then lay back in the tub and soaked. Her eyes closed as she imagined the way her day would be. She pushed her head back against the pillow that was attached to the tub and relaxed. She turned the Jacuzzi on and let it massage her body gently as she dozed off thinking of her beautiful day.

It hadn't been more than 30 minutes when she heard the laughter of children, which woke her suddenly. She washed her hair quickly and shaved her legs. She got out of the tub and applied her lemon lotion to her body. She knew Nicolas loved the scent of her lemon lotion. She grabbed the bottle of argon oil from the counter and poured just a small amount into the palm of her hand, applying it sparingly to her hair. This made her hair shiny and controlled the frizz in the humidity of Miami. Mia brushed her teeth and put on a black airy sundress.

She walked into the bedroom where the curtains were blowing with the slight breeze. She walked toward the center of the room and twirled slowly. "It's so beautiful," she thought. She walked around the big bed running her fingertips along the edges of the furniture that lined the walls and imagined herself with Nicolas. She couldn't wait to be together with him in their honeymoon suite.

Just then the phone rang. It was her grandmother. Ana asked, "Are you getting ready?" Mia said, "I fell asleep in the tub and now I'm rushing." Ana assured Mia she had time and didn't have to rush. She had three hours before the wedding.

Ana said, "I'll be up in about 45 minutes to an hour. I'm going to finish getting ready and then I'm going to talk to the caterers. I saw them when they came in and everything looks perfect. They have some things in the ovens and it smells delicious." Mia smiled.

"Ok, Gram, I'm going to start putting on my make up while my hair dries. It always comes out better when I let it air dry and today, it has to be perfect."

Mia sat on the bed and began to apply her make up as her hair dried. A friend of Mia's who was a make up artist was coming in to help her, but Mia always did a few things to her eyelashes. She would leave the eye shadows and final touches to her friend.

She heard a knock at the door. Mia turned to see Nicolas' mother, Sofia, and her grandmother enter the room. They were dressed in their beautiful Bordeaux colored dresses. Mia gasped and said, "You both look so beautiful."

Ana's dress hugged her body at the top and flared out at the waist. Nicolas' mother, Sofia, wore a wrap dress which was straight cut and fit her slender body perfectly. They were gorgeous. They had chosen the same color and had done everything via internet camera, since Sofia lived in Spain. Mia said they had done a wonderful job getting their dresses to match perfectly.

Suddenly, Mia heard the children playing in the gardens.

Nicolas' niece and two nephews had come with their parents from Spain. The boys were David and Andres, and the darling little girl, with curls that hung to the middle of her back, was Feliciana. Mia loved being around them, and she had only known them for two days. They were friendly, and very inquisitive. The boys, already in their suits, were chasing Feliciana in her satin, cream colored dress.

Mia walked toward the window to see what they were doing and she gasped when she saw them.

Nicolas' mother, Sofia, saw Mia's reaction and she noticed the children. Just as she was about to call out their names,

Nicolas ran out and scooped Feliciana up into his arms and told the boys to follow him into the house. They did as he said. Pushing and pulling each other playfully, they followed him into the house. Nicolas' mother said, my grandchildren are rather playful. Mia laughed and nodded her head in agreement.

Just then, Sofia saw Nicolas turn his head, looking up toward the balcony, as he walked toward the house. "It's Nicolas," she said and quickly took Mia by the arm and stepped back, pulling her away from the window so Nicolas and Mia would not see each other.

Although Mia did not believe in superstitions, especially the bad ones, she was relieved. She turned toward Sofia and smiled and said, "Thank you, thank you," then tightly hugged her in appreciation. Mia was not going to let this or anything ruin her day and was glad Sofia had pulled her away from the window.

Mia turned and walked toward the dressing table where she had placed her make-up and pins for her hair. The dressing table was a full size mirror with a silver frame and the table was placed in front of it. The bench in front of the mirror was upholstered in silver velvet.

Ana sat on the chair next to the bed. She stared at Mia's reflection in the mirror, while lost in thought. Sadness covered her face. Mia looked at her grandmother through the mirror and wondered what she was thinking. Mia watched her grandmother and remembered the look on her face. It was a look that was very familiar to Mia. She hadn't seen it for a while, but saw it often when she was a little girl.

Mia remembered her grandmother always looked this way when she told Mia the sad love story of a man and woman who had fallen deeply in love and because of circumstances beyond their control, they could never be together. Mia always thought it was just another fairy tale, like all the others her grandmother told her. But not until Mia was older did she realize her grandmother told this story with much more emotion than any of the other fairy tales she told.

Her grandmother never told her what the circumstances were or where the story came from, but Mia often wondered if the story was about her grandmother and someone she had always loved or someone she may have known very well. Mia had never asked her grandmother that question but someday soon she would. But, only when the time was right.

Mia then said, "I love you, Gram," and blew her a kiss through the mirror. Ana was stirred from her memories, and stared blankly forward, then blew a kiss to Mia, almost trancelike.

Then she walked over to Mia and put her hand on her shoulder and said, "Thank you for this beautiful day. I love you my niña and you deserve this day and every day from here on out to be as beautiful as you are, as beautiful as the two of you, together, are. You have found the love of your life and together, I know, you will build a beautiful and happy life. My dear, I have seen the way you two look at each other. And I know the type of love you feel for each other. It is a love that will last your lifetimes, and many lifetimes to come."

Ana turned her head quickly.   Tears had filled her eyes as she talked to Mia and she did not want Mia to see her cry. She turned toward the mirror and Mia saw her reflection. "Gram, don't be sad," she said. "I now realize the story you told me when I was a little girl, the story of a deep love lost was about someone you knew."

Ana smiled, but did not confirm what Mia said. She immediately stood a little straighter and primped her hair while looking at her reflection in the mirror. Ana took a tube of lipstick from her evening bag and applied it to her smiling lips and said, "Mia, this is your day, your day of celebration. There is no time for tears of sadness. The only tears today will be tears of joy."

Ana straightened her dress and confidently walked toward the door while stating, "I want to see the camera man. He should be here taking photos of your private moments before the ceremony.   I'm going to find him and I'll be right back." Her tone was joyful, yet a bit exaggerated. Mia curiously watched her disappear behind the door.

Within minutes Ana returned with the cameraman, both laughing as they entered the room.

Ana began directing the cameraman. Mia chuckled to herself and thought her grandmother was surely in charge. The cameraman began to take photos of everyone in the room. Four-year-old Feliciana, the flower girl had come up and was keeping everyone entertained. She sang songs and twirled around in her beautiful little dress. She stomped her feet on the hard wood floor, as the music spilled into the room from the gardens.

CHAPTER XIII

The room was filled with chatter from the women busy with the last touchups to their hair and to their make up.

Mia quietly walked out onto the balcony and closed the door behind her. She wanted to be alone for a few moments. She wanted to speak silently to her parents, as she always did before one of her big events or accomplishments. She stood in the center of the balcony, opened her arms widely and looked out toward the water.

"Mama, Papa," she said, "Please watch over Nicolas and me, today and everyday as we spend our lives together. Pray for us to have the love that the two of you had for each other, a love so strong, where nothing can separate us. I love you both, and I miss you. I know it was the two of you who watched over me, and led me to Nicolas, someone so special, someone who you would have loved as a son."

"I know you are here with me tonight and I know you are proud of me, and as Gram walks with me, I know you both will also be at my side. I love you mama and papa, and I miss you both with all my heart."

The tears began to run from her eyes… and she laughed, then said, "Mama, Papa, I'm not supposed to cry." She fanned her eyes and looked to the sky and blew a kiss into the air, whispering softly, "I love you." She closed her eyes and slowly turned. Mia straightened her shoulders and stood tall, regaining her composure, she confidently returned to the room.

Everyone was silent as she entered. She smiled, and said, "Why's everyone so quiet? It's time to get this party started." They all began to clap and little Feliciana began to dance around the floor again. Everyone laughed, which made Feliciana dance a little faster.

Sofia picked Feliciana up and said, "slow down my darling, you will tire yourself for your walk down the isle." Feliciana looked at her curiously and struggled to free herself from her grandmother's arms.

Mia, her grandmother, her Maid of Honor and bridesmaid were in the dressing room getting ready. The wedding was to begin in one hour. Mia's makeup artist applied a few more coats of mascara to her long eyelashes, brushed on another coat of the soft pink lipstick, then applied a thin coat of lip gloss.

Mia's hair was pinned up and held up by a sterling silver comb that had been her great grandmother's. Her mother and grandmother had also worn the comb for their weddings. This signified something borrowed.
Long strands of hair fell over her shoulders and down her back.

Mia put her dress on behind an old Victorian dressing screen. She had a pin of blue birds her grandmother had given her when she was little, and pinned it to her bra strap. She wore it to signify something blue.

Behind the dressing screen was a mirror. Mia was able to dress in front of the mirror. Everyone impatiently waited for her to appear from behind the screen.

Mia was ready. She stood in front of the mirror and touched her dress, running her hands, from her breast area, slowly downward. She stared at herself and smiled. She was so happy and knew Nicolas was going to love seeing her in the beautiful dress she had chosen. The dress, Mia knew from the moment she tried it on, was made especially for her.

She walked out from behind the dressing screen and walked toward the 3-way mirror in the corner of the room. She stood there for a few seconds looking at herself from head to toe, then turned toward everyone with her hands outstretched, and said, "So? Tell me? How do I look?"

Ana and Sofia reached for the other's hand and their eyes filled with tears at the sight of Mia. She was so beautiful.

No one said anything, as Mia stood there and smiled. "Someone say something," she said. Mia's grandmother said, "My dear, sweet Mia, you are the most beautiful bride I have ever seen. Your mother and father would be so happy."

Mia took her veil from the hanger at the side of the mirror and sat on the bench. She looked toward her grandmother and soon to be mother in law and said, "Would you both, please do me the honor and help me with my veil?" Ana and Sofia quickly and nervously approached Mia to help her with the sheer veil she had chosen.

She was breathtaking.

Mia stood up and took another look at herself in the mirror. She turned toward everyone, opened her eyes widely and said, "I am sooooo nervous." She began to laugh as she anxiously waved her hands.

Everyone laughed with her, as they too, were a bit nervous and knew what she must be feeling.

Ana offered her hand to Mia and she took hold of it and squeezed it. Ana led Mia out to the balcony. She handed Mia a small box. Mia looked at her grandmother and her eyes filled with tears. "Mia, please don't cry, you will mess up your make up." Mia laughed and said, "Gram, I love you so much." Mia remembered not long ago, she had her grandmother promise she would not let her cry on the day of her wedding so her make up wouldn't be ruined and so all the photos of the special day would be perfect.

Ana, kissed her and said, "Go ahead, open it." Mia opened the small box and inside the box was a necklace. The necklace matched the ring Ana had given her many years before. A round, deep red ruby sat in the same antique silver setting as the ring and hung on a delicate silver chain that sparkled. Ana said, "Something old," and she smiled.

Mia had never seen the necklace before, and it matched the ring perfectly. She knew it had to be a set with the ring Ana had given her a few years before on her birthday.

Ana told Mia, "Now all you need is something new."

Mia remembered the gift on the table next to the bed. It was a box wrapped in white satin material, which was not typical wrapping paper. Mia knew it was from Nicolas. He told her, he wanted to give her something new. Mia reminded her grandmother about it and they returned to the room. Mia picked up the gift from the table and began to open it. Inside the wrapping was a teal colored box. Mia knew exactly where Nicolas had bought it.

In the box was a diamond bracelet. "Oooooh, this is perfect," she whispered and looked at her grandmother and smiled. "Gram, help me please." She put out her arm and handed the bracelet to her grandmother. All the women in the room gathered to see her gift. It was a delicate bracelet of diamonds attached by slender pieces of antique silver. It was so dainty it could barely be seen. It was beautiful and matched her wedding ring perfectly.

Mia stood in front of the mirror admiring her bracelet. She was suddenly startled and turned quickly as one of her friends peeked into the room and without any warning said, "They're ready!"

Mia inhaled deeply and said, "I am ready too, let's do this!" Mia grabbed her grandmother's hand and they walked into the rounded corridor that led to an open door. Mia felt the breeze at it entered from the open doors.

They walked through the door that lead onto a balcony and walked toward the outdoor staircase. The view was breathtaking and the weather was perfect, Mia thought.

The city lights in the distance began to appear on the bay waters as the sun began to set, and as the sky turned orange. Mia could not be happier.

Mia stood outside for a minute and breathed in deeply. She closed her eyes and looked toward the sky and whispered, "Thank you," then walked toward the staircase.

Everyone took their place ahead of Mia.

Mia stayed back, so Nicolas would not see her until everyone had reached the bottom. She had planned it this way. She wanted him to see only her. She wanted to give him something he would always remember.

Today, their first day as man and wife would forever remain in their memory. And every detail, she had planned, had to be special and perfect. Just like she did everything else she did.

The music began to play. Everyone was quiet.

The stairs led to a small path lit with candles, which led to the crystal palace.

The bridesmaid began to walk holding Feliciana's hand until they reached the bottom. She let go of her hand, and bent down to tell Feliciana she could now begin throwing the rose petals. The Maid of Honor followed behind Feliciana, who had the crowd entertained with her innocence and dainty mannerisms as she gently tossed the rose petals from her basket.

When Mia approached the edge of the balcony, she heard the "ahhs" of the crowd below. Mia smiled and looked toward her grandmother and whispered "I am so happy, Gram, look at Nico, he is so handsome."

Ana stayed behind Mia so she would be the only thing Nicolas would see at the top of the stairs. She then took Mia by the arm to accompany her down the stairs, and said, "Yes he is! Very handsome indeed," Ana squeezed Mia's hand tightly and they began to walk.

They walked down the wide stairs, slowly. Mia and Ana held hands as they walked. Mia was nervous and fought off the tears that began to form in her eyes.

Nicolas, his brother Ramon, and Antonio all stood tall and looked so handsome. David and Andres nudged each other nervously.

As Mia and her grandmother walked down the stairs slowly, Mia looked into Nicolas' eyes. Their eyes locked. He looked at her the way he always had, with such intensity.

Nicolas thought, "There is no other woman more beautiful than Mia, and she will soon be my wife." Tears began to fill his eyes and he smiled.

When they reached the bottom of the stairs, Ana let go of Mia's hand and made her way to the front of the church to watch Mia walk down the isle. Mia stood at the entrance until their song began to play. Then she began walking toward the love of her life, Nicolas.

Mia walked down the rose petal covered isle. She walked slowly, her dress flowing behind her. Her veil gently lifted with the breeze from the bay, as she approached Nicholas.

Mia and Nicolas were lost in each other's stare as she walked. And, although the distance between them was filled with friends and family, it was just the two of them. Everyone around them had disappeared. Mia tilted her head, as she so often did when she felt that deep feeling of love and security he made her feel. Nicolas had always loved the childlike look that came upon her face when he knew she was happy.

Mia saw the intensity on his face as she got closer. His eyes were magical and told her she was the most beautiful woman in the world, to Nicolas, and she knew he would forever love her.

She walked slowly, staring into his eyes, never losing eye contact with the man she loved. Ana met Mia before she reached the altar and took her hand as they walked toward Nicolas. Ana kissed Mia on the cheek and said, "May you live happily always. I love you my niña," then placed Mia's hand into Nicolas' hand and said, "She is yours, love her forever."

Nicolas bent forward and kissed Ana on her cheek and said "Never worry, I will protect her and make her happy always, thank you, Ana, for allowing me to marry the woman of my dreams." He looked at Mia, who was smiling at him, and bent forward and kissed her gently on the lips. As he gripped her hands tightly, she moved to stand facing him.

At that moment, he saw in Mia's eyes, a love, so pure. A love, which could only come from the depths of her soul. At that moment he knew she was giving herself to him entirely and what he saw was the love he felt for her reflected. He knew she loved him more than anything. And, he knew he would never hurt her and would forever love her.

The preacher began...

"We are gathered here today to witness the joining of two people.

Nicolas Diaz and Mia Martinez.

We have come together to witness the union of a love, which began only a few months ago, but know will last a lifetime and beyond. Destiny brought them together to share a life of love and happiness always.

On this special day, they would like to recite their vows."

"Nicolas," the preacher said, and motioned so he would begin.

Nicolas squeezed Mia's hands and began…

"Mia, I've heard stories of love at first sight. I now know what that means, because on the first day I saw you, I loved you.

Every day since that day I have loved you more.
You have filled my life with smiles, and with happiness,
You have made me complete.
I want to take you by the hand, and lead you through a life
of happiness
Be my lover, my best friend, my wife, my everything.
So on this day, I promise I will forever love you,
And, will forever make you smile.
Mia, today, I am yours."

Mia bit on her lower lip then smiled, as her eyes filled with tears. She put her head down to regain her composure, then looked up at Nicolas as she began to recite her vows.

"Nico, my love, my lover, my friend,
When I began to write my vows I had so much to say, but didn't know how to put it all together because what I feel is more than words can express.
Nicolas, my Nico
Today I promise to love you
For as long as my heart beats
I promise to be yours
For all of eternity
I promise to make you smile
Until my very last breath
And after that
I will love you forever
Because in you I found
The part of me that I had, for so long, been searching for.
Nicolas, my soulmate, my everything... you complete me.
I am yours."

Nicolas wrapped his arm around her waist and pulled her into him. Just then Nicolas felt a nudge at his leg, it was David, pushing the rings toward him. The crowd began to laugh and Nicolas stooped down and thanked David, taking the pillow with the rings from him. He gave the pillow to Mia. She held it while he untied the rings. He returned the pillow to David and then looked into Mia's eyes and as he placed the ring on her finger, he said, "With this ring, I am yours." She smiled and took Nicolas' hand and placed the ring on his finger and said, "And with this ring, I am yours."

The priest quickly said, "By the power vested in me, I now pronounce you man and wife."

They began to kiss and the crowd went wild with applause and loud whistles.

They kissed for what seemed like minutes then realized they were in front of their guests and families. They turned to the crowd and Nicolas laughingly said, "Sorry, we forgot you were here." The crowd laughed and applauded the couple loudly.

The priest then said: "Family and friends, I present to you Mr. and Mrs. Diaz."

The crowd began to applaud and shout as Nicolas and Mia walked down the isle, holding hands.

The crowd followed them into the larger area of the crystal gazebo. It was decorated beautifully. Each table was covered with cream colored tablecloths, and each had a vase filled with calla lilies which surrounded candles at the base of each centerpiece.

The tall backed chairs were covered with cream satin covers and were tied with wide maroon ribbons. The tableware was cream with silver etching.

The wedding party and the guests all sat down. The tapas were brought out on platters and placed on every table. People began to eat and chatter as they ate slowly.

Red Sangria, White Peach Sangria, sweet tea and a white fruit punch for the children, were served

After the tapas were eaten. Dinner was brought out. Nicolas and Mia both had paella. They ate slowly and laughed and talked with their guests. Antonio, being the loudest in the group, talked about the time after Mia and Nicolas met. Everyone laughed as he described Nicolas as a lovesick puppy.

The crowd buzzed. Everyone enjoyed dinner, and when dinner was done, the band outside began to play. The bride and groom walked through the wide door into the area where they had recited their vows. Tables had been placed around a dance floor, which was installed while they ate. The music played loudly and everyone began to dance.

When it was time for the first toast, Ramon got up, since he was Nicolas' best man. He thanked Mia for taking his brother off his back. And the crowd burst into laughter. Nicolas just shook his head and chuckled.

Then it was Antonio's turn. He began by telling Mia that in the beginning he didn't want her taking his club partner away from him, but he got over it when he saw how happy she made his brotha. He then thanked Nicolas for taking himself off the market and leaving the ladies for him.   The crowd laughed at his humor.

Mia's best friend, Lauren, got up and quickly wished the couple a happily ever after. Then Nicolas' sister, Andrea, got up, and emotionally asked Mia to please take care of her baby brother. She cleared her throat and confidently stated she had no doubt Mia would. She thanked her for making her brother happy and was so happy to feel the love that spilled from them.

After the toasts, the crowd spilled onto the dance floor enjoying the modern dance music, most with a tropical beat typical to Miami, to traditional music from Spain.

At midnight, a bell was rung and the bride and groom were taken to a place at the end of the dance floor where the presents had been gathered. The card box was filled with cards and there were a few presents on the table and a large gift leaned against the wall.

Mia and Nicolas were told to open the presents and they could open the cards later.   Mia's grandmother began, "This one is from me!" as she handed them a box wrapped beautifully in dark maroon paper with small black ribbons. Mia and Nicolas looked at her and she smiled. She clenched their hands tightly and kissed them both then stood back and watched them as they opened their gift.

In the box was the deed to the condo apartment she owned in Spain. Mia excitedly said, "Grandma... it's my dream! Thank you, I love you." She stood up and hugged her grandmother tightly, then kissed her on the cheek. Her grandmother's eyes filled with tears. Mia said, "Don't cry Gram, we're all going to live happily every after, I promise." Nicolas kissed Ana on her check and thanked her for the special gift. Ana smiled and quickly wiped a tear that ran down her face.

Nicolas then opened a few other gifts, a juicer, crystal glassware, a 'his & her' package for a day at the spa, and a weekend stay at a hotel in the Florida Keys from Antonio. The last present remained, where someone had leaned it against the wall. Mia said, "We can't forget this." Antonio walked over to the wall for the gift and placed it in front of Nicolas.

Mia looked for the tag on the gift to see who had given it to them and couldn't find one. She asked, "Who is this from?" and looked into the crowd for the person who had brought the gift. No one answered. Nicolas laughed and said, "It must be a surprise." Mia smiled and looked at him curiously, thinking it had to be Nicolas, up to another of his surprises.

She began to carefully tear the paper from the gift. Under the paper was a scarlet colored velvet covering. Nicolas stood up and untied the black cord, which held the covering closed at the top. The covering slowly fell to the ground and Mia gasped.

It was a painting of the little girl in a white nightgown dancing under the moon and stars. It was the painting, which had been won by the bidder at the charity event. Mia's face turned pale and she suddenly reached for Nicolas.

Nicolas said, "Hey, the guy must have known you really wanted it," and laughed. Mia said, "No!" and looked at her grandmother. Her grandmother placed her hand to her mouth and shook her head slowly as she recalled Mia telling her of what happened the night of the auction.

Mia then instinctively looked out toward the water, and saw on the yacht, silhouetted by the city lights, a man, standing on the upper deck, who so closely resembled the man who had won the bid. She gasped.

"Nicolas, look, it's him," Mia said excitedly as she pointed toward the yacht. Nicolas turned toward the direction where she pointed and saw only the yacht. She pulled Nicolas close and said, "Never leave me, promise me." Nicolas said, "Don't worry mi amor, I promise I will never leave you."

Ana looked worried for she too had seen the man on the boat and remembered how Mia had described him. Mia looked at her grandmother. Ana avoided eye contact with Mia by putting her head down. She didn't want to worry Mia more because she also felt something was not right. Mia wondered why her grandmother had reacted so strangely and wondered if she knew something, but what? What could it be? Who could this man possibly be?

Nicolas yelled out, "What about the cake, I'm starving! And, I need to take my wife on a honeymoon." The crowd clapped loudly and began chanting "Cake, Cake, Cake." Everyone laughed as they neared the table where the cake was displayed.

The cake top and first layer were taken off and placed on the side to be enjoyed by Nicolas and Mia on their first anniversary. The cake was cut and served with small cups of coffee and small glasses of sweet liqueur. The guests mingled as they enjoyed the delicious cake.

It was a beautiful event. Everything had turned out perfectly, just as Mia and Nicolas had planned. Everyone was having a great time dancing, but Mia was worried. Why had this painting been given to them on their wedding day? She had to meet the man who did this and find out why he gave them the painting. What were his intentions, she wondered. Nicolas saw the look on her face and told her not to worry, he reassured her it was nothing and all he wanted was this day to be perfect for her.

At 2 a.m., everyone gathered to see Mia and Nicolas off, although, they were only leaving to their honeymoon suite in the grand house. Mia and Nicolas thanked their guests and walked up the steps to their suite.

As they walked up to the room, their guests shouted well wishes. When they got to the top, they turned and waved good-by and blew kisses to the crowd. The crowd clapped loudly and yelled, "Que vivan los novios!" and "Long live the happy couple!"

The crowd danced awhile longer until the band played no more. Everyone mingled after the music stopped then gradually began to leave.

After the guests had gone, Mia's grandmother went to her room and Nicolas' family went to their rooms. Everyone was exhausted.

Nicolas and Mia had been sitting on the balcony watching the moon and the water. Mia said, "The room is so romantic. Nico, you picked a perfect place for our wedding." Nicolas smiled and nodded in agreement.

During the wedding reception, the room had been cleaned and candles were lit throughout. The balcony was also lined with small white candles flickering with the breeze. The small white lights, which were hung around the arches and along the windows, lit the area romantically.

Nico pulled Mia to him and said, "May I have this dance my beautiful wife?" Mia said, "Yes, my love," and placed out her hand for Nicolas to take hold of it. They held each other closely. Nicolas began to hum and they danced under the moon. Mia looked up at his face illuminated by the moon. How could she ask for anything more, she thought. Everything had been perfect.

When Nicolas stopped humming they stopped dancing and stood under the moon. Mia looked up at him and he took her face, which lit up under the moonlit sky, into his hands and kissed her gently on the lips. She wrapped her arms around him and began to kiss him passionately.

Mia looked deeply into his eyes and said "Nico, I love you." Nicolas replied, "Mia, I have always loved you, from the very first moment I set eyes on you and I will never stop loving you." She kissed him and they stood there, slowly swaying and holding each other closely.

Suddenly, Nicolas scooped her up into his arms and said, "I have to carry you over the threshold my beautiful wife." Mia wrapped her arms around his neck and said, "Yes, you surely do, my dear handsome husband, that's what all those push ups were for, right?"

Mia held on tightly and as he carried her into the bedroom, she looked up toward the attic window. There was a light on in the room. It seemed to be a candle. She wondered who was there and hugged Nicolas tighter.

Nicolas carried Mia to the middle of the room and gently let her down. Mia then asked Nicolas to unzip her dress. He slowly did as she asked, taking in every part of her body as the dress opened up exposing her beautiful body. She was wearing a lace, cream colored bra with matching panties and a garter belt that held her thigh high stockings in place.

Nicolas ran his hands over her body slowly and began to kiss her neck. He kissed his way downward as her dress fell to the floor. Mia stood there running her fingers along Nicolas' arms as he dropped to his knees. He pressed his face into her body and quietly said, "Thank you Mia, thank you for becoming my wife."

Mia lowered herself to Nicolas. She gently pulled his face upward to look into his eyes. They were filled with tears. She pulled him closer and kissed him many times on his mouth, and between kisses she said, "I love you Nico."

Mia stood up and told him she had to bathe, because she had another surprise for him. He smiled and didn't say a word. He watched her disappear into the bathroom.

Mia bathed quickly. She got out and dried herself and played with her hair until it was perfect. She took her wedding nightgown from a bag behind the door and put it on. It was made of white delicate lace that hung to the floor. The sheer bodice made of stretch lace covered her breasts perfectly, making them look full and rounded. She stood in the mirror and saw her nipples harden. Her small nipples, the color of darkened raspberries pushed the lace forward. She touched them gently, then squeezed them. She thought of Nicolas and felt the awakening between her legs, while she pinched her nipples. She reached down to touch herself and she was wet, already.

She walked out and Nicolas was standing by the doorway looking out toward the water. He wore his white shirt, unbuttoned over his black pants. Mia stood at the door of the bathroom. She leaned against the edge and slowly applied her lotion to her body as she watched him. He was gorgeous under the moonlit night. She walked toward him quietly.

The night was still. He heard Mia approach and turned to see her. "Wow, you are beautiful. Do you know all I have ever wanted is you?" She smiled and slid her hand into her panties and touched herself, she was like a moist, ripened peach, so soft and so wet. She pulled her hand from her panties and slid her wet fingers into his mouth. Nicolas moaned as he sucked on the juices from her fingers. He lifted her and said, "Mrs. Diaz, you are mine."

Mia, whose face was near his neck, nodded her head slowly and he felt her smile as it formed over his skin.

He took her and placed her gently on the bed, then bent down and kissed her softly on the mouth. She sat up and pulled him into her. She fell back slowly bringing him down with her. He kissed her body from head to toe, as she moaned. She reached out to touch him, anywhere, and slid her fingertips over his skin. He saw her hard nipples protruding from the delicate lace of her nightgown and pushed his tongue onto her nipple then pulled gently with his teeth. Mia held his head as he sucked them softly. Mia then ran her fingertips along Nicolas' sides. He shivered and moaned deeply and began to slowly undress her as he kissed her gently.

She moved her hands slowly over his shoulders, as they kissed and pushed his shirt open and down his arms. Passionately they kissed, with their mouths never losing contact as they moved together, hungrily.

She ran her fingers through his hair as he mounted her. He placed his hands between her legs and felt she was ready. He lowered himself and slowly entered her. Their lips did not separate and with their hands lost in the other's hair, they moved together.

She arched her back and they began to move in a rhythm that shook their bodies. They became wild and Mia began to moan loudly as he pushed into her deeply and they began to move faster. She bucked her hips wanting to feel him deep inside her. She wanted to feel pain from his hard cock. She pushed and he moved faster. Mia grasped his hair in her hands and began to pull his hair and began screaming, "Nico, fuck me, please!"

He did as she asked, moving faster until he felt her body tighten. He pushed deep into her one last time as she began to shake, and with the force of her pulsing muscles, hc could wait no longer and in that instant he shot his hot load into her pulsing body. Breathing heavily, they held each other.

She whispered between her deep uncontrollable breathing, "I love you," he nodded in agreement as his weakened body lay covering hers. He remained there, gently kissing her chest and shoulders. Mia continued to tenderly play with his hair.

They fell asleep in each other's arms, without moving from the spot they had made love in.

The next morning, Mia woke up to the sound of footsteps in the room above. She saw the curtains blowing with the breeze that entered the room from the bay. It was so quiet she could hear the waves. She looked down at Nico who had his head resting on her stomach. She ran her fingers through his hair lightly. He stirred and then looked upward toward her. "Good morning Mrs. Diaz." She smiled and replied, "And a good morning to you Mr. Diaz." They laughed and he moved up to kiss her.

Nicolas looked at the clock and realized they were running late and said "Baby, we have to be at the airport by 12:00. We only have two hours, I have to get my bags packed and we should have breakfast before we leave. I smell the bacon, your grandma must be cooking." Mia said, "Yes, it definitely smells like Gram's cooking. Let's shower, pack our bags and then go downstairs to eat breakfast. When we are done, we can come back up and change and make sure we have everything before we leave."

They showered and dressed quickly. Nico, in shorts and a t-shirt and Mia wore a long black sundress. They hurried downstairs where the family was gathered eating breakfast.

Sofia heard them on the second floor as they were approaching the staircase and said, "Here come the newlyweds!" Everyone got up from their seats and went into the dining room near the staircase.

Feliciana, Andres, and David ran to greet them and tightly hugged them and said, "Buenos Dias." Mia and Nicolas replied "Good Morning," and Feliciana took Mia's hand and led her into the kitchen. Everyone clapped as they came into the room saying, "Good morning, Mr. and Mrs. Diaz."

Nico ruffled the boys' hair before they ran to the table where they had been eating homemade churros and chocolate that Ana had prepared. Mia and Nico walked in holding hands with Feliciana leading the way.

They sat at the table and Mia's grandma served the freshly squeezed orange juice and asked what they wanted for breakfast. "You have a choice of my special waffles, bacon and eggs, fruit, or toasted baguette with tomatoes." Nico winked at Ana and said, "I'll have everything, including your delicious churros and chocolate." Mia looked at him wide-eyed and said "Everything?" He said, "Yes, a married man has to eat." They all laughed. Mia said, fruit and a toast with tomato for me, Gram." Ana nodded and said, "Coming right up!" Nico said, "Now that's what I call service. I could get used to this!" Mia tickled him on his side and he moved in to kiss her, playfully.

They ate quickly. Nico said he had reserved the house for the entire week and wanted everyone to stay and enjoy it. He let them know the pantry had already been stocked for the week and so had the freezer. He told them the cars in the garage were there for their use. "We'll take a cab to the airport. Nico's dad said, "I don't mind driving you, son." Nico said, "No Pa, you stay and enjoy yourself by the water. Yesterday was so busy, you all deserve a day of rest. We'll get our sleep on the plane."

As she was eating, Mia remembered the light on in the third floor window and the footsteps that woke her. She asked if anyone had spent the night in that room. They all said no. Ana didn't say anything and turned toward the stove. Mia noticed her odd reaction.

After Mia and Nico finished breakfast, they went upstairs and double-checked the room, making sure they hadn't forgotten anything.   Mia quickly changed into the long black sundress and sandals she had left out. She had one pair of sandals with heels and the other were flats, just in case she got tired in the heels.

Nico changed into a pair of jeans, a black button up shirt and black shoes.

They were ready. Nico called the cab company and said they'd be ready in a half hour.

When they walked downstairs with their luggage, Ana told them she would take the gifts to her house until they got back. Mia said, "Gram, you can have them delivered to my apartment, you have the key, and it'll be much easier on you." Her grandmother agreed.

Mia then remembered the painting.   She looked toward the wall where it was leaning.   She loved the painting. But, she did wonder what it all meant.   She looked at her grandmother, who was gazing at the painting.   Ana looked away when she noticed Mia look toward her. She looked into her grandmother's eyes, which avoided her, and she knew her grandmother knew something, but why wouldn't she tell her? When Ana finally looked at Mia. Mia slightly tilted her head and looked at her with a questioning look.   Her grandmother nodded her head slowly and smiled.   Mia did not know what her grandmother knew or what she meant by the nod. But she was going to find out.

Mia followed her grandma into the pantry and as she began to ask her what the painting meant, Nico ran in and said, "The taxi is here. Let's get moving." He smacked Mia on her butt and said, "Let's go, let's go, we're going to be late."

Mia looked at her grandmother with the same questioning look then said, "Gram, we have to leave. I love you very much and thank you so much for making my day so wonderful. I will never forget it thanks to you. You made it more beautiful than I could have ever imagined."

Mia's grandma hugged her tightly and said, "I know you will always be happy." She placed her hand in her apron pocket and pulled out a set of keys and an envelope and said, "Here are the keys to the piso. Mrs. Espinoza, the caretaker and cook, will be there during your visit. She will take care of everything you need.

"In the envelope I have written everything. The blue key is to unlock the gate, the black key is to the front door and the silver key is for the garage. I also purchased a small car for you to keep there. Mrs. Espinoza has the keys."

Mia looked at her grandmother and said, with a lump in her throat, "Thank you, you thought of everything, you are wonderful.

Nicolas yelled, "He's here, Mia, he's here!

Mia kissed her grandma quickly and hugged her tightly while Nico told his parents, brother and sister, and their families goodbye. Mia quickly kissed everyone, then grabbed her purse and carryon bag. Everyone walked out into the yard to see them off. Nico kissed Ana on the cheek and said, "I'll take real good care of her, please don't worry." Ana said, "I know you will, Nicolas, for that, I have no worries." She placed her hand on his cheek and smiled. He kissed his mother and Ana on the cheek, hugged his dad, and helped Mia into the cab.

They waved as the newlyweds drove off.

CHAPTER XIV

Their plane touched down in San Javier at 5 p.m. They went out of the gated area where a driver waited for them with a sign that read DIAZ. He greeted them and introduced himself as Joaquin. He asked how their trip had been.

Joaquin, handsome and tall, with hair cut very short, led them to the car and began to put the suitcases in the trunk. Nicolas helped Joaquin pack the car with their suitcases while Mia got into the car.

The city was a 30-minute drive from the airport. Mia and Nicolas sat in the back seat. Mia sat in the middle leaning against him. She looked out the window and remembered the countryside. It was where she spent one week every summer with her mother's parents. She looked out curiously trying to identify sights she remembered from her visits.

Her grandparents had a home on a small farm, which seemed to be so very far from the city, she remembered. The farm and the beach, is all she knew of Spain. She loved it there, from what she remembered. Yet, now, she was so excited to experience the city life she had never experienced during her trips to Spain.

When they got to the city, Mia was amazed. She wondered why her grandparents had never taken her there since she now realized it was much closer to their home, than she had believed.

Joaquin drove through the narrow streets to the building where their apartment was located. It was located in La Plaza de las Flores, a small square lined with restaurants and outdoor patios and a bakery with wonderful pastries. Apartments, called pisos, were above the businesses and were where people lived. A church was at the entrance to the plaza. The plaza was a busy place where many people gathered to eat, drink and socialize.

Joaquin parked on the narrow street and began to take the suitcases from the trunk. He helped Nicolas take them into the elevator. The hallway was quiet. Mia could hear a television blaring from one apartment and a lady humming in another. She heard the cries of a baby from a far off apartment and smiled. She told Nicolas, "So this is Spain?" Nicolas said, "Yes, my darling, it is"

Mia replied, "This is nothing I experienced on my trips here throughout the years." He laughed and said, "What a shame, but baby, I'm sure you are going to love it."

Nicolas unlocked the door to the apartment, which opened into the living room furnished with old wood furniture from a few decades before. It looked as though nothing had been updated for many years. Nicolas said, "Wow, this is spacious, that's great." They walked into the living room and Joaquin and Nicolas placed the suitcases on the floor. Joaquin gave Nicolas his business card and told him if he needed anything to give him a call.

Nicolas reached into his pocket for some euros to tip Joaquin. Shaking his head and waving his hands, Joaquin would not accept the tip saying, "Sir, that has already been taken care of." Joaquin gave him a curious look and Nicolas insisted. Joaquin, again, did not accept, repeating everything had already been taken care of. Joaquin then asked if they needed anything else. Nicolas shook his head and thanked Joaquin. Joaquin said good-bye and quickly walked out of the apartment closing the door behind him. Nicolas thought it odd that he would not accept a tip. He shook his head, shrugged his shoulders in disbelief and took off his jacket.

The living room and kitchen were furnished with furniture from the 60s. The furniture was simple but very high quality. The legs and arms of the furniture were delicately hand etched. Mia opened the curtains, and to her surprise, was a direct view of the Plaza de las Flores, The Plaza of Flowers. She could not believe her eyes. She opened the tall wooden doors with wooden blinds. They opened out to a small balcony. The railing had wood boxes filled with beautiful red flowers.

The apartment was a corner apartment on the top floor of the building. It had two bedrooms, two bathrooms, and two balconies. One balcony entrance was from the living room, and the other from the main bedroom.

In the distance she heard the sound of someone playing beautiful Spanish guitar music. She loved the atmosphere. She wanted to go out and explore immediately. "Nico, when can we go out and explore this beautiful city?" she asked.

Nico said, "Why don't we shower, and rest up a bit. We can have something to eat, a small snack, and then we'll have dinner in the plaza later." Mia agreed knowing neither had slept very well on the plane. Nicolas took the suitcases into the bedroom while Mia went into the kitchen to see what she could prepare.

She walked into the kitchen. It was dark. She looked for the light switch and couldn't find it so she opened the curtains, which allowed the last rays of the evening sun to enter and light up the room.   She saw two aprons hanging on the hook next to the small closet and chose the shorter one and wrapped it around her waist.

She opened the refrigerator, which had been filled with fruits, meats, and cheeses. She grabbed a strawberry and began to eat it slowly as she began to rummage through the cabinets.

The cupboards had also been filled. Bags of potato chips, olives, canned vegetables, coffee, cookies, teas, and tuna were stacked neatly.

Mia was startled by a soft knock at the door and walked toward the living room, as she wiped her hands on the apron. Nicolas also heard the knock, and walked toward the door.   Nicolas opened the door to a woman, who appeared to be in her early 60s, like Ana, whose striking white hair was pulled back and placed in a bun behind her head. She introduced herself to Mia and Nicolas as Mrs. Espinoza.   She was the housekeeper Ana had talked about.

Mrs. Espinoza entered and took her sweater off as she began to congratulate them on their wedding. She hung her sweater in a small closet next to the door. She switched on the light switch, which was hidden near the closet. Mia laughed and told her she couldn't find it earlier.

Mrs. Espinoza slowly explained to them, she had taken care of the house since Mia's grandmother left Spain. "You two are the first to stay here in the home in over 30 years. I have taken care of this as if it were my own, never changing anything." Mia smiled and thanked her.

Mrs. Espinoza then walked quickly into the kitchen and took the other apron from the hook. placed it over her head and tied it around her waist tightly then, began to take things from the refrigerator.

She first pulled out ham and cheese and placed it on the counter, then took out a small bowl of crushed fresh tomatoes, which appeared to have been made that day. She took the baguette bread from the cupboard, cut it lengthwise and then in half and placed it in the toaster. When the bread was toasted she drizzled olive oil over the toast and spread the tomatoes over the bread. She did this quickly without talking. Mia watched her. She then placed the ham and cheese over the bread and slid the sandwiches in the toaster for a couple more minutes so the meat and cheese could warm slightly.

While the sandwiches were warming, she opened a can of olives, drained the liquid, and poured them into a small bowl. She also opened a bag of potato chips and put them in another bowl. She placed them both on the table and told Mia and Nicolas they could come and eat.

When the sandwiches were ready, Mrs. Espinoza took them out of the toaster and set them on a cutting board and cut each one in half. She placed them on the table and went to the refrigerator for a large blue bottle of water and two sodas. She put them on the table with two glasses. Mia and Nicolas ate, and when they finished Mrs. Espinoza cleared the table and began to wash the few dishes they had eaten on.

When she was done, she asked if they preferred to eat in or go out for dinner that night. Nicolas told her they had decided to eat out, because Mia wanted to see the city.

Mrs. Espinoza told them she would be there early the next morning to prepare breakfast. She also let them know, if they preferred to eat out while they were there, to let her know and she would not prepare anything for the meals they went out for. They agreed and thanked her.

As Mrs. Espinoza was about leave, she turned and told them the key to the attic loft was on the hook near the door and the keys on the other hook were to the car parked in space 4 in the parking garage. She told Mia the attic is where her grandmother Ana left her personal items, things from Mia's childhood and also items which belonged to Mia's father and great-grandparents. Mia thanked her. Mrs. Espinoza said good night and left.

That evening they got ready to go out. Mia put on a pair of jeans, a tight knit, light blue top, boots and a sweater.

Nicolas wore a dark blue shirt with light blue lines. They each took a light jacket because the weather was still not very warm and the evenings were chilly.

They walked into the plaza where a few people had already begun to gather for dinner at the restaurants. They continued to walk and came upon the Cathedral. There were restaurants open and people walking throughout the area. It was Monday night, not many people were out.

Mia and Nicolas held hands as they walked down the narrow streets of Murcia. They decided to keep walking so they could see more of the town before they ate. They came upon an arched walk way and entered the Plaza of San Juan. There was a church at the end of the Plaza and in the center was a large tree and under the tree were seats where people could sit. The lights in the buildings and streetlights lit up the small plaza.

They smelled the wonderful aromas of the Spanish delicacies, that awaited them, coming from a restaurant on the corner. Mia and Nicolas decided to eat there. They walked to the entrance and were asked if they wanted to sit on the terrace or inside. They chose to sit outside on the terrace as they wanted to take in the atmosphere of the plaza. The host seated them and placed two menus on the table in front of them.

Nicolas ordered water and a beer. Mia asked for water. The waiter came back with a basket of bread, Spanish olives in a small dish, a large bottle of water in blue glass and a bottle of beer for Nicolas. Nicolas asked what the waiter recommended.

The waiter introduced himself as Ginés, then recommended the lamb and grilled vegetables. Nicolas smiled, he loved lamb and that's what he asked for. Mia asked for only the grilled vegetables. She was still full from the sandwiches they had eaten earlier.

Their food was served rather quickly. They ate slowly, enjoying the atmosphere. They loved their meal. Mia took a bite of Nicolas' lamb and savored it. She said she would have the lamb they next time they came. Mia talked about her vacations to her grandparent's home when she was younger while they shared a piece of caked called tarta de la abuela (grandmother's cake). The cake was a rich chocolate with crème filled layers. It came with a side of ice cream made from fresh cream. It was delicious. They both ordered cortaditos, espresso with milk served in small glasses.

When they were finished, Nicolas asked for the bill. The waiter brought the bill and Nicolas placed the euros in the small plate which had the bill clipped to it. Nicolas left Ginés a tip, and he happily thanked him. In Spain it was customary not to leave a tip, but Nicolas always left something wherever he went, whether it was customary not to leave one or even when it had already been added to his ticket in Miami. He did this because of his experience in the restaurant business.

They slowly walked back toward the cathedral, hand in hand. The streets were quiet, although the spring fiestas had already begun.

It was getting late, and most people had to work the following morning. Mia wrapped her arm around Nicolas' waist and he hugged her over her shoulders as they walked.

Mia was fascinated by the city. She loved the architecture and the way the lights lit up the hollowed narrow streets leaving some areas so darkly shadowed, giving it an almost eerie feeling, she thought.

They got to their apartment and went in.

Mia went to the restroom and took her nightgown out of her suitcase. She had been tired earlier and hadn't unpacked. She thought she would do that in the morning. She washed her face and brushed her teeth.

When she went into the living room where Nicolas had turned the television on, she saw he had fallen asleep, still in his jacket. "My poor baby, you're so tired." Mia said. "It's been such a long few days. She pushed his hair back from his forehead, kissed him and said, "Baby, wake up. Let's get to bed." Nicolas slightly opened his eyes and smiled. He pulled her down and kissed her. "I was dreaming of you," he said. "And I woke up to my dream come true."

Mia jokingly said, "Now you can sleep comfortably in bed and dream all night. Now come on, let's go to bed! I'm exhausted!"

She grabbed Nicolas' hands and pulled him toward her so he could stand up. He stood up and took his jacket off, and laid it on the back of a chair near the sofa. He went into the restroom and brushed his teeth then joined Mia, who was already in bed.

The bed, king sized, had six big fluffy pillows. The sheets were cold and so fresh. Ana had a new mattress and new bedding delivered for the couple. She had also given them a check from her Spanish bank account, to buy furniture if they wanted to change anything or if they saw things they needed while shopping.

"Brrr baby, it's cold under here, hurry up so you can warm me up," she told Nicolas. Nicolas, dressed only in his shorts, smiled, lifted the blankets and got into bed. Mia snuggled up against him then turned her back to him and he wrapped his arms around her. He moved the hair from her neck and kissed her.

He asked her if she liked the apartment. Mia said she loved everything. Then she asked him, "Do you know what I love best, though?" Nicolas did not reply. "Baby, do you know what I love best. Nicolas? Are you awake?" She turned her head slightly and saw he was already asleep. She turned her body slowly, not to wake him up and kissed him on his lips. "Sleep tight, baby," she whispered, snuggled in closer and then said, "And, what I love best is you." She pressed her face against his chest and kissed him softly, snuggled even closer and fell asleep.

CHAPTER XV

Mia woke up with the sun coming through the window. Nicolas had his arm over her. She moved it gently so she wouldn't wake him and got out of bed. She went to the window and opened the tall brown door, which was accented with black etchings.

The smell of the fresh air was welcoming. She took a deep breath and breathed it in. The air was cool. The birds were singing in the trees and some were flying in a circular motion in the plaza, chasing each other playfully. She saw the beautiful flowers in the flower boxes on the balconies of the buildings that surrounded the plaza. She bent down to smell the flowers in the flower box of their balcony. They smelled wonderful and were so vibrant, standing up with their faces open toward the sun as the rays began to peek over the buildings.

People walked busily through the plaza, on their way to work. She saw people who had gathered at the café across the way. There was a group of men at the counter, drinking their coffee, talking and laughing loudly. There were three women sitting at a table, talking rapidly and smoking as they drank their coffee.

Mia smiled. She felt she was finally home. This is where her father had grown up and she had always been curious to see the city. She never knew why her mother's parents had never brought her here. Mia sat and watched the people and noticed the women's styles. The styles were not much different from Miami, although they were a bit more conservative.

Mia let Nicolas sleep. She knew he was tired. He hadn't been able to sleep much on the plane and the days before the wedding had been so busy, not only at the restaurant but also getting everything perfect for the wedding. Mia smiled and watched him sleep. He is so ambitious she thought, when he sets his mind to something, there is nothing that can hold him back. He pushes until he accomplishes what he set out to accomplish. At that moment, Mia smiled as she realized just how proud she was of her husband.

Mia got into the shower and showered quickly. She got out, dried herself and put her hair up in a towel. She put her robe on and went out into the living room and placed a chair near the balcony. She applied her cream to her body as she watched the people outside.

She could hear Nicolas moan and turned toward the bedroom door. She saw he was waking up. She scurried into the room and jumped onto the bed, and said, "Good morning sleepy head." Nicolas rubbed his eyes, smiled and said, "I see you beat me today."

Mia replied, "I thought I'd let you sleep. I wanted you to catch up on your sleep so you wouldn't feel the jet lag too much and so we can go out and have fun discovering this beautiful city."

"Thanks baby, I definitely needed it," he said.

Just then they heard noise in the kitchen, which caught them off guard and scared them a bit. Mrs. Espinoza had let herself in through the kitchen door. They also began to smell the coffee. Mrs. Espinoza had prepared coffee and had put out a plate of small pastries. She also sliced apples and placed them in a plate with the biggest green grapes Mia had ever seen.

Mrs. Espinoza then began to clean the bathroom and tidy up the living room. Mia told her she would take care of the bedroom, since they had to still had to unpack.

Mia and Nicolas ate their breakfast. Mrs. Espinoza had picked up a newspaper on her way in, which she left on the table for them to read. Mia ate quickly and thanked Mrs. Espinoza. Nicolas stayed at the table eating the leftover pastries as he read the paper.

Mia went into the bedroom and placed her suitcase on the table near the closet. She began to remove her clothing from the suitcase, placing her underwear and folded clothing in the drawers and hung her dresses and jeans in the small closet.

Then she started unpacking Nicolas' suitcase. She put his t-shirts and underwear in separate drawers and hung his jeans and shirts in the closet next to her clothes.

She took his shaving kit into the bathroom and unpacked it and placed it neatly on the higher shelf. Then, Mia placed her toiletries on the shelf below.

Nicolas could hear her humming from the kitchen while he ate. Mia's humming was always one of the best things about their mornings together, he thought. They had only been married just a couple of days, but he hoped every morning, for the rest of their lives, would be so peaceful.

After things were put away, Mia told Nicolas she would like to go to a shopping center to pick up a few items she loved having and always missed from Spain. Things she remembered her grandmother always had when she arrived. Certain cookies, crackers, chocolate bars, and crème filled licorice.

Nicolas asked Mrs. Espinoza where they could find a shopping center. She pulled out a map from her bag and wrote on the map as she explained the route to take to two different shopping centers at the end of town. She gave him the map and told him it was very easy and shouldn't take them long to arrive, "15 minutes at the most," she said.

Nicolas thanked Mrs. Espinoza and kissed her on the cheek. He asked her if she could think of anything they might need for the house or something she needed. She pursed her lips and shook her head. Nicolas printed his number for his mobile telephone on a paper and gave it to her, in case she needed to reach them or thought of anything they may need in the house while they were out.

Nicolas grabbed the keys from the hook where Mrs. Espinoza had placed them and told Mia he would be waiting for her downstairs. He went to get the car and drove it out onto the street and waited for Mia to come out.

They drove through the town. Buildings of no more than 20 stories, and most with less than 10 stories lined the streets. Mia loved the town. She asked Nicolas if the town he grew up in was similar. He said yes, although it was a much bigger city.

Driving in Murcia was different from the streets in the United States. Mia laughed as they drove through the rotundas. Nicolas was used to the driving in Spain, as he often visited to see his old friends and his family and mainly because it was where he had learned to drive. Although after being in the United States and coming back, it took him a little while to get used to the rotundas and the different street signals and signs.

They arrived at the store. Mia found the items she loved and could not find in Miami. She remembered her grandmother would receive packages of their favorite things from Mrs. Espinoza at different times of the year.

Nicolas followed her around patiently as she walked down every aisle, looking at the products and talking about the differences from back home. She placed red candles in the basket. Then she found whipped cream for the strawberries. Nicolas bought some crackers he remembered eating when he was a boy and craved from time to time

They went home and put the items away. Mrs. Espinoza helped. She did things quietly and didn't talk much. When Mia asked her questions, her answers were short and simple.

Mia then asked her what she recommended for lunch. Mrs. Espinoza told them of a restaurant in La Plaza de Las Flores. She said the squid, which was called pulpo in Spanish, and the tapas called marineras were wonderful there. Mrs. Espinoza explained that marineras were potato salad placed on a small circular cracker with an anchovy on top. She told them there were various restaurants, but the restaurant at the corner was well known for these two tapas.

Mia told Mrs. Espinoza they would go there for lunch today. Mrs. Espinoza asked if they would like to have dinner in or have dinner out for the evening. Mia said she would ask Nicolas, who was again asleep on the sofa. Mia looked at Mrs. Espinoza and shook her head as she laughed. "Jet lag," Mia said. She slightly smiled at Mia and nodded in agreement.

Mrs. Espinoza grabbed her sweater and told Mia she would stop by later to see if they would have dinner in or would be going out. Mia thanked her as she left.

While Nicolas slept, Mia began to look at things in the house. There was a shelf with old books. She took them down and saw they had been from her grandmother's younger days. Just as she was going through the books, the telephone began to ring loudly, which startled Mia. The phone was an old phone with the circular dial and when it rang, it was loud. Even from across the room, it caused Mia to jump.

"Hello," she said. "Mia, my dear, it's me." Mia heard her grandmother's happy voice on the other end of the phone. "Hi Gram, how are you?" She asked. "The place is beautiful, thank you so much." Mia continued before her grandmother had a chance to reply. She spoke rapidly, telling her grandmother of how beautiful the city was. And how the condo was perfect and in a perfect location.

Nicolas woke up and heard Mia talking to her grandmother. He asked to let him talk to her as well. Mia told her grandmother and handed him the phone. "Thank you Ana, for everything. The place is beautiful. And thank you for sending Joaquin to pick us up. We were going to take a cab."

"Joaquin?" asked Ana.

"Yes, the driver, who picked us up at the airport," Nicolas replied. "He said the cost had been taken care of already, and I assumed it was you, who had requested he pick us up."

Ana was quiet for a second then she calmly said, "No, it wasn't me." Nicolas, not thinking anything of her denial, imagined it must have been Mia's mother's parents who had requested this. They were the only ones who could have done this, as they were the only ones who knew Murcia, besides Ana. Nicolas thanked Ana again for everything and handed the phone back to Mia. Mia told her grandmother she'd call her tomorrow to let her know all they had done. She told her she loved her and hung up the phone.

Mia told Nicolas Mrs. Espinoza would be calling to see if they'd be eating in or out that evening. She also told him about the restaurant she recommended in the Plaza de Las Flores, and it was where they could eat lunch. Nicolas asked Mia, "In or out tonight?" Mia said, "Your choice." Nicolas said, "In. Is that ok?" She replied, "Yes, I know you are tired and we still have a week. I want to get rested for the festivities tomorrow. They should be a lot of fun."

Mia began to get ready for lunch. Nico changed his shirt and then went out to the small balcony and leaned on the railing. He watched the people gathering in the square and looked at the various restaurants that lined the square. It reminded him of his hometown. It's what he missed most about Spain. And it's what he had hoped to bring to his restaurant when he opened Nico's, yet hadn't quite accomplished it.

Mia came out of the bedroom. She was wearing a blue dress with a black belt. Nicolas whistled as she walked out. She smiled and said, "Let's go baby, the plaza will be filled with people because of the fiesta." Mia took a sweater from the closet and tossed a light jacket to Nicolas. They locked up and walked down to the plaza.

They walked slowly around the plaza to see the other restaurants. The plaza was already filled with people. Nicolas smiled as they walked toward the crowd, holding hands. He said, "I really miss this Spanish lifestyle."

They walked toward the corner restaurant and were asked if they wanted to sit inside or on the terrace. Nicolas asked for a table outside. The tables and stools were high. Mia ordered a glass of wine and Nicolas ordered a beer. When the waiter came, they ordered the tapas of pulpo and marineras that Mrs. Espinoza had recommended.

They ate their tapas, and the waiter came with the menu. Nicolas ordered a plate of salmon and Mia ordered two more portions of squid and another marinera. Nicolas also ordered another beer to drink with his meal.

The order of squid and marineras Mia ordered came first and they shared them. Then the salmon and potatoes were brought out. They shared it as well. In Spain, it is customary for various plates of food to be ordered and shared by the people at the table.

They ate slowly and watched the people in the plaza. Everyone seemed so happy, and the buzz of conversation was like the buzzing of a million bees, Mia thought. She asked for another glass of wine and Nicolas ordered lemon sorbet and cortados, espresso with milk, which they finished slowly, as they watched the people in the plaza.

People gathered and laughed, and talked as they shared small plates of tapas. Mia loved the atmosphere. It was nothing like she remembered. Her summers here were usually spent on the farm with her grandparents. When she was a teenager she was able to visit friends who lived near, or they were taken to a small town near the beach to get ice cream.

Mia loved her time here when she was young, and always wished she could have stayed longer than a week. She remembered thinking she never had enough time to really get to know her mother's parents. She realized her grandmother Ana was afraid of loss, just like Mia was. And because of this, Mia always felt she, in a sense, had to take care of her grandmother as her grandmother took care of her and it was why she never asked to stay longer.

Mia and Nicolas finished up their meal and paid the bill. They walked through the town's crowded streets. People were everywhere because of the fiesta. Later that evening there would be a parade. Mia was excited to see the parade, especially one at night, which she had never seen before.

When she mentioned it to Nicolas, he reminded her they told Mrs. Espinoza they would be having dinner at home. Mia said, "Oh, what if she wants to attend the parade with her family?" Call her and tell her we will eat out. It'll be more fun with all the festivities and people in the streets."

Nicolas called Mrs. Espinoza and told her. She thanked him and said she would also be attending the parade with her family. Mia and Nicolas were glad they had decided this, because it also gave Mrs. Espinoza some time with her family.

They went home and slept the siesta. When Mia woke up, she kissed Nicolas who was still asleep. He woke up slowly. "Baby, it's dark outside, we overslept. We need to get to the parade route." Nicolas got out of bed and went into the bathroom and threw water on his face. He brushed his teeth, as Mia hurriedly got ready. She then brushed her teeth and put some lipstick on her lips.

Mia grabbed a sweater and a jacket for Nicolas from the closet and stood by the door waiting for him. He was putting his shoes on, tying them slowly. Mia said, "Baby, come on, we're going to be late."

"Here I come," he said and walked toward the closet for his jacket. Mia waved his jacket so he could see she had it. He winked and said, "You think of everything." He took the jacket and kissed her on her forehead. She smiled and walked out the door hurriedly. Nicolas followed behind trying to keep up with her quick pace, and then she suddenly stopped and grabbed his hand so she could pull him along so he could keep up with her.

They walked swiftly, holding hands, looking for the street where the parade would pass. Mia saw a group of people walking and pulled Nicolas in that direction. He followed. She was determined to get to the parade as soon as possible. She did not want to miss a thing.

The group of people turned the corner, and Mia said, "Hurry, we'll lose them." Nicolas laughed and said, "We'll make it baby, don't worry." Mia said, "This is my first Spanish parade, and I'm not going to miss a thing."

They turned the corner where the crowd they were following had turned. When they looked down the street, they saw the large crowd of people who had gathered for the parade. Mia sighed deeply and said, "We're here!"

Mia pushed through the crowd, excusing herself as she pulled Nicolas by the hand. The people she passed looked at her strangely. Mia was determined to get to the front. Nicolas, speaking in Spanish, apologized to the people, letting them know it was her first parade in Spain. The people laughed and smiled and let them in without hesitation.

Mia stood in front with Nicolas standing behind her, hugging her tightly. She turned and looked up to him and said, "I love you Nicolas, thank you." And she pushed her lips out so he could bend down and meet them with his. The parade was amazing. The floats were decorated with lights and intricately designed with flowers. It was the spring festival and the floats were dedicated to spring.

Mia watched in amazement at the floats rode by. There were groups of beautiful women dressed in clothing only covering the most intimate parts of their bodies. There were groups of people, dressed in customary costumes for the region, who, danced and sang.

She was amazed by the length of the parade and with the amount of people participating in the parade. There was a car with people who threw out candy, and all the children and even some adults ran to gather the candy, putting it in bags they had brought to the parade, hoping they would be gathering a lot to take home.

Mia bent down to pick up the few pieces that had fallen between her feet. She opened one and took a bite, then pushed the other half toward Nicolas' mouth. He took it and ate it. She stood on her tiptoes and told Nicolas, "This is magical, Nico. I love it. I'm so glad we are here." Nicolas agreed.

When the parade was over, Mia and Nicolas walked home and on the way there, they decided to get something to eat. They walked into a small restaurant. The bar was on one end of the narrow room across from small square tables that seated only two per table. They sat at the counter.

The waiter asked what they wanted to drink. Nicolas ordered a beer and Mia ordered a cola. The waiter brought their drinks and asked what they wanted to eat. Mia ordered a tuna sandwich and Nicolas ordered steak with potatoes. Potato chips and olives were placed on their table before the meal. They ate them and talked about the parade.

It took longer than usual for their food to arrive. When it did, Mia said, "Mmmm, it all looks so good," as the waiter placed her sandwich in front of her. She opened her sandwich to find flakey tuna, olives and red peppers on baguette bread. Nicolas' steak was cooked perfectly and the potato wedges seasoned with parsley were delicious. They finished their food and Nicolas ordered a dessert typical to the region.

He ordered paparajotes, which were lime leaves covered in batter, deep-fried, and sprinkled with sugar and cinnamon. They were served with chocolate sauce for dipping.

The trick to eating them was to take a bite of the battered area without biting through the leaf. The leaf was to stay intact. Mia remembered eating these when she visited her grandparents. She loved them because they were light and also fun to eat. They had coffee with their dessert and ate slowly as they talked mostly about the parade.

They finished and paid and walked home slowly, enjoying the night air and the ambiance. Groups of people gathered along the street and in the cafés after the parade. Nicolas hugged Mia as they walked slowly, home. She looked up at him as they walked and said, "I love our honeymoon." Nicolas agreed by nodding his head and said, "Yes, Spain is perfect."

They went home and cuddled in bed while they watched television. Mia fell asleep first. Nicolas turned off the lights and TV, kissed Mia and hugged her closely. He fell asleep soon after.

CHAPTER XVI

Mia woke up not feeling well. She turned over and told Nicolas. He asked her what bothered her. She said, "My head hurts and my stomach is queasy." Nicolas got up from bed and went to get a bottle of water and two aspirin. He handed them to Mia. She took them and swallowed them hesitantly. She hated taking pills.

"Mia, why don't you get some rest? I'll close the curtains so the room is darkened. You are probably tired from the trip and all we've done over the last days. You really haven't slept much."

She agreed and got comfortable in bed. Nicolas pulled the covers up over her shoulders and bent down and kissed her.

"I'll be in the living room. Mrs. Espinoza is preparing breakfast. If you get hungry let me know and I'll bring you something, ok?"

"Yes, Nico, I'll let you know." She turned over and closed her eyes and he walked out of the room.

Nicolas ate a few cookies as he drank his coffee. Then went to the pharmacy to buy more aspirin and cold medicine for Mia. When he walked out of the pharmacy, he noticed the supermarket across the street and decided to go in to pick up more fruit and things Mia might want to eat later.

While Nicolas was out, Mia woke from her nap feeling better. She went to the kitchen to warm some water for tea and on the table was a note. "Going to Pharmacy and Supermarket, I'll be back soon. Love you, Nico".

She opened the refrigerator to see what was left over from breakfast. She grabbed two cookies and began to eat them slowly as the water warmed. She opened the cupboards to see what else she found and when she closed the last cupboard door, she noticed the key to the attic. She prepared her tea, picked up the key and walked into the bedroom.

The door to the attic was at the corner near the bathroom door. She unlocked the door and looked up. A long string hung from the light bulb on the high ceiling and she pulled it. The darkened staircase lit up.

She held onto the railing as she climbed the narrow stairs toward the attic. When she arrived at the top, she smiled and scanned the room slowly. It was beautiful, she thought, and what she always imagined an attic to look like. It was filled with old pictures. Some hung on the slanted ceiling and some on the floor, leaned against the wall. Mia thought, all that she saw were small treasures from her family's past. She saw knick-knacks that must have been her great-grandmother's because they seemed to be very old. She also noticed how clean the room was and knew Mrs. Espinoza had kept it tidy over the years.

She opened a box nearest where she stood and in it saw porcelain dolls, which must have been her grandmother's. There was also an old dollhouse with small furniture, which had been placed toward the back corner of the room. The nostalgic pieces from her grandparent's past filled the room. Then behind the boxes she saw, small trucks and a train. She knew these had to be her father's toys. She picked up the small red train and rolled it over the palm of her hand, then hugged it closely. "Daddy, I miss you," she whispered.

She began looking through a box filled with pictures. She was amazed at all the photos her grandmother had left behind. Why had she not taken these important things to the United States with her? It was as if she had left suddenly, intentionally leaving her past behind. Was it because it had been so painful? Mia wondered what the reason could have been to make her want leave everything so important behind.

At the bottom of the box was a book. It was her grandmother's baby book. The first page said, "For my darling princess Ana, I will love and cherish you always." It was signed by her great-grandmother. The album was filled with photos of her family and notes of different events, which must have been important to her great-grandmother.

Under the baby book was another book with a photo on the cover. The photo was one of a very beautiful woman. This was not her grandmother. She took the book out and there were photos of her grandmother as a child with her parents. The beautiful woman was her great grandmother Daniela. Mia flipped through the pages. There were newspaper clippings as well as photos and letters. She opened one letter and read it.

My beautiful, my love,
I am leaving to work in my father's company in
Barcelona. It weakens me to know that I must
spend one minute, much less 6 months without your
beautiful face before my eyes. I will write to you
each and every day. My heart is saddened because
you cannot come with me. I will love you every
minute of every day, and will soon be back so that
we can marry. Enjoy your studies. Please know
that every moment that passes, you are on my mind.
I love you from the most profound depths of my
soul. Never stop loving me, as I am now, and will
always, be yours. Yours truly,

A smudge remained where the signature had been and Mia
could not make out the name.

She imagined it must have been her great-grandfather's
love letter to her great-grandmother and imagined the
smudge was the result of her tears falling to the paper as
she read it over and over again. Mia smiled.

There was also an article of her great grandmother,
Daniela's death. The cause listed as unknown. Mia
wondered what happened. Her grandmother had never
mentioned how she had died. Mia dug deeper through the
box of papers and photos and found a journal.

She opened it and skimmed through the pages noticing the
beautiful penmanship of the passages written. She began
to read the first page when she heard, "Mia, I'm back,
where are you?" She heard Nicolas calling her name and

stood up quickly and said "I'm here baby, in the attic, come up, I want you to see something."

She heard Nicolas open the door and begin to climb the stairs. She stood up after neatly placing the things back into the box.

Nicolas stood at the top of the stairs and said, "Cool, antiques! I bet you're loving this." Mia grabbed the journal and hugged it to her body and said, "Yes, it's all a part of my family's past. There are so many beautiful things here and also things that belonged to my father... small trains, cars, and paintings that must have been done by him." She closed the box, leaving the journal out, then she picked it up and began to follow Nicolas toward the stairs.

As she neared the stairs she noticed a small black trunk decorated with scrolls made of wrought iron and on the top was a plaque where MIA was engraved in beautiful lettering. "Wow, this is beautiful! Nico, look! Is this for me? It has my name on it!"

He turned back and looked at the trunk she was kneeling by. She shook it a little. There was something inside She then tried to open it. It was locked. "Nico, I wonder where the key is" she said. "I want to open it." Nico shrugged his shoulders and said. "Maybe Mrs. Espinoza knows where it is."

"Yes, I'll ask her, and Nico, please take it downstairs, it doesn't seem very heavy."

Nicolas picked up the trunk, which was no bigger than a small suitcase yet heavier than it appeared to be. He walked down the stairs slowly, trying not to hit the walls in the narrow stairway. Mia followed him. He placed it by the window. Mia stood above it with her hand on her hip. "What a curious trunk. I have never seen anything so pretty. I wonder if my grandmother had it made for me? I will call her later to ask what this is." Nico smiled and winked at Mia.

Mia, realizing she still had the journal in her hand, placed it in the drawer of the nightstand next to the bed.

Nicolas hugged her and said, "Feeling better?"

"Yes," she said, "a little better."

"I'll warm up the chicken soup Mrs. Espinoza left so you can get something in your stomach. Why don't you lie down and I'll bring it to you in bed, if you'd like."

"Thanks baby," Mia said and went into the bathroom.

Nicolas warmed the soup and took it to Mia in bed. She sat up and ate it slowly. He turned the television on, and lay down beside her and watched a game of soccer. Before Mia finished her soup, she noticed Nicolas had fallen asleep. She finished and then placed the bowl on the nightstand. She opened the drawer where she had placed the journal, took it out and began to read.

August 16, 1964

It's been 2 months now. I am not sure what is ailing me. I have been to many doctors here and in Barcelona. They tell me they are not sure what has made me ill. I have been given penicillin, with hopes that this may cure me. My illness is nothing they have seen before. The doctors have told me, my blood has been poisoned. I am not sure what they mean by this. I have been to curanderos for a natural cure and witch doctors, because I was told it could have been a spell placed upon me by someone who does not like me, or someone who may want my husband. They too, have not been able to cure me or tell me why I am sick. As each day passes, I am weaker. Today I can hold the pen for only a short while. I am saddened to see my beautiful daughter Ana suffer by seeing me as I weaken. It hurts me to cause my family such great pain.

August 17, 1964

My dear Francisco has come to me today with news from the doctors in Barcelona. What they have realized is, I have an incurable disease in my blood. Why did one day they call it a poison in my blood and today they call it an incurable disease? Francisco has told me, he was told there have only been 4 known cases of this illness in Spain. Why me? What caused this to happen? I cannot leave my dear husband and my daughter alone. I have to live and be with them as we have always been. I am weak now, I will write more later.

August 18, 1964

Today, I am not well. I am weakening more and more with each passing day. I have little strength and cannot stand on my feet. It is killing me to see the pain in my loving Francisco's face. I cannot leave him alone, because I know how deeply he loves me, and without me he will be alone and lost. Taking care of our beautiful Ana, my sweet, sweet beautiful Ana, so young and so in love. In a relationship with someone I do not approve of. He has changed since his move from Murcia and I no longer approve of her seeing him. I no longer approve of their love. I see in her eyes, the deep love she feels for him. But I will not allow her to marry this man, who's name I will not mention, because he has broken her heart. I will fight until my very last breath to keep her from him.

It was the last entry her grandmother wrote. Mia then looked at the newspaper article she had taken from the baby book. It was dated August 19. The article had the date her grandmother died as August 18th. August 18th was also the day she wrote the very last entry in her journal.

Mia was sad. She wondered about her great grandmother and how she must have suffered knowing she was dying and was leaving behind her daughter and husband.

Mia also wondered if her great-grandmother's dying wish had come true and her grandmother Ana had not married the man who had moved away, the man she did not want her daughter to be with. She had married her grandfather Jose, but had never heard of him living in Barcelona. Ana wondered if this man could be the man in the sad love story she told Mia. Was he the man she talked about in a roundabout way? Was he the man, she so often spoke about, as the example of a long lost love? Was he the person she referred to when she spoke of love lasting a lifetime for some, and also the unfinished love that forever lived in so many people's hearts?

She placed the journal back in the side table and cuddled up to Nicolas. She lay in his arms staring at the TV, not able to concentrate on the movie that played, yet wondering about what she had just read.

When Mrs. Espinoza came later that day, she walked into the living room and saw the trunk and gasped. Mia noticed her reaction and asked about the key for the trunk. She replied, "You will have to ask your grandmother," and quickly walked into the kitchen. Mia called her grandmother later to ask about the key, and got her answering machine. She left a message telling her why she had called.

The following day they would be returning to Miami, Mia took the journal and baby book and packed them in her suitcase. She and Nico had also found a box in which to pack the trunk. She hadn't spoken to her grandmother, but she would return with the trunk and hopefully her grandmother had the key. She was certain the trunk was hers because her name was etched on the small plaque.

CHAPTER XVII

When Mia and Nicolas returned home, things went back to normal. Mia moved into Nicolas' condo and rented hers to a nice couple with a small child.

The days went by, and Nicolas worked the restaurant. Mia also helped him during the evenings when he was busy. Mia eventually quit her job to dedicate herself to working on her designs and to helping Nico with his business. She also helped him at the restaurant with the bookkeeping. She wanted to be near him, and with his long hours, this is what she chose to do. He loved her helping at the restaurant. It kept her busy and they were able to spend more time together and also share in the success of the business.

Seven months after the wedding, Mia's designs were complete. They had been sent to the factory for completion. She would soon have the clothing line and would begin to market it. This made her so happy. It had always been her dream and it was now coming true.

A few days after celebrating their first wedding anniversary, Mia received the first shipment of her designs. She was so excited. She packed a bag of dresses and took them to the restaurant so Nicolas could see them. Nicolas was so happy for Mia, as she was now ready to plan the grand opening of her shop.

One morning, while brushing her teeth, she started to gag. She ran to the toilet and vomited. She was ill. She brushed her teeth trying not to gag, but she had to get the horrible taste of vomit from her mouth. She then went to the refrigerator and served herself a large glass of orange juice. Nicolas had already left to work. She sat at the table slowly drinking the juice, hoping the nausea she felt would subside. She did not feel well at all.

She found some crackers they had brought from Spain and began to eat them slowly while she lay on the sofa. She began dozing off. She was so tired. She dozed off for a few minutes. When she awoke, she sat up suddenly and thought, "How can I be so tired, I just woke up from 8 hours of sleep?" She wondered about it and lay down again. She didn't think much more about it and was soon asleep again.

Every morning for the next week, Mia felt the same. Sick to her stomach, and she could not eat much during the day. The only thing that did not cause nausea was bread, and she drank an unusual amount of water or anything to quench her thirst. The thought of meat and cheese made her gag. Nicolas started worrying about her and told her he was taking her to see her doctor so she could be examined.

The appointment was Friday and it couldn't come soon enough for him. In the doctor's office, Mia explained her symptoms. The doctor said the first thing he wanted done was a pregnancy test and handed Mia a cup and pointed toward the restroom.

Mia went into the bathroom and filled the cup as the doctor ordered. She placed it in the small window, which was connected to the laboratory and went back into the room to wait for the results. About half hour later, the doctor entered the room with the results.

"Mr. and Mrs. Diaz, I want to congratulate you," he said. "You are going to be parents." Nicolas jumped up and picked Mia up, swinging her around. Then he slowed down, realizing he could hurt her. They all laughed as he tried to make her comfortable again.

The days went by. Mia always seemed to be tired. She began to stay home more often. Nicolas worked his schedule together with Antonio's so he could be home more with Mia during the evening

On the day of her first ultrasound, Nicolas took the entire day off. He wanted to take Mia out to lunch at a small restaurant in the midtown area. Mia loved the sandwiches there and Nicolas was sure she would find something that was appealing to her weird pregnancy appetite. When he told her this, she laughed.

They left to the hospital early. Mia had to drink a big bottle of water so the ultrasound would work correctly. The ultrasound technician walked in, gave Mia a gown, and told her to strip from the waist down. Mia took the gown and went into the stall and did as the technician said, then returned to the room where Nicolas was waiting.

Mia placed her clothes on a chair next to the entrance to the bathroom. She walked slowly, trying to keep the gown closed in the back, just in case the technician walked in. When the ultrasound tech entered, she motioned so they would follow her and they followed her into a darkened room where the ultrasound would take place.

Mia nervously lay on the bed with her hands crossed, twiddling her thumbs. Nicolas sat patiently at her side. She looked up at him and he played with her hair, running his fingers through it slowly. She looked up at him and didn't say anything. She just looked deep into his eyes and smiled. He smiled, then leaned forward to kiss her on her forehead. "I love you Nico…you know?" "I know baby, and I love you too," he replied.

The technician sat on a stool at Mia's side. She placed a jelly like liquid on her stomach warning her it may feel cold. She shivered as the technician applied it. Nicolas held her hand. The technician then placed the cold ultrasound wand on her stomach. They immediately heard what they thought could be a heartbeat. Mia smiled when the technician confirmed the echoing sound they heard was the baby's heartbeat. "That's our baby, Nico," she whispered. Nico kissed her. And kept his hand on the crown of her head.

They both watched the screen as the technician moved it around slowly, then clicking on areas of the screen. Then she stopped, and concentrated on the screen with what seemed to be a worried look on her face. She moved the wand again and told the couple she had to find the doctor and left the room.

Mia looked at Nico and said, "What could it be, is there something wrong with my baby?" Nico said, "Don't worry, everything is ok. The tech probably just needs to verify something with the doctor." They waited quietly for a few minutes, which seemed much longer. Worry came over Mia's face. Nicolas touched her softly and reassured her everything would be ok.

They heard footsteps in the hallway and the doorknob slowly turned and Mia's doctor and the technician entered the room.

The doctor said, "Hello Mr. and Mrs. Diaz, lets see what we have here." The technician began to move the wand around again, and she and the doctor looked at the screen. The doctor asked her to move a little to the right, and she did as he asked. The doctor nodding his head said, "You were right," as he looked at the technician. "Mr. and Mrs. Diaz, I would like to be the first to congratulate you on the twins you are having."

They looked at each other in shock. Mia's mouth hung open and her eyes opened the size of large marbles. Nico smiled and kissed her. The doctor said, "Look, you can see the two of them, very close together." It was hard to see them as they are huddled so close. "Listen and you can hear the two heartbeats." They listened and heard the echoing heart beats of their babies. The technician pointed out the tiny movement of both hearts. They saw the tiny organs of their babies move as they listened to the echoing of their hearts beat.

Mia and Nicolas left the clinic without uttering a single word. They were in shock and could not believe they were having twins. On the way home Mia nervously talked about names and wondered if they would be boys or girls.

Mia's pregnancy was not easy. She was sick often.   Her grandmother reassured it was normal. She remembered Mia's mother being sick throughout her entire pregnancy. One Sunday, while they were home, Nico was refinishing a small chest of drawers for the babies' room. He heard Mia humming her song as she cleaned the kitchen after they had eaten breakfast. Mia stood at the sink looking out the window at the beautiful bird feeder with the bronzed lady, and she watched two blue birds land on her outstretched fingers. She watched them, as she washed the glass in her hand slowly, so very slowly, feeling as if time were standing still. Then suddenly she saw the eyes of the bronzed woman look directly at her, she stepped back, and her head began to spin.   She felt herself falling and grabbed for the counter, but she fell and hit the floor, shattering the glass she held in her hand.

Nico heard a thump and ran. He found Mia lying on the floor. He called the ambulance.   He stayed there with her, talking to her as she lay there unconscious.

The paramedics took her to the hospital where she was admitted.   They ran tests, and said she was low on iron. The doctor ordered her to stay there over night so they could monitor her.

She looked at Nico sadly when the doctor told her she had to remain in the hospital.   Nico assured her that everything was going to be ok, and she could get some rest by spending the night there, while they administered iron through the IV's.

The nurse told Nicolas he could stay with her until visiting hours were over. Nicolas put on a movie they both liked and he sat by her bed holding her hand.

Her doctor came in later and told Mia he would like to see her weekly. He told her this was not uncommon since she was having twins. She was only four months pregnant, but due to her low iron levels and pregnancy with twins he thought it best to see her weekly. Mia held Nicolas' hand tightly and nodded in agreement as the doctor spoke.

Mia was placed on higher doses of iron. But she still had no energy and was not well. She slept most of the day. Ana came from the farm to stay with Mia and Nicolas to help take care of her while he worked.

Mia's doctor began to worry because she was not gaining weight. The babies were getting bigger but she had not gained any weight. He was very worried, as Mia was always tired. Mia told her doctor she ate regularly, although she did avoid meats. She did eat everything else when she had an appetite. Mia's doctor gave her orders to drink smoothies made of fruit or vegetables three times a day to help with her weight gain. Mia did as he ordered, but still did not gain any weight. It seemed like the babies got bigger as she got thinner.

After the fourth weekly visit and no success in her gaining weight, he ordered numerous tests. He also ordered Mia to be admitted to the hospital for a week. He wanted her on an IV to make sure she was getting all the nutrients she and the babies needed. He knew weight gain was crucial to the delivery of twins as well as to the health of the mother. He believed it was the best solution for increasing her weight and her strength.

On the fourth day of her stay, Mia's obstetrician called Nicolas and asked if he could be at the hospital in an hour. Nicolas panicked and immediately left the restaurant, which was only 15 minutes from the hospital.

Nicolas rushed to Mia's room. She was asleep when he arrived. He brought in a teddy bear that he bought the night before when he left the hospital. He sat on the chair and watched her sleep. He could see the babies moving inside her. He wondered why the doctor wanted him there and this made him uneasy and anxious to speak to the doctor.

There was a knock at the door, and the doctor peeked his head in and said "Hello, Mr. Diaz. It looks like Mia is sleeping. She's doing a lot of that lately." Mia stirred as she heard them talk. She slowly opened her eyes and slowly sat up. Nicolas stood up and kissed her and said, "Hello sleepyhead."

"Hi baby, I missed you," Mia replied.

The doctor sat at the foot of Mia's bed and asked how she felt. "Fine," she said, "just tired."

The doctor pulled out her chart and as he looked down at the results of her tests, he began, "Mia, we ran numerous tests on your blood a couple of days ago. In the tests we found something in your blood. It appears that you have a rare case of an illness that dates back to 1950s Spain. It is very rare, and we are now in the process of communicating with doctors in Spain to find the research they have done on this illness. There are no other prior cases we have found besides those in Spain. We have no knowledge of it ever occurring in another part of the world." Mia turned pale and looked at Nicolas. She gasped and said, "My grandmother, Daniela!"

Nicolas said, "Don't worry Mia, we don't know yet." Mia began to cry uncontrollably. Nicolas hugged her and rubbed her head gently as she shook in his arms. "Don't cry baby. I promise everything will be ok," he said as he remembered the story Mia told him of her grandmother's illness and death.

She calmed down, as she noticed the crying made her extremely tired. Nicolas sat on the bed and lay back with her, holding her thin body in his arms. She fell asleep on his chest and he slowly got up to let her sleep more comfortably. He walked into the hall where the doctor was waiting.

"Doctor, can you please tell me the area this disease came from in Spain?"

"Southern Spain," the doctor replied.

Nicolas turned toward Mia's room. Then he began to cry and slammed his fist onto the wall, saying "NO!!!!!!" The doctor calmed him and took him to the waiting room and gave him a cup of tea. Nicolas sat there and drank the tea slowly.

Nicolas calmed down. He sat in the chair with the tea mug in his hands. His head hung and he looked into the cup of tea and began to talk. He told the doctor of Mia's great grandmother. He explained they were from southern Spain and she had died in the 1960s of a blood disease. Nicolas did not know the name but told the doctor he would get more information from Mia's grandmother.

The doctor let Nicolas know that he had already contacted hospitals in the region to see if they had any record or knowledge of the disease and was waiting for an answer. Nicolas thanked the doctor and the doctor walked out of the room.

Nicolas sat there, staring into the cup not knowing what he would do. Wondering if there was anything he could do.

Nicolas placed the half full cup of tea on the table and returned to Mia's room. He told the nurse he would be staying with his wife tonight. She began to tell Nicolas he couldn't stay after visiting hours. Nicolas said, "If you don't allow me to stay with her, I will have her taken out of this hospital and placed in one where I am allowed to stay with my sick wife." The nurse said, "Don't worry Mr. Diaz, I'll get clearance," and she walked away.

Nicolas sat at Mia's side all night. He watched her sleep. The only thing he could think was what they learned today could change their lives forever.

How could she have been diagnosed with this blood disease? Was this the same disease that took her great-grandmother's life, the incurable blood disease, which Mia too, could die from?   If so, how had she contracted the disease?   Nicolas placed his face in his hands and asked "why?" and began to sob quietly.

CHAPTER XVIII

Mia woke up that morning and saw Nicolas asleep in the chair. His body twisted and his head hung to the side. "My poor Nico," she thought, and whispered, "Baby, wake up."

Nicolas woke up and sat there and stared at Mia, he smiled and said, "Do you know you are the most beautiful thing I have ever laid eyes on?" Mia blew him a kiss and said… "I Love you Nico…so very much. Please hold me, I am so scared."

Nicolas stood up from the chair and went to the bed. He sat on it and pulled Mia close. She began to sob. Nicolas tried to be strong, yet his eyes filled with tears. Mia felt his tears touch her neck as they fell from his face. They held on to each other tightly as they both imagined the worst.

A knock at the door caused them to sit up and wipe away their tears. It was a nurse with release orders from the doctor. "Mrs. Diaz, the doctor is releasing you and will be in shortly to explain your prescriptions." Mia and Nicolas both thanked the nurse and she left.

Dr. Thomas came into the room a short time later and reassured them they would get information from Spain and begin treatment as soon as an answer was obtained. He gave Mia prescriptions for nutritional drinks, vitamins, and iron. He advised her to rest and told her she should eat eight small meals throughout the day. Mia and Nicolas thanked the doctor as he left the room.

Mia got dressed, with Nicolas helping her. The nurse then came in with a wheelchair and Mia got into the chair and she was wheeled out. Nicolas walked at her side, holding her small suitcase and purse.

On the drive home, they held hands. They were silent. Mia thought of her babies. What would they grow to be, without her? How could she leave Nico alone with the babies? They all needed her. What about her grandmother, how could she go on without her? Mia was all she had.

Nico's heart was breaking inside. He knew he could not live without Mia. How would he raise two babies without the most special woman as their mother and the only woman in this world as his wife? Mia was the true love of his life. He was strong but he was angry, and wanted to punch anything and everything near him. He lifted Mia's hand to his mouth and kissed it gently, lingering on her soft skin, then moved it to his cheek and he held it there. He then squeezed it firmly shaking it and said, "We have to be strong Mia, everything will be ok...I promise...it has to be."

He held Mia's hand tighter and as he caressed it with his thumb, she started to cry and choked out between her sobs. "Nico...stop the car. Please!" He pulled over to the side of the road and pushed the gear into park.

She looked at him and said, "I don't want to die, I have too much to live for. I want to be with you 'til we grow old. And what about our babies? What will you do without me? What will I do, without you?" She shook as she cried from the pit of her stomach. He held her tightly and could not hold back his cries. They cried and clung to each other until they could cry no more. They stared out into the world, a world now so cold and so very unfair. The world as they had once viewed it was now different. All their dreams had come true and now, this unfair life was taking it all away.

Mia had lost strength from crying. Nicolas held her and rubbed her head, softly pushing his fingers through her hair. He pulled her close and kissed her forehead.

"Mia, don't worry, my love, I will find a way to make you better. Nearly fifty years have gone by since your grandmother died. There has to be a cure, something that they've discovered. I won't stop looking 'til you are cured. We can't lose hope, my love. When we lose hope, we have lost everything. Promise me you will keep the hope and faith alive." She promised Nicolas, with only doubt running through her mind.

Mia said, "I believe in you Nico, and I have faith in you and I know you will find something." She began to put her seatbelt on and Nico reached over and kissed her on the mouth, then moved down to kiss her stomach and lingered. He sat up straight, putting his seatbelt on with a sense of conviction, gaining his composure he put the car in drive and headed home.

When they arrived, she went to the babies' room and arranged things nervously. He stood at the door watching her. She hummed the song she always hummed. He couldn't take his eyes off her. At that moment, he swore to himself he would do anything and everything in his power to find a cure for her illness. He was not going to lose the love of his life, not now, not ever. So many things ran through his mind, but the only thing he knew was, he would do whatever it took to save her, even if he died trying.

CHAPTER XIX

That night they lay in bed. He rubbed her back lightly and was quiet. Mia was still.

"Nico, I'm scared," she said. Nico replied, "Mia, please don't be scared, I will do everything in my power to find a cure for you. Let's please not lose hope."

"Nico, I love you, never forget it, please."

"Mia, I will never forget, for as long as I live, I will never forget, because you will be here with me always reminding me that you love me."

She smiled. She saw the tears fall from his eyes, as the light from the muted television reflected on his face. She pulled him close, and he held her tightly, kissing the top of her head.

Mia fell asleep after a few minutes. He felt her steady breathing, and heard her moan slightly as she slept. He touched her hair gently and kissed her.

The tears ran down his face. He didn't know what to do. Where would he start? How would he find a cure? Could he find a cure? He lay there looking up toward the ceiling lost in thought planning the exact steps he needed to take. He would start by researching what happened to her grandmother and whomever else this had affected. He wanted to know where else this had happened. Yes, that is where he would start.

Nico lay awake most of the night, thinking of how he would handle both restaurants. He would leave Antonio in charge while he took care of Mia and while he looked for a cure. He could not lose her. He wouldn't let this illness take her life, as well as his.

He decided he would get as much information from Ana tomorrow, when she returned to stay with them. She had gone home for a couple days to make sure everything was ok and to take care of a few things that needed her attention.

Nicolas fell asleep with the TV on. He was exhausted.

Nicolas woke up after a couple hours of sleep when he heard Ana preparing breakfast. He couldn't believe he had slept so late. He looked over at his phone and had numerous missed calls and text messages from Antonio.

He got out of bed quietly and went into the bathroom to wash his face and brush his teeth.

He went into the kitchen where Ana was now washing dishes. He kissed her and poured himself a cup of coffee and sat at the table. Ana began telling Nicolas about a hanging flower pot that had fallen because of the wind while she served a plate of eggs and potatoes.

When she turned to place the plate in front of Nicolas, she noticed he was not himself. She saw his eyes were swollen and wondered what was wrong.

"Nicolas? Is something wrong?" He looked up at her and his eyes filled with tears. She grabbed onto the chair and her knees weakened. She knew something was horribly wrong just by the look on his face.

Nicolas quickly stood up to help her. She pulled out the chair next to Nicolas and sat down. He pushed his chair closer to her and took her hands into his and held them firmly.

Nicolas began, "Ana, yesterday we were told Mia has a blood disease. "

Ana gasped and turned ghostly white. She pulled her hands from his and began to sob into her hands. "No, no no, not my Mia," she continued to say as she shook her head. Nico tried to calm her and reassure her everything would be ok. She stopped crying after a few minutes and stared blankly toward the floor as visions of her mother's last days became so vivid in her mind.

She remembered her mother and how she suffered before she died. Then she looked up at Nicolas, and asked if they named the illness? "No, they did not, they said the only other occurrence was in Spain over 50 years ago. Dr. Thomas told us there were only four women who contracted the disease."

Ana again began to cry softly, whispering, "No, not my niña, not my Mia." Nicolas comforted her.

Nicolas told her he was going to do everything in his power to find a cure for Mia. And he would never stop until he found help for her.

Ana placed her hand on Nicolas' face and gently caressed it, saying "Mia is so lucky to have you."

Nicolas smiled and said, "I am the lucky one." He began eating his breakfast when he heard Mia call his name. He stood up quickly and ran into the room.

She was sitting up, leaning back on her pillow. She was beautiful and so vibrant this morning. Nico said, "You look so beautiful this morning. You must have had good dreams."

"I did, I could see myself playing with the babies in a big field and I could see a small house in the distance, where you were. It was a happy dream, baby."

Nicolas said, "I can't wait 'til it happens. We'll be with the babies, here in this house, it's going to be amazing Mia." Mia smiled at him, but in her eyes he saw sadness. He knew what she felt, just by looking into her eyes.

She looked down and held back her tears and slowly nodded in agreement.

She had been sitting in bed, thinking about her disease. She remembered Nico's words last night, "We can't lose hope, we can't lose faith." She had always read books on positive thinking, and she knew that with this knowledge and her religious faith, it was how she would have to live…with hope and also knowing they would find a cure for her. She had to believe she would be with her babies and watch them grow.   She knew that whatever was going on with her, she would fight with every ounce of her being. She knew she would be ok, and she could not let Nicolas suffer because she couldn't bear to see him sad.

CHAPTER XX

One evening as Mia lay sleeping, Nicolas sat in front of his computer, searching for answers to her illness. He found the illness had lain dormant for many years. The last recorded case was in 1964 in a town in southern Spain.

It was also believed to have been the cause of an epidemic in the late 1800s, which had taken the lives of the majority of the women in a small farming community in the southeastern region of Murcia.

As he searched he found a page on urban legends and read that during the time of the deaths of these women, it had been said there had been a spell cast upon the town. A spell cast by a woman who had been believed to be an evil witch. The woman had an affair with a married man and fell in love with him and he would not leave his wife for her. The wife of her lover was the first woman to contract the disease. She carried on with the married man as the wife wasted away. After that, many women of the town were also affected. They all eventually died. The woman, who was called the witch, was not affected by the illness. She was one of very few who had survived, but because of the belief that she had cast the spell to kill the wife of her lover, then spreading it to the beautiful women of the town, she was cast out and told never to return. When she was cast out, she vowed the town would forever suffer because of her fate.

Nicolas looked for the area on the map but there was no name for the farming community. He would later find out the town was abolished, because of the illness and the woman's threats.

The area was not far from where Mia's grandparents lived, where she visited throughout her life. It was also not far from where they spent their honeymoon.

Why? He asked himself. Could she have contracted the disease when they were there? Was it hereditary? He had to find out. He would leave to Murcia on Monday.

Nico made reservations for the flight online. He would stay in their apartment. He went to bed and lay awake looking at the ceiling. Mia slept soundly. He wrapped his arm around her. "She seems too fragile for me to hold," he thought.

Mia had not gained much weight. She ate what was prepared for her, which were the prescribed meals by the doctor, in order to keep her strength up as well as to nourish the babies. She usually struggled trying to get the food down, but she always said she did this so she would be able to be with the babies when they were born and so they would be born healthy.

Nico lay next to her and held her fragile body close. He knew he had to leave her tomorrow. He hadn't been away from her since they were married and hated the thought of leaving her now more than ever. He knew her grandmother would be with her and also knew Antonio was nearby if they needed anything. But, he felt so helpless, leaving her alone. He touched her hair softly, not to wake her and pressed his face into her hair and neck to inhale her fragrance. He was going to miss her so much. He fell asleep lying close to her.

Mia woke up early and needed to go to the restroom. Her belly was swelling and it put pressure on her organs making her go to the bathroom often. Mornings were the worst. She opened her eyes, and realized Nicolas had his arms around her. "Baby, Baby, wake up," she said and nudged Nicolas a few times with no reaction from him, then slowly he moved his arm and turned onto his back.

"Hi beautiful," he said.

"Hi baby, you were knocked out. You must be so tired, you wouldn't budge." Nicolas laughed and said, "Yeah I guess I was tired, I stayed up late getting things done."

Mia anxiously said, "Baby, help me to the bathroom or I'll pee in my pants." Nicolas jumped up and helped her to her feet. He placed his arm around her waist and she placed her hand into his free hand. They walked slowly to the bathroom. Mia then brushed her teeth and washed her face. Nicolas stood by her and also brushed his teeth, making faces in the mirror to get her to smile. She laughed at his silliness.

"Will you help me shower Nico?" she asked. "Yes, my love, let me get it warm." Mia leaned back against the counter to stabilize herself as Nicolas got the towels and placed them on a bench near the shower. He made sure the water was perfect and undressed first. Then he helped Mia remove her nightgown and underwear and helped her into the shower.

Nicolas washed his hair, while Mia let the water run down her body. It relaxed her. She held onto Nicolas' hips as he washed his hair. He washed and rinsed himself quickly. Then he took the soap and put it on a washcloth and began to rub it over Mia's body. Her stomach was so round and big. He bent down and kissed it and then looked up at Mia. She smiled and said, "I was so lucky to have found you." As she said that, her eyes filled with tears. She was so beautiful. Nicolas stood up quickly and pulled her into his arms. "Mia, don't worry please, everything will be just fine, I promise." Then Mia began to sob, and she fell to her knees. She slipped right through Nicolas' wet hands and he quickly bent down and sat in front of her as she cried.

"Nicolas, how am I not supposed to worry? Tell me!!! I promise, I'm trying. But, I can't stop thinking that I may never see my babies, and if I do, it will only be for a short time, and then I will die. How am I not supposed to worry that I may soon leave you… alone? I can't be strong, I want to be with you and our babies and I don't know what to do about it."

Nicolas held her as the tears that fell from his eyes melded with the water that ran down her back. She sobbed in his arms, and he held her tightly, trying to remain strong, but the pain he felt was more than he could ever remember feeling. He wondered if he could handle the pain he knew losing Mia would cause him. He had to, he knew, but felt so weak. He felt as if his every strength had been taken, and at this moment he did not know how to regain it.

"I love you my sweet, sweet Mia, I live for you, every breath I breathe is because I want to be with you always. You have become my reason for living, and I will find a way to make you better. Or your last breath will be my last breath… if I don't have you, I would rather be dead."

Mia kissed him and said, "I love you Nico, please never ever forget."

Mia tried to stand and Nicolas helped her up. He pulled the towel from the bench and helped her dry herself off. She was a bit clumsy and he didn't want her to slip or strain herself.

Nicolas helped her dress and then carried her into the bedroom. He placed her on the bed and positioned her pillows so she could sit up. He knew breakfast would soon be ready and he wanted to tell Mia and Ana, together, about the decision he had made the night before.

Nicolas opened the door for Ana, he knew she would be entering soon with the tray of breakfast for Mia. No sooner had he opened it and she was there with breakfast. "Good morning you two, I hope you slept well."

Nicolas took the tray from her and placed it at Mia's side. Her belly was too big to have it comfortably placed over her legs.

Mia was more hungry than usual. She began to eat the fruit. Sliced bananas, strawberries and pieces of mango. She also had a glass of freshly squeezed orange juice, a piece of toast, and oatmeal. She was eating and talking.

Nicolas sat and watched her. When she was done eating, Nicolas took the tray and placed it on a chest of drawers near the doorway.

Nico then said, as Mia lay back on the fluffy pillows, "I found some information on the internet, about this illness, last night, and I've made plane reservations to go to Spain for the next four days. I have to go there and talk to as many doctors and historians as I can find. I have to find a cure, or the reason for this illness, and then maybe I can find something that will cure you." He also said he had things to take care of at the restaurant, and would be home later, but he said he would be leaving the following morning.

Mia smiled at him, she had no strength to do anything else. When she ate she usually lost her energy. She lay on the bed on her side with her eyes closed. Nico lay behind her, and rubbed her stomach. He felt the babies move.

She was six months pregnant now, and due to her illness and because she was carrying twins, she had been placed on bed rest. Mia began humming her song and placed her hand over Nicolas' hand. Nico kissed her neck and shoulders and said, "I love you Mia." Mia nodded her head slowly and said, "I know baby."

When Nicolas got home that evening he began to gather his things for his trip. Mia sat up in bed and watched him. He saw her reflection in the mirror watching him. She was so serious, looking at him, lost in thought.

Then out of nowhere, she began to talk.

"Nicolas, please promise me something." Nicolas looked at her curiously and nodded his head, "What baby?" He asked.

"Promise me that if I am not with you and the babies, that you will live your life for them. Promise me that you will do everything in your power for them to have happy lives. You must promise me that you will find happiness and the will and desire to breathe again because of our children. I don't want our babies to grow up to be sad adults. Take them everywhere we have gone, show them everything we saw. Tell them stories about me. Tell them things to make them laugh, the things that made us laugh. Promise me you'll be happy, because I can't die knowing you will be sad, because I will live an eternity of sadness. Please, Nico, Please. Promise me?" Mia tilted her head as she pleaded with Nicolas.

Nico looked deeply into her eyes, he took her chin in his hand and said "Mia, if you are gone, I have no idea where I will find the will to live, the will to smile again, the will to laugh. You are everything to me, and what you have brought to my life is, I now know what feeling complete truly means. I don't need or want anything or anyone but you. My heart will die if you are not here, I will be empty and lost in this world, forever looking for you. And I won't be whole again, until I am dead and by your side."

"Nico, I know what you are trying to tell me, because I too, don't know how I will live an eternity without you. Because when I'm gone, I will not be whole again until you are with me. But, we have two little babies who need their mommy and daddy. Their mommy might not be here, but you will be."

Mia took Nicolas' hand and placed it on her belly and said, "These two little babies inside of me, these tiny little babies are a part of you and a part of me. You are the only one who can protect them and teach them and let them know how much I loved them, and how much you and I love each other. You have to look at them and know I am there. If I am gone, you must always know I will be right there with you. I will always be at your side pushing you and giving you strength when you can't find it. Baby, my heart and soul will always be with you. Never doubt it. But please choose to be alive for our babies. Please Nico, I beg of you, please!"

Nicolas placed his head on her belly and began to cry. She pushed her fingers through his hair and began to hum her song, hoping it would calm them both.

Nicolas then said, "Mia, I will be all that you ask, I will be the father you wanted for your children. And our children will know the person you are, and how much you love me, and how much you love them. Mia, this I promise to you... everything you ask, I promise I'll do."

That night, after Mia fell asleep, Nico went into the kitchen where Ana was cleaning up after dinner. He took a beer from the fridge and sat at the table. He stared at the bottle, lost in thought. He began to lift he label from the bottle nervously. He was looking down at it, and the tears began to fall from his eyes. He slammed his fist against the table, Ana turned, and he cried out, "WHY?"

Ana went to him and bent down and held him as he sobbed into her shoulder. Ana rubbed his back lovingly. She felt as if she were holding a small child as he sobbed uncontrollably.

When he stopped, Ana remained at the table with him. She took his hand into hers and confidently said, "Don't worry Nicolas, everything will be ok." He shook his head and said, "I don't know." He stood up and went to the fridge and brought Ana a beer. "Ana, I know I am very optimistic when I talk to Mia, but I have no idea where I'm going to look, and don't even know what I'm looking for." He quickly finished his bottle of beer and went for another. He asked Ana if she knew anything about her mother's illness.

Ana looked down and began, "I was young, when my mother became ill, I didn't know the gravity of this illness. In the beginning I was never told why she died, only that she had died of an illness which spread through the town. I never asked questions, I thought it was an epidemic. My mother and I were not close at the time of her death. It was a very sad time."

"She had become very controlling. She did not want me to marry the love of my life. She forbade it. She had forbidden him from visiting me. I was miserable when I was away from him, only until we would steal time and risk everything to be together. My mother was also miserable, as I refused to talk to her and had become very defiant."

"My mother died a very sad woman, because I would have nothing to do with her. And, when my mother died, it was I who became a very sad woman. And, on the day she died, due to my regret for distancing myself from her, and for defying her wishes, I promised I would fulfill her dying wishes and I would not marry the love of my life. And, because of that decision, from that day forward, I have lived a very lonely life."

Nico looked at her, questioning what she had just said. "You didn't marry the love of your life?" he asked. "No," she said. Ana shook her head slowly and looked away as she smiled a sad, sad smile.

"Does Mia know this?" Nicolas asked.

"She knows bits and pieces, but not the whole truth. I've told her stories, but never said the stories were about me," Ana replied.

Nicolas nodded, as he realized what Mia had talked about previously. He now understood.

Nico looked down at his bottle. He then said, "If there hasn't been an outbreak or known case of it since the 1960s, maybe there is a cure for it. There may be an immunity now in the town. I have to go there and find out."

Ana said, "There is a doctor there who I went to as a child and until I left Spain. He is about 85 years old now. I have heard Mrs. Espinoza speak of him often. He may be able to answer questions you have. His name is Dr. Francisco Garcia."

Nicolas packed his bags quietly as Mia slept. He would leave at 10 a.m. the next morning and wouldn't arrive for 12 hours.

He took a quick shower, and then confirmed his reservation and checked in online. He got into bed quietly so he wouldn't wake Mia. She felt the movement and turned toward him, still asleep.

He saw the babies moving as she slept. He got as close to her as possible and could feel the babies kicking. He smiled at the movement. Those were his babies. Those were their babies. And he rubbed her stomach and said, "Hey babies. This is your daddy talking, and it's time to let your mama rest." He rubbed her stomach and the babies settled down. This made him smile.

Earlier that day, they received a call from the hospital confirming her second ultrasound. Nicolas thought about Mia's excitement when she heard, as he lay back on his arm, looking up toward the ceiling. She was so excited to find out the sex of the twins.

She told him they could go and buy the last things they needed and buy the babies clothes, and she would finally know the names of the twins, because of their sex.

When he saw Mia so happy, it always made him happy. He told Mia as soon as he found out the twin's sex, since they were identical, he would finish their room. Mia was so excited.

He woke up early. Ana made him breakfast and was preparing a small breakfast for Mia. Mia's appetite was not very big, so Ana prepared her several small meals throughout the day. She had cut up watermelon, cantaloupe and peaches for her to eat and prepared a glass of milk with the vitamin drink mix the doctor had recommended so she get all the vitamins she needed for herself and for the babies.

Mia sat up in her bed and ate her fruit as she watched Nico get ready for his trip. "Baby, I'm going to miss you," she said. Nico said, "I have the phone, you can call me anytime and please don't worry, I'll be home in a few days."

Nico was ready. He sat on the bed next to Mia and kissed her. He pushed her hair back and ran his hand down the side of her face. Then she said, "Lay with me before you go." He got into the bed and held her. The twins were moving again and she moaned as they kicked her ribs. "These little monkeys love to keep mommy awake," she said as a weakened laugh escaped her.

Nico kissed her lips and then kissed her stomach twice, once for each baby. "Mia, I have to leave now," he said. "I love you Nico, call me when you get to a place you can call from. I'll be waiting." Nico said, "The first chance I get I'll call you." Mia said, "Baby?" "What?" he asked.

"Can you call me before you board the plane, so I can kiss you before you leave the ground?" Nico said, "Of course I will." He bent down and held her face in his hand and kissed her lips quickly and forcefully, one, two, three times. He held her face and looked directly into her eyes and said, "Baby I love you, never forget it." She said, "I love you, and always will." He grabbed his bag and before he walked out the door, he turned and looked at her. She was watching him leave. He blew her a kiss and she blew one back and waved good-bye.

Nico drove to the airport and parked in the extended stay parking lot. He rushed to get to the gate as he was running late. He got there on time and before he boarded the plane, he called home. Ana answered, and said Mia was asleep. "Can you wake her, I promised I'd call before I left the ground." Ana said, "Sure," and woke Mia.

Mia and Nicolas told each other bye and they loved each other. Before they hung up, Mia reminded him that the day after he arrived, they had the ultrasound to find out the babies' sex. He told her he couldn't wait to get back. Nico hung up, turned his phone off, placed it in his bag and boarded the plane.

CHAPTER XXI

The flight was long, 10 hours to Madrid. Nico slept for a couple hours, then researched more on the Internet. The plane was quiet, everyone slept except him.

When they landed in Madrid he looked for a restaurant and had a sandwich and a beer. He sat staring at his sandwich, concentrating on what he might do when he got to Murcia, and then he looked up. There was a beautiful woman staring at him. She had long black hair, and piercing brown eyes. She smiled and he half smiled and looked down at his sandwich as he took a bite. He looked up toward the woman as he chewed. An uneasy feeling came over him as he watched the woman. He finished his sandwich and beer quickly and grabbed his bag and walked down the long station looking for the gate.

While he waited for the boarding announcement, he turned and saw the woman, from the restaurant, sitting behind him. She looked away as he looked at her, yet momentarily caught eye contact before she quickly turned her head.

When they landed at the airport in San Javier, Murcia, he quickly walked outside to find a taxi. There were no taxis, and as he waited, he saw Joaquin, the driver who had picked him and Mia up when they came for their honeymoon. Nico waved him down. "Hey, Nicolas, como estas? – How are you?" Nicolas asked him if he was going into the city. Joaquin said he was on his way there now. "Want a ride?" Nicolas said yes, and got into the car with Joaquin.

Nicolas saw the strange woman at the entrance of the airport and when he got in the car he looked back and she was getting into a black Mercedes with dark black windows. The car she was in drove slowly by Nicolas and Joaquin, keeping the same pace for a few minutes, then speeding up, it drove off quickly.

The drive was close to 45 minutes to the city. Joaquin stopped at the door of the building where Mia and Nico had the condo. Nicolas took out his bag and thanked him and took out his wallet to pay Joaquin. Joaquin said, "Don't worry, it's already been taken care of." He then quickly corrected himself and said, "Don't worry, I mean, I was on my way into town anyway."

Nicolas remembered the last time he took them into Murcia. He remembered Joaquin said it had already been taken care of, and remembered thinking it was Ana who had paid for the car. He would have to ask Ana again, if she knew Joaquin.

When Nicolas walked up the stairs to the apartment. He ran into Mrs. Espinoza. "Hello Nicolas, Ana told me you would be here, and I just took up some groceries. If you need me to cook, please call me. I will be here when you need me." Nicolas thanked her.

As she continued down the stairs, Nicolas shouted down to her, "Do you know Dr. Francisco Garcia?" Mrs. Espinoza stopped suddenly and looked up, then quickly turned away as if she hadn't heard him and continued down the stairs without answering, "Is he close by?" Nicolas asked. Mrs. Espinoza said, "I will talk to Ana to see if she remembers his address, and I will let you know." Nicolas thought she acted strangely and also remembered Ana mentioned Mrs. Espinoza had talked about the doctor and it was why she knew he was still alive. He continued up the stairs. He had no time to waste. He would find Dr. Garcia himself.

Nicolas took a quick shower, and changed his clothes. He picked up his agenda where he had written his notes of things to do while he was there, and he walked out the door.

He walked to a small restaurant in the plaza, where he ordered a beer and a sandwich of serrano ham and manchego cheese. He sat there eating. Then he began talking to the waiter. "Do you know of a doctor named Dr. Francisco Garcia?"

The waiter said, "Yes," and went on to explain Dr. Garcia no longer practiced, but his son did. He began to tell Nico the reason he was still at the clinic was to make him believe he was still capable of practicing medicine. Then he laughed and said, "But everyone in the town knows he'd better not be the one to practice on them, he is too old to be practicing." The waiter continued to laugh as he walked away. Nico slightly shook his head and chuckled… not at what he said, but at how the waiter, so casually, told the story to a stranger.

Nico walked through town. It was quiet. He walked about two blocks and saw "Medico" (Doctor) sign on a window. He walked in and asked for Dr. Garcia. A young man in his 30s walked out and said, "Hola." Nico said, "Hola." Nico asked, "Are you Dr Garcia?" "Yes, I am" said the doctor. Nico asked, "Is your father in?" "Yes, but my father doesn't practice," the young Dr. Garcia replied.

"I've come to see your father, because he may know of a rare illness my wife has contracted. Her great grandmother died from the illness in the 60s. It was an incurable blood disease that killed women in this town." Dr. Garcia turned away nervously. Nico asked Dr. Garcia, "May I speak to your father?" Dr. Garcia said, "Why would you want to know about something that happened over 50 years ago?" Nico, holding back his emotions, blurted out, "Because my wife has contracted the same disease and she is dying." When Nico said that, Dr Garcia turned and looked at him with panic in his eyes.

Dr. Garcia said, "I don't know anything about it, but my father has talked about it often over the years. I will bring my father here tonight at 7:00." Nico thanked him and said he would return at 7:00.

Nico left and went to the apartment. He needed to get some sleep. He was exhausted. He went home and slept for about two hours, and when he woke up he felt like he hadn't slept more than five minutes.

He got ready and went to the plaza near the doctor's office and went into a restaurant to kill time. He ordered a cortado; he needed something to wake him.

There weren't many people there, it was still the hour of siesta, the afternoon break time. He ordered some tapas, and a beer and sat down to eat. There was a beautiful woman, with long brown hair, sitting by the window. She smiled at Nico as she nervously played with her napkin. Nico smiled and turned away. When he looked back toward her, she was gone.

Nico finished his coffee, paid his bill, and left. He walked through the town and saw the people as they began to come back into the street after the siesta. He remembered this so well when he was a child in the city. When he first arrived in the United States, it was one of the things he missed most, and although he had gotten use to it after almost nine years, he still at times missed it.

Nico walked toward the doctor's office. He knocked on the door and the younger Dr. Garcia unlocked and opened the door quickly. Almost as if he had been waiting at the door for Nicolas. The older doctor was sitting at a table. He looked up at Nicolas over his glasses and said, "Hola."

Nicolas said, "Hola." Dr. Garcia looked down toward the table and said, "My son said your wife has contracted the blood disease that killed many women many years ago and also killed her grandmother in the 60s."

"Yes," Nicolas said.

"I was a young doctor then, I had just finished studying. There was only one case, that year, of the epidemic. Daniela Sanchez. The very last case I have knowledge of."

Nicolas asked, "Do you have any knowledge of it ever being contracted other than here?" Dr. Garcia shook his head and said he was not sure how it had been contracted by the women and went on to tell him he had researched it for many years and could not find where it had come from, if it was hereditary, or just an exposure to something that no longer existed. He told Nicolas what he remembered was the townspeople did not want it mentioned. They spoke of it as an old wives' tale and thought speaking of it would cause it to reappear. Although, they spoke of it only as a fable and not as something that had actually happened, it was something taboo.

Nicolas told him Mia was diagnosed with the disease a month ago, and she was pregnant. He told Dr. Garcia, Mia's great grandmother was Daniela Sanchez, who had died from the disease. Dr. Garcia looked at Nicolas in disbelief, shook his head, and said "I'm sorry my son. I don't know what to tell you, and can't give you an answer to your questions. After many years of researching the disease, I stopped. One reason being, it was the last case recorded and because I could not find any results or link it to any other illness I had ever researched, I stopped."

Nicolas grabbed Dr. Garcia's arm and said, "You have to help me. There is no one who can help me. The doctors give her no chance of living more than six months, and the babies are killing her slowly. Please! I need your help!!"

The younger Dr. Garcia stood up and firmly said, "Please, you need to leave. My father is not well." The older Dr. Garcia put his head down into his hands and shook his head. "I can not help you my son." The younger Dr. Garcia insisted, "Please leave, he is not well."
Nicolas agreed to leave. But before he left, he took a pen from his pocket and pulled out his business card. He placed it on the table and wrote his home phone number on the back. He said, "Here is my card, it has every number where I can be reached. If you think of anything, please call me. I will do anything to save my wife's life. Anything!"

When he said this, Dr. Garcia looked at his son, directly in the eye, and the son turned away quickly.

Nicolas felt they had to know something and didn't want to tell him. Nicolas said, "I am staying at the address on the back of the card. I will be there until tomorrow at 6 a.m. when my flight leaves. I am begging you, please help me."

"Son, I have nothing to share with you, and no way of curing your wife," said the older Dr. Garcia, then he slowly stood up, grabbed his cane and began to walk toward the back of the house.

Nicolas said "Thank you," and walked toward the door. He stood outside the building in the hot evening sun. Nicolas feeling hopeless, looked up toward the sky and said "God, I need your help, please send me something, I can't live without her...I won't live without her."

The tears started to fall from his eyes. He grabbed his sunglasses and put them on and walked toward the Cathedral. He wanted the hours to pass so he could be home.

He walked around the plaza, watching people coming and going. The crowds of people were laughing and seemed to be enjoying life. He noticed the couples together and realized there was a chance he would never be like that with Mia again. He felt desperate. What could he possibly do?

He walked through the town, wandering the streets and came upon a new age store, which said herbs and vitamins on the window. He walked into the store where the strong smell of incense filled the air and seemed to make the air almost thick inside. As he walked in, a woman handed him a card for tarot readings. He told her he wasn't interested and handed it back to her. She insisted, pushing the card onto his chest and said she had something important to tell him. He refused. The woman turned quickly and the card fell to the floor. Nicolas bent down to get the card to return it to the woman but when he stood up, she was gone. He placed the card in his pocket and smiled and shook his head wondering how she had escaped so fast.

The store was long and narrow. It was dark with small vintage lamps positioned on each wall above the shelves. The walls were paneled in dark wood. Sepia colored bottles filled the shelves behind the counter. The bottles were filled with herbs and oils. The lighting was dim.

Nicolas looked around for someone then knocked on the counter. A beautiful woman stood up from behind the desk.

She said, "Hola guapo." He said, "Hola." Then he started talking in English. "Have you ever heard of an incurable blood illness in the 60s that killed some women here?" The woman said, "I have heard something about it, but thought it was an old wives' tale, but I don't know much about it. There is a gentleman who will be here next week who may be able to tell you more. You can come back then."

Nico said "But, I don't live here, and I am leaving tomorrow at 6 am. Is there any way I can see him today? I live in the United States and my wife has contracted the illness and is not expected to live more than six months. She is also pregnant and the babies are taking the life from her faster."

"Babies!" she said, shaking her head. "Yes, Nico said, "she is pregnant with twins." The woman smiled and congratulated Nicolas.

The woman then went on dusting the bottles and without giving him eye contact, she said, "I am sorry, but the gentleman will not be back for another week." Nico said, "Ok, then I, too, will be back next week."

The girl said, "ok," and turned her back to him as she continued to dust the bottles. Nicolas thanked her and began to leave. She did not respond.

Nicolas walked out onto the street and began walking without direction, then remembered he had forgotten to ask for the gentleman's name. He turned around and walked back toward the store, when he arrived, the shades had been pulled down, the closed sign was out and the door was locked. He thought it was strange, but thought it may be customary for that type of store to close early.

He walked to the restaurant where he and Mia had eaten. The waiter who had served them together was there. Nicolas called him by his name, Ginés, and the young man, surprised he had remembered his name, began to attend to Nicolas even more efficiently. Nicolas was relieved he had gotten there before it closed and relaxed into his chair.

Nicolas ordered a small steak and baked tomato. He loved baked tomatoes. They reminded him of home when he was a child growing up in Spain. He ordered a beer and sat there thinking.

The noise of the people in the restaurant did not bother him, he welcomed it. He began to eat the fried almonds that had been placed on the table, thinking about the conversation he had with the woman at the store. The waiter soon appeared with his food. It looked and smelled delicious he thought. He began to eat, savoring every bite. He hadn't realized just how hungry he was. As he ate slowly, he felt someone staring at him and he looked up and saw a beautiful woman.

Long black hair framed her face and her enticing red lips on her white skin were like a magnet, drawing his attention toward her. She was strangely beautiful he thought. She stared at Nicolas, with the most seductive piercing black eyes. He stared at her, almost entranced. She touched her hair as she watched him watching her. He grabbed his beer and took a quick drink, breaking the trance, then nervously cut into his steak, keeping his gaze on his plate as he began to eat more quickly. He remembered the other women he had seen since he arrived in Murcia, all strikingly beautiful. Nicolas then reached for his beer and before it reached his mouth, he glanced back at the woman. She was gone.

Nicolas ordered another beer and sat back in his chair and drank it slowly. The sun was beginning to set and the plaza was filling with people. He watched a family enter the tented area for dinner with the children happily laughing and the parents holding hands as they waited to be seated. Then he turned to where the beautiful woman had been sitting and caught a glimpse of the woman who had given him the card for tarot readings.

She stood in the shadows at the edge of the building. She was an older woman, wrinkled from the sun, who wore a colorful scarf on her head. She was reminiscent of the gypsies who lived in the nearby neighborhood when he was growing up. Women dressed in flowing dresses, scarves, and jewelry…. lots of jewelry, bracelets, necklaces and big earrings, which as a small boy, he found fascinating.

She leaned against a wall, and played with her cards. She glared at him, avoiding eye contact and continued what she was doing, fanning herself with her cards, and pressing her finger through them to make a shuffling sound. He also avoided eye contact with her. He wondered what she meant when she said she had something to tell him. Could she have an answer, he wondered. He had never liked anything to do with the supernatural or occult. He remembered his grandmother's warnings against these things. But now, in his desperation, he was willing to listen to anyone and everyone.

He finished his meal and ordered a coffee. He drank it slowly. He watched the woman and was growing more curious as to what she had to tell him. The waiter brought him the bill and he put the money on the plate and thanked Ginés, then decided he would approach the old gypsy woman.

He walked toward her. The old woman glared at him with wide open eyes and quickly turned and walked away. She walked swiftly, then turned into a dark narrow alley. He followed her, and as he approached her, she quickly turned and again pressed a card onto his chest. "Beware, my son," Nicolas said nothing as she continued. "All that is around you is not as it seems. Betrayal comes from the most unlikely. You will be given a choice, do not make it in haste, as you may regret the decision you take for as long as you live." Nicolas listened carefully to her every word. She continued. "Go now, your heart will tell you, and you must listen to you heart, your heart will not deceive you. Listen to it, it is the only thing you know to be true." She turned and walked away quickly. Nicolas walked behind her asking her to explain what she meant. "Go, go now!" she said forcefully, "I cannot be seen with you." She walked quickly and disappeared into the large crowd of people.

Nicolas stood in the crowd, as people went by, some brushing against his statuesque body. He was confused. What did she mean? After losing sight of the woman, he sat at an outside café and ordered a beer and watched the people pass as he wrote what the gypsy woman had said, he couldn't forget her words. He wrote and underlined the words three times. Then remembered her last words, "I can not be seen with you." Why? He wondered.

He drank his beer slowly, looking from his written words to the people in the crowd. Laughter rang through his ears, which was painful, as he thought of the sadness that now lived within him. Thinking he could lose Mia, he wondered how he would ever laugh again, without her.

Nicolas paid and began to walk home slowly. He was tired and had to get to the airport by 4 a.m. He was exhausted. His body and brain hurt. But, his heart was about to explode from the thought of losing Mia. He couldn't lose her and would do anything and everything to save her, or lose his life, trying.

Nicolas fell asleep as soon as he hit the pillow. And woke up at 3:30 a.m. with just enough time to get to the airport. He wished he had had time to go back to the herb store before he left. But, he knew he would be back.

He got to the airport and purchased a return flight for the following week. He was coming back to find the man at the new age store to see if he could possibly help Mia.

The flight took forever it seemed. He read, and tried to sleep. He read his written words of the old gypsy, over and over again. He connected to the internet to research more and to see if he could find something, anything, but found nothing new.

He arrived in Miami at 3:00 that afternoon. He got into his truck, and drove home. He was tired, but he had an adrenaline rush that hadn't stopped since he found out she was sick.

He drove home, not realizing the distance he had traveled or anything he passed, until he was home. He parked in the driveway, pulled out his bag and walked inside.

When he entered the kitchen, he saw his mother washing dishes. Ana was at the table peeling apples for an apple pie. His father was watching TV. They had arrived while he was in Spain without his knowing they were coming to visit. Later he found out Ana had told them of Mia's condition and they wanted to be near to help in whatever way they could.

He said hello quickly, kissing his mother and Ana as he went through the kitchen and walked directly to their bedroom. The TV was on. One of Mia's favorite soap operas was on. He looked toward the bed and she was asleep. He turned the volume down and sat on the bed next to her. He touched her hair softly, taking a few small strands between his fingers, feeling the silkiness of her beautiful hair and he slowly let it slide from his grasp.

He had missed it. She opened her eyes slightly and looked up. "Nico, baby, you're home. I missed you so much."

He lay beside her and pulled her into his arms. He kissed the top of her head and he listened to her questions. "Did you have a good flight? Did you eat good food? Did you meet nice people?" He heard her questions, but his mind was far... far away, he just nodded in response to her questions. He wondered how he was going to tell her he had come back with nothing.

He answered her questions quickly, then, changed the subject. "I brought you something." She looked up at him, wide eyed, with the look of a little girl, when she was excited.

He got up from the bed and went to his bag. He opened it and pulled out a small silver jewelry box with a small ruby in the middle. He said it was to place the babies' first locks of hair. Mia loved it. She held it in her hands and inspected it carefully, then looked up into his eyes, with a questioning look.

He kissed her on the lips and said, "Baby, I have to go back next week to meet with someone who might know something about helping us." Mia smiled, and said nothing. She looked down at the jewelry box and slowly traced the etchings with the tip of her finger, then said, "Thank you Nico, I love you more than I know how to express." He kissed her, and said, "I know baby, it's exactly how I feel."

They lay in bed and fell asleep together. Nico, still in his clothes, was exhausted.

Nico woke up awhile later and was so happy to be home. He looked down at Mia's stomach. The babies were moving. He put his hand on her stomach gently and could feel their feet and arms as they pushed outward, stretching her skin. She moaned. He rubbed her stomach and then put his head next to it and talked to them. "Hey you little babies, you need to let your mommy rest. She's tired and she needs all her strength." He started humming the song she always hummed, and rubbed her stomach. It was as if the babies heard him hum, and they stopped moving. As he hummed, he knew he could never forget the song, and he knew if Mia were gone it would be the only thing that calmed their babies. But in his heart, he knew only Mia humming the song would be what calmed him.

Nicolas got up from bed and went into the bathroom. He looked into the mirror and examined his bloodshot eyes. For the first time, he realized not only how exhausted he looked but actually was. But he wouldn't stop. He turned on the shower and took off his clothes. He stepped into the shower and let the warm water run over his body. He began to cry, as he so often did, when he got into the shower and was alone. It was his safe haven. The place he knew no one could hear or see him.

When he got out, he shaved, brushed his teeth and wrapped the towel around his body. He walked out and Mia was awake. She smiled as he entered the room. "Baby, she said, I miss you, and I want you." You look so sexy. Will you help me into the shower, so I can be clean for you?" He nodded his head and helped her up from the bed. He held onto her as she walked slowly into the bathroom then helped her undress.

She was beautiful. Her stomach was big, and her body was thin. Her breasts were full and beautiful. He looked at them and touched them gently with his fingertips. "Hold me Nico, I want you to make love to me, I missed you so much."

He turned the shower on and helped her in. She stood there as he washed her hair. He made lots of suds and placed it on top of her head. He got the loofah sponge, and poured her favorite soap onto it and washed her body gently. She stood there hanging on to him. He washed her slowly. He got down on his knees to wash her legs and feet. She held onto his head. He looked up and saw her looking down at him. Her stomach was between the two of them. He washed up her legs then put down the loofah and with his hands, began to lather between her legs. Then he reached for the hand held shower attachment and rinsed her body. He held her, and placed the showerhead between her legs. He sucked her nipples and let the water spray and tickle her. Mia held him tighter, and he knew what it meant, she suddenly weakened and fell deeper into his embrace from the orgasm, which resulted from the water touching her so gently.

He wanted her badly. He was hard. She said, "Baby, I need you." He hugged her and she groped him, and slid her hand up and down his stiffness. Nicolas kissed her, taking her mouth into his. He loved her so much and the love that once resulted in pleasure was now filled with pain.

Mia looked into his eyes and saw his pain. She wanted him to be happy and began to crack simple childlike jokes. He laughed and it made her happy.

He rinsed the soap from her hair and suds from her body then helped her out of the shower and dried her off. He helped her put her robe on and they walked to the room. He pulled out her favorite pink nightgown and put it over her body. She laughed and said, "You didn't think I'd get so fat that you'd have to dress me did you?" He laughed and said, "No, I didn't, silly!"

Then he thought of something. He knew how much she loved the movies and said, "Hey, I have an idea for tonight. How about we go to the drive in. We can make a bed in the back of the truck, take snacks and watch the movie."

Her eyes lit up with his suggestion, and she started to do her little bounce she always did when she was extra happy. "It'll be fun," she said. "What will we watch?"

Nicolas told her they could head out to the drive-in at the end of town, the one that plays the classic movies on Wednesdays. She said it sounded like fun. But she needed chocolate covered raisins for the movie. He laughed and said with a broken southern accent, "Anything you desire, ma'am." Mia laughed.

"I'll go out and get the things we need, and I'll be back in awhile," he said. She told him she'd be ready when he got back. He said, "It's a deal." She smiled and blew him a kiss. He got into his shorts and running shoes, put on a t-shirt, kissed her and left.

Mia called her grandmother and asked her to help her get ready. Mia asked for the pink dress she bought when she first got pregnant. She hadn't worn it before. She thought Nico would love her in it because he always said he loved her in pink. She put the dress on and sat up on the bed and put her make up on. She combed her hair and put it up in a ponytail, then decided to let it down. She knew Nicolas loved playing with her hair and she wanted to look beautiful for Nico.

She sat up waiting for him as she watched her soap opera. She laughed as she realized she never watched soap operas until she got pregnant. She rubbed her belly and laughingly said, "See what you kids are doing to me, you're making me into a housewife who watches soap operas."

Ana peeked from the bathroom, as she was cleaning and saw Mia laugh. She smiled at Mia and blew her a kiss. "I love you Gram, she said." Ana replied, "I love you mi niña."

Nicolas went to the grocery store, got ice for the cooler, water for Mia, and a couple of sodas for him to drink with the popcorn. He got a big bag of chocolate raisins so they could share. He also picked up some peaches and strawberries. He knew, now that she was pregnant, she craved refreshing fruits and water.

He got home and put everything together in the cooler. He pulled out some blankets from the closet and grabbed the pillows from the extra bedroom.

He walked into the room where she was sitting with her back against the bed. She looked so beautiful in her pink dress.

Her hair hung down over her breasts, it had grown so much. "She is so sexy," he thought. Mia had applied light pink lipstick to her lips, which made them sexier. She looked up and smiled when he entered. He looked at her with an intense look, the look she knew so well, the look that affirmed his love for her and showed how much he desired her.

Nicolas winked at her and she smiled and said, "Do you like it?" as she extended her hands so he could see her dress. "I wanted to be pretty for you." Nicolas smiled that sweet sad smile, and said, "You're always pretty Mia." Mia smiled back at him. She's happy, he thought, and that's all he really wanted for her. He asked, "Are you ready?"

"Sure am," she said. He helped her stand up, grabbed her pillow and the pillow support she used to sit up in bed. They walked to the truck. He picked her up and sat her in the truck. She pulled him and kissed him as he helped her place the seat belt over her big stomach. She giggled and

said, "Almost getting too big for this seat belt, huh baby?"
Nicolas smirked as he struggled to get it fastened.

Nicolas drove to the drive in. When they arrived, he
opened the back of the truck, and arranged the blankets
and pillows, making it as comfortable for Mia as he could.

"Let's get popcorn before the movie starts," he suggested.
Mia said, "Yes!" He helped her out of the truck and they
walked to the concession stand. There was a bench in the
concession stand where Mia sat, so she could wait for him
as he stood in a line with 10 people ahead of him. "Baby,
do you want a hot dog, burger, or nachos?"

"I'll have a burger and fries. Only tomatoes and mustard
please."

He got to the head of the line and ordered two hot dogs for
himself, a hamburger for Mia, and a large bucket of
popcorn. As he was paying, Mia asked for cotton candy.
He ordered the cotton candy, paid, and helped her up.

They slowly walked to the truck as the sun was setting
behind the large screen, leaving a sunset of orange and
pink across the sky. They could hear families laughing,
teenagers talking and two little boys were running and
shooting each other with water guns. Mia looked at them
and then looked up at Nico with a strange look.

"What's wrong Mia?" he asked. "Nothing, I'm just
watching the little boys play, thinking about our babies.
Tomorrow, we'll be able to know if our babies are boys or
girls." "Yes, mi amor," Nico said. And then kept quiet.

He didn't want to think of what could happen. He only wanted to enjoy her, every minute he could, now that he was here. He would leave to Spain and find the person who knew how to cure her. He believed it in his heart. And he would not stop until he found something, or he would die with her.

When they got to the truck he helped her up, put the pillows around her to support her, and placed the soft blankets and foam behind her, so she would be as comfortable as possible. He got into the truck and arranged the food and drinks around her so she wouldn't have to move if she needed something.

She pulled out the hamburger and started eating it, ate two bites, then started on the popcorn. She took about three handfuls, and asked for the chocolate raisins. He opened her water and put it in the cup holder near her. He laughed at her because she was eating everything around her, going from the raisins to the popcorn, to the hamburger. He laughed and she then realized what she was doing and said, "Well, I was hungry." They both laughed.

The movie started; it was an old movie from the 70s. It was near Halloween and the line up was horror stories. Mia leaned against Nico and he held her. They watched the movie together.

Nico leaned back and got comfortable and Mia rested on him. He worried that the back of the truck might be too hard for her and she would not be able to sleep later. He pushed the remaining pills behind her.

Ten minutes hadn't gone by when he noticed her steady breathing. She was asleep. He could see her face with the light from the movie screen. She was so beautiful. He stared at her and gently touched her cheek, then pushed away the hair that had fallen onto her face. He watched her and lightly touched her hair as he trailed off in his thoughts.

His thoughts went from the day he first saw her walking in South Beach, lost, then he reminisced of the day they got married, remembering how beautiful she looked as she walked down the stairs. He ran his fingertips over her arm softly. She was so thin. It scared him to realize just how thin she had gotten. He couldn't stand seeing her waste away. He couldn't stand seeing her suffer.

They lay in the truck until the movie was over, then Nicolas woke Mia. He helped her into the front seat and they drove home, holding hands.

CHAPTER XXII

Friday, the day of her appointment, Mia woke early   She was so excited to find out the sex of the babies.   Nico helped her out to the car and they drove to the doctor's office.   His parents and her grandmother stayed at home and waited for them.   They thought it would be better if they had this special time together and alone.

The doctor's office was busy with pregnant mothers, their husbands, parents, and new mothers.   Nico let the receptionist know they were there.   The receptionist let Nico know Mia had priority and they would call her in next. They called Mia after about 10 minutes.   The ultrasound tech prepped Mia.   Nico loved seeing Mia so happy, and all he could hope for is that this would never end, but a voice in the back of his head reminded him they had very little time together, unless he found a cure.

The ultrasound technician began the procedure.   She pointed out the babies' hands and feet, and told them she couldn't see between their legs--they were hiding. "They're modest," she said, and laughed.   Mia smiled and looked up at Nicolas.   He knew she was nervous, almost as nervous as he was.

The ultrasound technician put her cold hand on Mia's stomach so the babies would move, and as she did, baby A's legs opened.   Nico's eyes widened and said, "It's a boy!!!"   Baby B then pushed his way and Nico said, "Another boy!"   Mia started giggling nervously, then whispered, "Oh my God, they are boys!" Her eyes filled with tears.

Nico covered her face with kisses and she looked at him so seriously and said, "Nico… they're boys and we still haven't chosen another name. Michelangelo is all we have," then she started crying. Nicolas laughed and reassured her they would find one soon, and not to worry. He told her it was what she could do, while he was in Spain.

Nico was so happy they were going to have two sons. "Wow, I can't believe it," he said, then thought about Mia's reaction and chuckled.

"Now we have to buy boy clothes, can we stop at the mall to buy two little outfits?" She asked. Nicolas nodded.

Mia talked nonstop on the way to the mall. She talked about her identical twin boys. "Nico, will they have the same personality, will they be completely identical?"

Nico said, "I suppose so, but we can research all about identical twins tonight." He hadn't read much about twins and had never known any identical twins, only a couple sets of fraternal twins growing up in Spain.

When they got to the mall, Nico requested a wheelchair, which was given to them immediately. He pushed Mia through the mall and headed directly to her favorite department store. He knew they had to do this quickly as she tired so easily and he also wanted to spend time with her at home before he went back to Spain.

Mia found two small onesies with little bears embroidered on the front and two matching hooded sweat jackets with small bears on the pocket. She picked out two pair of matching baby blue booties with small brown bears on them as well. She also bought two blue blankets, one dark blue, and the other light blue, which would go well with the theme they had chosen for the babies' bedroom.

When they were done, Mia asked if Nicolas would take her to have frozen yogurt. Lately she had begun craving anything cold and refreshing. Mia chose the coconut yogurt and added chocolate sprinkles. Nicolas had a mix of strawberry, chocolate, and coconut in his bowl with assorted toppings and topped it off with whipped cream. Mia laughed when she saw how full his bowl was. They sat and ate their yogurt and Mia talked nonstop about the babies.

Nicolas ate his yogurt slowly as he listened to her talk. She was so happy today. He realized, just knowing the babies' sex had completely changed her mood. She hadn't talked about her illness all day.

He knew he had to leave Mia in a few days. And now knowing about his baby boys, everything seemed even more real. He knew he had to find a way to cure her. But...how?

Nicolas tried to concentrate on what Mia said. He knew he had to remember everything, for if he were to lose her, he had to have everything engraved in his heart and mind. Not only for the babies, but for himself in order to go on.

His mind was not fully there, as he thought about Spain and what he needed to do as soon as possible. He sat back on the couch they were sitting on and Mia sat back leaning into him. She continued talking about their baby boys.

They went home and Mia organized the blankets on the beds and placed the little outfit above each one. Nico stood at the door leaning against the entrance. He watched her as she did this, humming her song. Then she turned, and looked at him in a panic with her eyes wide open.

He got frightened and ran to her, thinking something was wrong. But she said "Nico, my love, we need another boy's name." He looked at her and laughed. He approached her and pulled her close. She looked up into his eyes and said, "Help me, please. What name goes well with Michelangelo? Nico responded, "Mitchelangelo?" and laughed.

"Nooooo," Mia said. "That's horrible!" "Marco Polo?" "Nooooo," she said laughing. "I don't know baby, let's "think about it." She pouted and said, "This might be a hard one." Nicolas smiled and kissed her forehead then said, "Don't worry about it, we still have time and like I said, it's something that can keep you busy while I'm in Spain."

The remainder of the weekend was spent at home with Nico's parents and Ana. It was quiet. Mia tired more easily lately. Nico read a lot, spending all his time with Mia in the bedroom, only taking her out to eat lunch and dinner, and when she woke up he usually took her outside where she loved to be in the garden. Nico also knew she needed the sun and the fresh air. It made her vibrant. Also, during the evening, if she was not too tired, they all went out and spent time telling stories on the patio and laughing.

Mia was happy. She talked about the babies' names and wondered what they'd be like. Nicolas silently watched her, most of the time. He saw the happiness in her, and from time to time, he saw her fade into the distance. Her expression would change to a look of sadness, and despair. He knew where she was when her thoughts trailed off. He knew she was thinking she would not be here to enjoy her boys.

Nico talked about things they had done before she got sick, when he saw her lost in her thoughts. It seemed to bring the smile back to her face, because she always added special things she remembered about those days.

Sunday night Nico got his bags ready. He had scheduled an early flight because it had the shortest layover time in Madrid. He needed to get to Murcia as soon as possible.

The following morning, after breakfast, Nico's father put the bags in the car and waited for him. Mia woke up when she heard Nicolas gathering his personal items for the trip. She sat up in bed and watched him get his computer and place it in his carry on bag.

He sat on the bed beside her and said "Mia, I'll be gone for a few days. I am going to speak to the man at the herbal store. He may have an answer to what we're searching for." She kissed and hugged him tightly.

He held her frail body close and hugged her gently. He then placed his hands on her face and held it and looked into her eyes and said, "Don't forget how much I love you, and don't forget that everything will be ok." She looked at him and said, "I love you Nico, and I believe you. Please hurry home. I can't be without you for long. I feel so weak without you."

They kissed, and he got up and turned away. She watched him as he walked away, and before he made the turn to leave the doorway, he looked back and winked at her; he needed just one more look. Mia kissed her fingers and then made a fluttering motion with them, and when he turned she blew kisses, and whispered quietly, "I love you Nico."

His flight seemed like it would never end. He couldn't sleep. He'd fall asleep for a few minutes, but would wake to dreams that did not make any sense. He could see Mia, cured from her illness and with two identical baby girls. They were far off in the distance and he could not reach them. He jumped and woke from his sleep. The lady sitting next to him asked if he was ok. He said, "Yes, just a bad dream." He stood up from his seat and went toward the lavatory. He stopped by the flight attendant station and ordered a coffee.

Nicolas looked out the window of the plane. Farmland, mountains, and small towns scattered the countryside, which were noticeable because of the cluster of lights seen from above.   Then the three towers in Madrid appeared. He knew he would be there soon.   His layover was three hours.   He would have a sandwich and something to drink while he waited.

At the Madrid airport he looked for a quiet place to eat. He found a diner that served sandwiches and other dishes customary to Spain.   He picked up a bottle of water, a sandwich, and a slice of Spanish tortilla made of egg, potato and chorizo.   He sat down at the table furthest from the entrance.   He ate quickly because of the impatience he was feeling.   He just wanted to get there.

He boarded his plane on time, and during the plane ride a woman who sat next to him began to talk.   She asked him where he was from, he answered.   She asked if he was on vacation or in Spain for business.   He told her his reason for going.   She was quiet after that.   They arrived at the airport and the lady smiled at him and slightly nodded her head saying, "Good luck, I hope your wife feels better soon."   He thanked her.

Nico hailed a taxi that drove him to Murcia. He arrived at their apartment during the time many businesses were closed.   He walked to a small restaurant and had a salad with tuna.   He had water and a coffee after his meal so he could kill time.

At 5:00, he walked to the herbal store   It was open.   There wasn't anyone in the front area of the store, but the door had a chime, which sounded when anyone walked in.   The same woman, who he had talked to, came out to attend to him.   She said immediately when she saw Nicolas, "He was here earlier and has already left for the day. He knows you were here and the reason, and he instructed me to tell you he has no answers to your questions, and he has never heard of any such disease."

Nicolas shook his head and asked for a pen, he took his business card out and wrote his address and number in Spain on the back. He said, "Here is my number and the place I am staying. Please have him call me if he can remember anything." The girl took the card, looked at it carefully and said she would tell him. She placed the card on the cash register without looking up at Nicolas.

Nico left the store very discouraged and walked slowly toward home. He stopped at the patio of a small restaurant and ordered a cortado. He sat there and drank it slowly, wondering what his next step should be. He pulled out a small book and pen and started to nervously write. He wrote the name of Dr. Garcia, the Drug store name, and other things he didn't want to forget. He wrote down everything he had been exposed to here. He had to make sense of it all. And he wondered if anything could be connected.

Nicolas noticed the streets were quiet. He walked through a narrow street. He didn't want to go far from the pharmacy, just in case the gentleman would call him. He saw a light in one of the shops. It was a tattoo shop. The door was covered with black Spanish style wrought iron bars, as were the windows. He could hear music coming from inside. He opened the door. There was a slender woman with long brown hair and piercing golden colored eyes, standing behind the counter. She introduced herself as Yolanda and asked if she could help him.

As she finished asking him, a man walked out of a back room wiping his hands with a black rag. "How can I help you, man?" The man asked this in English with a strong Spanish accent Nicolas thought, similar to his when he first moved to the states. Nicolas replied "I just came in out of curiosity. I heard the music, one of my favorite songs, so I decided I'd come in and see where it was coming from."   The receptionist kept her head down with only her eyes lifted looking at Nicolas, her hand frozen with the pen she had been using to write when he walked in.

The handsome, green eyed, tattoo artist continued to wipe his tattooed hands and said, "Are you interested in getting something done?" Nicolas sat on the sofa and put his head down and said, "Never thought about it."

"Never?"

"Nope, never!" Nicolas replied.

"I'm the best in town, so if you decide on something let me know." Nicolas shook his head.
The tattoo artist said, "I'm Jack," and stuck out his hand. Nicolas took his hand and shook it. "I'm Nicolas," he said.

You look like you need a drink. Nicolas shook his head and said, "No thanks."

Jack sat down on the chair next to the sofa and placed his arms on the armrests then sat back casually. "You don't look like you're doing very well. A lot of people come in here pretty happy, it's not often I get people who wander in here looking like you."

Nicolas smirked and said, "It's that obvious, huh?"

Jack said, "Yes! Very!" Nicolas laughed. "Where you from?" Jack continued.

Nicolas told him he was from Spain but lived in Miami.

So what's bothering you buddy?

"My wife is sick, not doing well, and we think we're going to lose her." "Wow," Jack said. "Pretty bad, huh?" Nicolas nodded slowly.

"I'm here looking for a cure. This is where it started. Many years ago, there was an epidemic here. It killed many women. There's an old wives' tale that said it was a witch who put a curse on the women."

Jack sat forward resting his arms on his legs and said, "I've heard wives' tales about witches, but not here in the city. I've heard of them coming into town from other villages. Story is, they'd come here enticing men and take them back to their villages where they would bewitch them and they would never return."

"I've heard it many times. People get carried away talking when they are drunk and getting tattooed. I listen but don't comment. A lot of people talk about it, mostly the younger generation. I think they do it to scare each other."

Just then the doorbell rang as the door opened slowly, then stopped before it opened completely. The door then suddenly began to close but remained slightly ajar. Jack stood up, and as he neared the door it swung open rapidly, almost hitting him. Again, the bell rang, and Jack opened the door to see what was going on. A tall blond walked in quickly. She was pale and said someone had been following her, she wondered if she could stay there. Jack asked her to come in and offered her a drink to calm her. He explained it was wine he made himself. He bragged about the recipe being in his family for generations and boasted it was the best in the area. She gladly took it.

She began to tell them she was walking toward her hotel room and noticed a man following her. A man she had previously seen in the restaurant where she had lunch. She felt she was in danger and this was the only place she saw open and it was why she came in. She finished her drink quickly then asked for another.

Nicolas noticed she was drunk after her second drink. She sat next to Jack and began rubbing his legs. Nicolas was quiet and watched Jack and the blonde interact. She began to touch his arms and ask the stories of his tattoos. She placed her leg over his as she leaned into him. She asked him if she could get a tattoo. He said "Sure," and asked what interested her. She said, "I want a broken heart tattooed on my lower back." Jack said, "Are you sure? That sounds a little drastic." She said, "Yes, of course, it's why I came here, to forget the love of my life and a broken heart seems appropriate for a first tattoo."

She opened her purse and took out her wallet and said, "How much?" Jack said, "150 euros." She agreed and placed it on the table. "Let's get ready." Jack told Nicolas he could watch if the blonde gave permission, but it had to be from behind the glass, because he was allowed only to have the person receiving the tattoo in the room for sanitation purposes.

Nicolas watched Jack as he prepared the equipment for the tattoo. The blonde lay on her stomach looking intoxicated. Nicolas remembered his friend getting a tattoo when he got engaged, but never wanted one himself. He saw Jack connect the gun, and pull out the ink.

He began to trace the edges of the heart on the woman's back. While tracing, he used a suction to suck the blood that emerged from the area. Nicolas wondered why she bled so easily. The blood was sucked up into a vacuum tube, almost like something used in a dentist's office. He remembered the blood being wiped off with a rag when his friend got his tattoo. He thought this procedure was strange, but then realized it could be a rule, in the country, regarding tattoos.

He watched the tattoo as it became more visible, and noticed the vacuum lead to a small bag, which looked like the bags of blood in hospitals. He also noticed the bag was beginning to fill with the blood coming from the tattoo. Nicolas thought it was strange. Jack looked up and noticed Nicolas staring at the bag and quickly positioned himself to cover it.

Jack began to talk nervously and called his assistant, Yolanda, who was at the front counter. She walked in and began to clean things around the area. Jack whispered something to her and she turned and looked at Nicolas, then closed the curtain to the window. She came out and said, "he needs privacy for the rest of the tattoo." Nicolas said, "Tell Jack I said thanks for everything and I'll see him around." The attendant nodded her head.

Just as Nicolas was walking out the door, two beautiful women with long dark hair dressed in Victorian style tight fitted dresses, stepped out of a black Mercedes G class. They each carried two black briefcases, one in each hand.

Nicolas stood there for a moment, looking into the Mercedes and noticed a shiny reflection on the driver's seat. It was so difficult to see who was inside, because the windows were so darkly tinted.

Nicolas turned and began to walk away slowly. He had a feeling something was not right and decided to head back to the apartment. He didn't know where else to go. Everyone he had searched for, to talk to about Mia's illness, had no information for him.

Nicolas stopped and looked back toward the shop before he turned the corner and saw the women enter the shop. When the first woman walked in, she went toward the window and closed the shades. The other woman pulled down the shade on the door. Nicolas then again looked into the Mercedes and could see the shadows of a man's face. A face he recognized. The man sat back further in to the shadows of the vehicle and Nicolas could no longer see his face. Joaquin, it was Joaquin the chauffeur, who had picked them up at the airport, Nicolas realized. He was sure of it.

Nicolas felt defeated. He went back to the apartment and sat at the table staring out the window. He could see the highest point of the cathedral from the window. He looked at it and then suddenly stood up and put his jacket on.

He walked out into the plaza, where there were people gathering for the evening. He walked toward the cathedral determined to get inside. He didn't know why, but he felt as if the cathedral was somehow calling him.

He walked into the cathedral pushing his way thru a large crowd of people who were leaving the church. Nicolas hadn't been to church since he left Spain to move to the United States. He looked around.

The small chapels, which circled the bigger chapel in the center, were dark. The gates had all been locked. It was near closing time and the cathedral doors would soon be locked to the public. Nicolas sat in the last pew and began to pray. He wanted to be there as long as he possibly could. He now felt peace. But as he continued to pray he began to sob uncontrollably.

He heard the heavy doors close and heard the keys turn, locking him inside. He heard footsteps but continued to pray. He prayed for a miracle, for a cure, he could not lose Mia. He stood up and took a few euros from his pocket, went to the candle table and knelt down. He lit four candles, one for each baby, one for Mia, and one for himself and as he was about to blow the match out, the hot tip broke off and fell into another candle and accidentally lit another one. He smiled slightly thinking it had to be for good luck. Nicolas put his head down and placed his face into his hands and prayed silently as he continued to sob.

He heard the footsteps approach him and before he could look up, he felt a hand on his back. He lifted his head and turned. There was a priest standing behind him. He looked at Nicolas compassionately and asked, "What is troubling you my son?"

Nicolas stood up and began to explain why he was there. The priest began to walk and Nicolas walked at his side, through the walkway. They passed every chapel, lit only by candles. The priest told Nicolas he had heard of the illness. He had also heard the tales of the witch who had cast a spell because of her lover.

After Nicolas told the priest of his reason for being there, the priest said, "I know of only one cure that is spoken about, but this is against the beliefs of our religion." Nicolas looked at him and said, "Please tell me what this is." The priest said, "I cannot my son, for it would be sacrilegious if it were to escape my lips, for it is forbidden."

Nicolas got on his knees and took the priest's hand into his and held it firmly begging for an answer, then asked, "If it is forbidden to save a person's life because of an evil spell, you are condoning this spell."

The priest said, "They are but only wives' tales my son, just wives' tales. Don't trust in what you've been told, as I have never known of proof of these tales. Have faith and what our father wishes, shall be. You must be strong for yourself and for your family. Pray, and have faith, and she may be healed by a miracle." Nicolas reluctantly nodded his head and thanked the priest. The priest hugged him and blessed him and told him to go with God.

Nicolas left the cathedral and walked into the plaza where many people had gathered. He felt hopeless and felt as if he had no strength to continue. He lifted his arms toward the sky and yelled, "Why, Why, Why?" then fell to his knees, crying into his hands.

The people around looked at him and walked away from where he stood.

He remained there for a few moments sobbing into his hands, until he quieted himself and regained his composure. He stood up and looked into the blank, scared stares of the people who remained around him. He placed his hands on his hips, looked around and began to walk.

He looked at his watch. 9:00 pm. 3:00 in Miami. He promised he'd call Mia at 2:00 Miami time. He pulled out his cell phone and dialed the number.

"Hello," he heard her say softly.

"Mia, it's me, I'm sorry I didn't call earlier."

"I waited for you Nico," she responded. Nicolas felt a knot in his throat and the pain he felt in his heart, just hearing her weak voice, was unbearable. She sounded so weak. She told him about her day, and he listened as he began to walk. When Mia asked if he had found anything, he changed the subject quickly and said he had to hang up. He could not break her heart and would only tell her of his findings when he got home. He knew he couldn't stay away much longer and would have to return to Miami as soon as possible. He stood tall and slowly began to walk. Not knowing where he was going, he walked… just walked.

CHAPTER XXIII

Nicolas walked aimlessly after he talked to Mia. He felt helpless and all hope he once had, remained no longer. He had nowhere to turn, and had no idea how he could save Mia. He walked without direction, not knowing where he was or where he was headed.

The streets were darker than the central part of Murcia. He heard people talking and laughing. He heard the sounds of life as he walked through the streets, lost and alone.

What stood out more than anything he heard was the laughter coming from the homes that surrounded him. He knew that soon he would be walking alone with his sons. He knew he would be alone in a world turned cold without Mia, a world with no meaning. He wondered how in his life, without Mia, he would ever be able to laugh again.

He walked and thought. He did not want to be an injustice to their sons. He knew if he lost Mia, his will to live, and the reason driving every aspect of who he had become since he met her, would be gone. Every desire and dream he had would fade to nothing. Without Mia, he was nothing.

How could he go on? He knew he had promised Mia, their boys would be the reason for going on. But the reason seemed so empty knowing that without her, life would never be the same. He knew he could not live without her.

Nicolas noticed the time – 11:45 pm. He decided to get something to drink and maybe a bite to eat, as he had not eaten dinner, and would then return to the condo to get some rest and start early tomorrow.

Nicolas then remembered what the priest told him of a forbidden cure for the blood disease. Tomorrow he had to find someone to help him. Nico, feeling desperate, knew whatever the cure was, forbidden or not, he would find it.

Nicolas heard music coming from down the street and walked in the direction of the music. The street was dark and at the corner was a dark red light near the entrance to a small bar.

The bar was empty of customers. On a small stage at the back of the bar, a woman played a haunting song on the piano. The bartender was a thin man. He stood behind the counter washing glasses.

The bar was decorated in a Victorian theme. The chairs were upholstered with dark wine colored velvet material. The tables were old, and Victorian style chandeliers were hung over every table. The bar area was lit dimly with blue lighting.

Nicolas ordered a beer and a piece of Spanish tortilla. He waited at the counter to be served and then took what he ordered to the table by the window. He drank the beer and stared at the plate of food. He wasn't hungry, but knew he should eat something.

Nicolas drank his beer and forced a bite of his tortilla. He ate slowly and picked at his food with his fork. His head hung low. He lifted his hand to ask the bartender for another beer. When the bartender placed his beer on the table, Nicolas lifted his head to thank him and saw a man at the table next to him. The man sat motionless in the shadows at the corner table, then Nicolas saw his finger tapping the rounded silver top of a cane he had at his side.

Nicolas hadn't seen the gentlemen when he sat down and hadn't heard him enter. He knew he was tired, but hadn't realized just how tired. He knew he had been lost in thought, but didn't realize how lost he had been until he realized he hadn't heard the man enter the bar.

Nicolas watched the gentleman lift his glass to his mouth. The silver ring on his finger glistened in the shadows reflecting the light from the chandelier above. The man nodded as to say hello. Nicolas mimicked him.
"Hello my name is Meseguer," the gentleman said.

Nicolas introduced himself.

"Are you from Spain?" Meseguer asked Nicolas.

"I am originally from Spain, but have spent the last eight years of my life living in Miami. I was born in Barcelona, and my parents moved us to Cartagena when I was 3, and later we also lived in Valencia."

Nicolas asked Señor Mesesguer if he was from Murcia. He told Nicolas he had lived there most of his life.

"Have you returned to Spain to visit or have you come back to live?" Sr. Meseguer asked.

Nicolas replied, "I am here to research an illness that my wife has contracted... an illness that has only been documented in this region. I've come to find someone... anyone, to help me. The only reason I'm here now is to find a cure."

Sr. Meseguer nodded and asked, "Have you found anything that can help her?" Nicolas shook his head slowly in apparent defeat.

Sr. Meseguer then said, "I see the pain in your face. You must love her very much."

Nicolas shook his head and said, "I can't live without her. I'm desperate. I feel I have run into walls every which way I have turned. She has filled my life and I don't know if I can go on. She is pregnant with our babies. I don't know if, even for our children, I can go on without her. I am not strong enough."

Nicolas explained she was pregnant and if he didn't find a cure he would not only lose his wife but could lose their twins, as well.

Sr. Meseguer nodded his head slowly, as he listened to Nicholas. He knew Nicolas was hopeless and had lost his will as he was slowly losing his wife. The anguish he saw on Nicolas' face reminded him of the pain that never subsided for him because of the love he had lost so very long ago.

"I think I may know what you are feeling right now, my son," Sr, Meseguer began.

"I too lost the love of my life. I did not lose her to death. I lost her to a greater loss than death. I lost her to an eternity of suffering and emptiness. Because in this world I have looked… I have searched for just one woman to give me all that she did, and in my travels to the furthest corners of this world, I have found no one to replace her or the love I felt for her. I have finally conceded to spending eternity alone."

"Eternity?" Nicolas asked. Sr. Meseguer said, "I meant, I must spend the rest of my life alone."

Nicolas did not understand what Sr. Meseguer was referring to.

Meseguer saw the confusion in Nicolas' face and went on. "Many years ago, I left the love of my life to work for my family. Our company opened a new branch in Italy. I was assigned there to teach the new managers the business process. I was to only have remained one month. During my stay there I became ill and became a different person. I was lost in a world of darkness, which kept me there for much longer than my initial appointment."

"When I finally returned to Spain to marry her, she had met someone else. She did not know what had happened to me because I had been gone for so long. During my time away, I knew I loved her. I loved her like no other."

"She felt betrayed because I had not contacted her, and when I returned she was engaged to be married. I asked her then to marry me and I told her of my illness. She refused and told me she never wanted to see me again."

"Night after night I watched her through the window. She had prohibited me from entering the property. I could not see her or talk to her. I watched her for years. She married and then had her child. I watched her with her husband, I saw her tenderness with her child. I was obsessed with her for many years."

"Then one night she saw me standing in the shadows. She approached me. She fell into my arms, and said she had never stopped loving me. She told me of the emptiness she felt with her husband, and when she looked at her child, she wished I was the father. I told her I could not forget her and it was impossible to find anyone to fill the emptiness I felt without her. She told me she knew I was near and wanted me to know she would never truly be happy without me."

"I realized my presence was what she felt and knew it was the reason she could not live the life she had chosen. I left that night. And, I didn't go back. I left because I could not see the pain she felt any more. I left to find something to fill my life and to let her live the life she deserved. I loved her so much and I forced myself to leave her. She is no longer here. And I will forever be alone."

Nicolas wondered what he meant by this. He didn't ask, he let the gentleman continue. He spoke of their time together as teenagers. He told of the moment he first laid eyes on her. He spoke of the love he felt from the moment he saw her. As he talked of the last days of her life here, his eyes took on a look of immense pain, and as Nicolas saw the eternal pain on the gentleman's face, he knew this too would be his destiny. Nicolas felt as if he were staring in the mirror of what the future had in store for him if he were to lose Mia. He knew Señor Meseguer knew, too well, the pain he was facing if he were to lose her. He also felt, at that moment, that Meseguer was placed in his path to help him. How? He did not know, but sensed it to be so.

Nicolas watched the man as he continued to speak of his lost love. He looked into his eyes as he described first the love and happiness he shared with this woman, and then the pain as he spoke of the loss of her. He told Nicolas he not only lost her once, but twice. The first time I lost her to another man, the second she was lost to eternity. Nicolas knew she must be dead, because he referred to eternity over and over again.

Nicolas saw the unbearable pain in his face, as if his own pain was reflected in Meseguer. Nicolas felt his pain, as he continued to speak. He knew he too would feel the pain that painted the anguish on Meseguer's face, because he too could lose Mia forever.

A feeling of desperation came over Nicolas. He knew he could not live without Mia a single day--much less until the end of his life. He could not fathom the pain of losing the most precious thing in his life. The person who brought joy, happiness, passion--everything to him. He could not live without her and knew he would not.

Sr. Meseguer talked more, reminiscing of the time with his love, so long ago. Nico felt very sorry for him, because there was nothing he could do to bring her back. Nico, on the other hand, knew he had to find the way, even if it was the most impossible or the most forbidden thing imaginable.

When Sr. Meseguer finished, he was quiet. Then Nicolas spoke. "If you know anything I can do to save her, please, help me. I can't lose Mia. I cannot go through life feeling the pain I see in you… the pain I feel through you."

Sr. Meseguer put his hand on his chin and looked at Nico. He nodded slowly as he stared into Nicolas' eyes. He realized the desperation painted on Nicolas' face and became quiet.

After a few minutes of Nicolas explaining all he had done during his trips to Murcia to find anything that could possibly help Mia, Sr. Meseguer stopped him. He told Nicolas he knew of someone who might know of a cure for her.

Nicolas grabbed Sr. Meseguer's hand as his eyes filled with tears, "I am begging you, please help me save my wife, she is my life. I will do anything!" Sr. Meseguer then told Nicolas he would meet him there the following night at midnight and he would have an answer to what he was searching for.

They walked outside together. They shook hands and Nicolas thanked Meseguer.

Nicolas turned to walk away, then suddenly turned around to ask him if it could be sooner. Señor Meseguer was no longer there. Nicolas stared into the darkness of the street. The hollowness of the street left a heavy, empty feeling in his heart as he realized he was alone. There was silence, only silence and he stood in the dark shadowy street, alone.

Nicolas walked to the apartment through the dark lonely streets. He walked up the stairs to the apartment instead of taking the elevator. He opened the door and walked through the rooms without turning the lights on.

He went into the bathroom, washed his face and brushed his teeth. Then he lay in his bed looking toward the ceiling as he pictured her face and heard her laughter and could almost swear he smelled her scent.

The moonlight shone on his face through the lace curtains on the window. He dozed into a light sleep, tossing and turning, as he dreamt she was running, running from something dark, trying to escape, she tripped and then looked up into the eyes of evil and screamed. The face of evil belonged to Señor Meseguer… smiling wickedly. Nicolas jumped to consciousness.

He turned toward the window and stared at the moon, confused as to why in his dream Meseguer was something he had not sensed when they were together, something evil.

Nicolas got up from bed and went into the kitchen for a bottle of water. He stood at the door in the living room, looking out over the plaza, which was now quiet. He drank his water and looked out into the darkness, with the evil face of Meseguer etched in his consciousness.

He went to bed and consoled himself knowing the same moon that lit the sky would soon be guarding Mia. He searched for her scarf and held it closely. Staring at the moon, he dozed off with her in his arms.

Nicolas woke to the sounds of people on the street. He could hear the sounds of waiters and waitresses positioning the chairs at the tables of the outdoor cafés.

He sat up and reached for the telephone. He dialed home hesitantly as it was only 6 a.m. in Miami. His father answered. "Nico son, we were waiting for your call. They have taken Mia to the hospital. She is not doing well. She is there for observation, as they feel it is much safer if they keep constant vigil over her, due to her illness. Her grandmother and your mother are with her. I was there most of the night with them and she was very worried about you not knowing she was there, so I promised her I would come home and wait for your call."

"Call her, Nico. She is waiting for your call."

Nicolas searched for the number in his phone and called. "Saint Joseph Hospital, may I help you." Nicolas asked for Mia's room. The phone rang, Nicolas' mother, Sofia, answered the phone.

"Hi Mom, it's me Nico, how is Mia doing?

"She's the same, honey," she replied. "Dr. Thomas was here earlier and he said Mia is stable, and he is recommending they perform a cesarean birth, as the twins are taking her strength." Sofia heard Nico sigh.

"Nico, the doctor advised you make the decision as soon as possible and you must come home as soon as you possibly can. Nicolas, she is asking for you, she needs you, I think you should come home."

Nicolas asked her to put the phone near Mia's ear. She did as he asked. He said, "Mia… Mia my love. I am here, and I will be there soon, I won't be long. Get some rest and I will call you later. I can't wait to be home, so we can be together. Wait for me, please, I love you." With the little strength Mia had, she said, "Nicolas, I need you and I love you, please come home, I miss you."

"And, I miss you and please remember I love you Mia, forever." Nicolas placed the phone on the receiver and leaned forward, placing his arms on his legs. He got an adrenaline rush and realized he couldn't wait until midnight. He would go to the bar today and find out where Meseguer lived.

Nicolas showered and got ready to go out and eat breakfast. When he arrived he told Mrs. Espinoza he wouldn't need her to cook while he was there.

He left and went to the café across the plaza. He ordered a café con leche and toast with tomato spread, ham and cheese. He sat and ate slowly as he watched the people walk to work and the kids walking to school.

He paid the waiter, then headed toward the bar where he met Sr. Meseguer. He arrived much sooner than he remembered it to be the night before. When he got there, the door was locked. He heard noise through an open window and shouted in, "Can you help me?"

The old bartender asked what he needed. Nicolas asked if he knew where Sr. Meseguer lived. The old guy said he had no information about the gentlemen and went about his duties.

Nicolas headed back toward home looking at things in the small shops, things he knew Mia would love. He stopped at one on a corner, which had so many things it was hard to concentrate on anything. It was one of those stores you had to take extra time to find something, which some might consider a small treasure. He looked around and found a table with sterling silver items. He picked out a small, silver trinket box, and a beautiful silver necklace with earrings to match, thinking he'd place them inside. He also bought a bag of red licorice and left.

The day was perfect. The sky was covered with white billowy clouds where only hints of blue escaped the few open areas. Since he met Mia, he noticed the sky more than ever before or at least was more conscious of what he saw, because she so often pointed out shapes in the clouds and now he also had begun to look for them.

He walked slowly toward the river. He sat on a bench and stared at the water while he ate his licorice. He listened to the laughter of the children playing close by and imagined himself with Mia and their twin boys playing in a sandbox. Thoughts of conversations they had about their soon-to-be-born twins flashed through his head. He knew he would give everything up, if he could only save her.

He wandered around the town until evening came, the stopped for tapas and a beer. The bar he chose was filled with people. A group of guys began to talk about soccer and Nicolas listened in then, decided to leave and go to the apartment and wait. It was close to 10:00 and he was restless.

He had left the television on earlier and he grabbed a beer from the refrigerator and sat on the sofa thinking that watching it would make time pass faster. He had about an hour to waste and just wanted it to pass quickly. He faced the television screen. He was lost in thought and looked at the clock above the television set every few minutes, only making time pass slower.

His long fingers tapped the arm of the chair impatiently. He could not sit still any longer. He put on his jacket and walked toward the door. He turned to look at the clock one more time. 10:30. He turned toward the door and reached for the knob, it was so cold. He grasped it firmly and slowly turned it. He opened it hesitantly and stepped out and as he turned to close the door, he glanced back at the clock. 10:32.

Time was not passing fast enough for the pools of anxiety that filled his every cell. He stared down the long corridor. Emptiness.

He looked at his watch. 10:33. Time was crawling. He walked toward the elevator anxiously and pressed the button forcefully. Nicolas looked down at the carpet while he waited for the elevator to slowly arrive. Memories of his and Mia's first day in the apartment filled his thoughts.

With his hand in his pocket he grasped her scarf and whispered, "I will never let you down, Mia." He knew he would do everything possible, even if it took everything he had. He knew he would give his last breath to save Mia and felt optimistic that Señor Meseguer held all the solutions he was looking for.

He pulled from his pocket her scarf and placed it to his lips. He smelled her and he missed her so much. The scarf he held was the one she had given him when he was leaving, asking him to hold it close, like he always held her close, whenever he needed strength and promised she would be near.

He pressed the elevator button again. The elevator was old, and he heard it creaking as it slowly arrived. When the door opened he stepped inside. The elevator walls were mirrored. He looked into the mirror and saw himself. His eyes were bloodshot and he looked tired although he was not. He knew the adrenaline, which built up from the anxiety of finding an answer, was what was pushing him.

He hadn't slept a full night for weeks. Since he learned of Mia's illness, he lay up many nights wondering and worrying. He leaned against the back of the elevator as it crept its way slowly, stopping at the floor below. He held the scarf to his face and felt as if time was standing still. He needed to go. Now. He desperately needed to solve everything. Now!

The elevator stopped on the third floor and Nicolas saw the exit door at the end of the hallway, the drawing of a staircase was calling him. He pressed the scarf to his mouth, and inhaled deeply then returned it to his pocket. Then, he instinctively stepped out of the elevator and quickly walked to the exit.

Without hesitation, Nicolas pushed the door open and ran down thc stairs, knowing the moments would move at a faster pace than they had crawled only a second ago.

When he got outside, he began to walk in the direction of the cathedral. He thought he could make it there faster if he took a shortcut. When he crossed the main street after the cathedral he cut onto a dark alleyway. He knew the bar was in this direction but after a few minutes realized he was lost. He continued to walk. He remembered he had walked for so long the night before and had gotten lost on the way home. He began to walk quickly. He only had an hour to find it and couldn't bear the thought of Sr. Meseguer leaving if he wasn't there on time. He began to walk faster wishing he had taken the path he took earlier in the day.

He began to run down the darkened streets. Lights flickered behind the sheer curtained windows. Running, he felt a million eyes upon him. Whispers in the wind brushed the senses of his hearing and far away he heard the slight laughter of a child, and then the cries of a woman. As he ran faster, the cries began to roar louder in his ears.

He stopped and put his hands to his ears, while at the same time closing his eyes. Nicolas slowly removed his hands from his ears and looked around. The crying had stopped and only the far off laughter of a child could be heard.

He opened his eyes to the darkness that surrounded him. The stillness of his surroundings eerily gave him the sense of time standing still. He sensed he was not alone. Were the eyes he felt upon him coming from the now darkened windows? What was it he sensed coming closer?

He placed his hand in his pocket, searching for his reason to move forward. He wrapped his fingers around the softness of Mia's scarf. He kept his hand in his pocket and walked slowly trying to regain his sense of direction. He gripped the cloth tightly in his hand.

Hearing voices in the distance, he picked up his pace. He approached a dark narrow street and saw a group of ladies standing near an open doorway.

He turned in their direction, and as he approached the group of ladies they began to whisper amongst themselves. Then one yelled out "Lost, handsome?" He waved and shook his head and continued walking.

As he went down the darkened street, he noticed a dim light in the window where the street ended. He was not sure what direction to take. When he reached the corner, the window went black. He stopped and looked to the right and saw another window with a light on inside and decided to walk in that direction. He continued to walk and the street became dark.

He began to run and noticed the reflection of the moon on the now darkened windows. Nicolas looked at his watch – 11:15. His pace picked up, as he was not sure how far he had run. As he turned the final corner he recognized the almost cryptic music that spilled from the café. He had arrived. The music he heard was just the way he remembered it when he first met Sr. Meseguer.

The door was open. He stood at the door and looked in. The bartender continued what he was doing. He didn't look up. Nicolas cleared his throat to get the bartender's attention. He looked up slowly avoiding eye contact. "Has Sr. Meseguer arrived?" Nicolas asked. The bartender shook his head slowly and continued what he was doing.

Nicolas approached the bar and asked for a drink. The bartender poured the rum into the glass, slowly. It almost appeared to Nicolas, that the rum entered the glass a drop at a time. Then he opened the bottle of cola and filled the glass, the fizz of the soda sounded so loud in the empty bar. He pushed it toward Nicolas without looking up. Nicolas put 2 euros on the counter and walked toward the window. He stood there and looked out into the darkness wondering why it was so eerily quiet that night. Then, he took a seat at the table where he and Sr. Meseguer sat the night before… and he waited.

"Why is it that everything appears to be happening as if I were suspended in time?" he thought. He could hear his heartbeat, which also seemed like a slow beat of a drum, telling a story of something wicked as it approached.

He stared out the window through the lace curtains, looking out toward the street. There was no one on the street. He saw the faint flicker of light coming from the apartment windows above.

Nicolas continued gazing hypnotically out of the window. He wondered why there were no people out at this time. This was not typical of the Spanish town where he grew up, it was not what he remembered. Usually, at this time on a Saturday night, the streets were filled with families strolling through the neighborhood after dinnertime. Teenagers with their friends and the older kids waiting to get into the bars were seen everywhere. It's what he remembered--why would this Spanish town be so different?

The pianist continued playing the slow cryptic music. Had it been the only song she played? What she played seemed to go on and on. He looked up at the clock near the door. 11:30. He quickly looked at this watch to confirm the time. His watch read 11:56. The clock above the door seemed to have stopped at 11:30 or was running behind.

Nicolas turned his chair toward the door to see Sr. Meseguer when he walked in. Nervously, he began tapping the empty glass in his hand against the table. Nicolas knew Mia could not hold on much longer. He nervously whispered, "Where are you, Meseguer?"

Nicolas asked the bartender for another drink. The bartender served it slowly and delivered it to Nicolas. Nicolas felt as if time were not advancing.

He looked down at his glass, and as he lifted the glass toward his mouth, he realized Sr. Meseguer was sitting in the chair across from him. Nicolas, moved his head backward in surprise asking himself, how he had not heard him arrive, yet was so thankful he had.

"Good evening, Nicolas," Sr. Meseguer said. "Good evening," Nicolas replied. "I didn't hear you come in."

Nicolas looked around, and the bartender continued what he was doing and the pianist played the only song he'd heard her play. Sr. Meseguer smiled confidently as he watched Nicolas.

Filled with desperation, Nicolas began speaking rapidly. "The doctor says they have to deliver the babies, they are draining her of her strength. If they don't, we could lose her and the twins. Please let me know what you can do for her. I need to get back to her as soon as possible. I need to go home today."

He begged, "Please, please, help me!" Meseguer looked at him and smiled, and said "Don't lose hope my son, there is time. You must come with me and all your worries will be solved."

Nicolas asked him to take him now! He could not wait any longer. Meseguer stood up from his seat slowly. He buttoned the front button on his coat. Grabbing his cane, he motioned for Nicolas to follow him. Nicolas did as he ordered.

Meseguer walked slowly. Nicolas walked at his side, wanting to run. His legs felt heavy, as they moved in sync with the motion of Meseguer's legs. Nicolas felt his legs motionless, yet knew they were moving. He felt as though he was floating. He looked down at his legs and saw them moving, slowly.

When they got to the edge of town in the distance, Nico saw a horse and carriage. There was a dim light coming from within the carriage and inside he saw two women. They resembled the women he had seen the day in the Mercedes at the tattoo shop. The women wore cream colored, lace veils, which covered their faces.

They were the women he had seen. He knew it, although their faces were hidden behind the veils. They approached the carriage and Meseguer opened the door. The women immediately put their heads down, and sat further back in their seats plunging deeper into the shadows of the carriage. Because of the lighting, their faces could not be seen. They were quiet and motionless. Meseguer signaled Nicolas to enter the carriage and Nicolas did as he asked.

Nicolas observed the women, who remained still as they rode into the night. He noticed their clothing, which appeared to be made of high quality silk woven lace and, their hands covered by lace gloves reaching half way up their arms.

Each wore a ruby ring. The ruby ring was similar to what Mia wore, Nicolas thought. He wondered why they would be wearing something so similar to what she had. He didn't think much of it, because he remembered Mia say her grandmother had given it to her and her grandmother had come from this region. It may have been a ring design for the region, as he remembered on a trip he took once to the island of Ibiza in the Balearic Islands, a ring typical to the island he had visited. This may have been the same type of ring for this region.

Meseguer said nothing as they rode quickly through the night. Nicolas could hear the whip as the driver lashed at the horses. He looked out into the night. The moon was full. The light of the moon lit the countryside and all he could decipher in the shadows along the road were tall trees lining their way. They rode swiftly into the darkness.

The horses then suddenly began to slow down, and Nicolas caught sight of a large house at the end of a road. The horses walked slowly toward the home then stopped suddenly, jerking the carriage. The women remained still, even with the movement of the carriage.

Meseguer straightened his hat.

Nicolas looked at his surroundings. He had no idea where he was. The flickering lights from the small towns seemed so far away. Had they really gone this far in such a short time, he thought? Guitar music could be heard in the distance. "Where has Meseguer brought me?" he wondered.

Nicolas then realized they were not far from the shore, as the sound of waves crashing into the rocky shore could be heard from where they were. The shore was at least 40 minutes by car from Murcia. He wondered how they could have gone so far in such a short time. Suddenly, the loud laughter of women could be heard over the music that played. He turned to the carriage and the women were gone.

Nicolas smiled as he listened to the laughter. The laughter was enticing and it stirred hungry thoughts and feelings through his body, awakening it sexually.

In the distance, behind the immense trees, etched by the light of the moon, appeared a high wall. The laughter seemed to be streaming through the wrought iron gate, which enclosed the silhouette of an ancient villa. It seemed to be protected from the world by the tall wall around it.

As they approached, Nicolas began to see the dim lighting from the lamps in the courtyard of the grand villa.

As they neared the wall that surrounded the villa, Nicolas noticed the delicately etched faces on its surface. Faces, almost angelic, looked directly at him. The faces of painful stares entwined by vines and delicate leaves decorated the wall. Nicolas wondered what this meant. He felt the eyes of the many faces staring at him, in horror. The faces glowed in the moonlit night as he approached. As he got closer, he looked into the eyes of the agony drenched faces. So beautifully etched, yet horridly portrayed. For a minute he was frozen and he fearfully sensed the faces were in someway warning him not to enter.

Nicolas closed his eyes and shook his head, as if to convince himself that what he felt was only fear of the unknown. Sr. Meseguer had not yet mentioned anything that could be done to save Mia. Nicolas knew the only reason he was here was because he was desperate and had not found any other clues as to how it could be done.

He could not turn back even as he sensed what lay before him was something so forbidden it may be the thing he regretted most in his life. He took a deep breath, stood tall, and walked through the open gate following Sr. Meseguer. He held his breath and knew the fear he sensed could be stifled only by his love for Mia.

The courtyard was dimly lit. Statues lavishly decorated the vast area. The laughter was now louder as it poured from the open windows. Meseguer walked toward the door, Nicolas followed close behind. Meseguer pushed against the heavy wooden doors. They swung open slamming against the wall then came to a sudden stop, as if they had been held there.

The door echoed in the hallway and the laughter stopped. Nicolas stood there hesitantly then walked into the house and all that remained was blood curdling silence. Nicolas sensed at the moment he would never be the same again.

Nicolas and Sr. Meseguer stood in the foyer. The décor was Victorian. The curtains fell to the floor in heaps of rich scarlet velvet.   Paintings of people who must have been ancestors hung on the wall.   The antique furnishings were etched to perfection with delicate designs.

Meseguer motioned for Nicolas to enter the room behind the doors. Nicolas obeyed.

Nicolas entered and Sr. Meseguer followed. The large room was empty but for three women, who sat near the fire.   The women were dressed in clothing of another time, just as the décor of the home depicted something from a time now past. The women looked nervously at Meseguer, and appeared to avoid eye contact when he looked toward them.

Suddenly two beautiful women with long black hair entered the room from a dark hallway. They turned and looked at Nicolas. The one to the right smiled at Nicolas and looked into his eyes, almost trancelike. She began to twirl her finger through her long strands of hair. The other licked her lips as she scanned Nicolas from head to toe. The women's sensuality awakened something in Nicolas and he nervously looked away.

Toward the end of the room, near the corner was another woman with long black wavy hair seated with two younger girls.   One with firey red hair and the other had hair the color of honey.   The oldest of the three stood from the chaise, pushing the other two younger girls from her legs, where their heads had rested.

She stood up and turned to look directly into Meseguer's eyes then confidently walked toward him.

She was dressed in a black lace dress, which fell ever so delicately from her shoulders. The lace draped along the length of her back and traced her neckline softly exposing her plump breasts as they filled the fabric. She approached Meseguer. She did not look at Nicolas.

She threw her arms around Meseguer and he pulled her close to him and their mouths met as they kissed passionately. He then grabbed the back of her hair and pushed her away. The other girls quickly stood from their positions, bowing their head and standing as still as stone. They were all beyond beautiful in an almost enticingly forbidden way and all were so different, except for two.

Meseguer said, "I would like to introduce you." He pointed to the two almost identical, with long black hair. Nicolas wondered whether they could be twins. He approached them and took their hands into his and kissed them. Their faces were beautiful, angelic and identical, except for their eyes, he noticed.

"This is Alesandra and her sister Angelina," Meseguer said. They lifted their eyes and stared deeply into his, without lifting their heads. Alesandra had eyes the color of the dark blue sea, and Angelina with eyes the color of the dark night sky. It was the only thing that differentiated them. Their milky complexions were highlighted by the faint color of pink in their lips. They nervously smiled, imitating the other's gestures.

"This is Ivona," Meseguer continued. She was tall and her dark red hair fell into long spiral curls, which hung over her bare shoulders. She looked up and looked at Nicolas seductively as she traced her chest with the tip of her finger. A small smile appeared over her full lips. She looked at him slowly caressing his body with her stare. He felt his body heat as she looked at him from head to toe and as her eyes traced his body, he felt a warming sensation, almost as if her eyes were actually touching each spot they gazed upon.

The fourth had long hair the color of honey. Her eyes were big and almost hollow. She looked sickly. Her lips were dark red as an overly ripened cherry. Meseguer said this is Amora. She lifted her head and her mouth smiled widely, as the look of anguish remained in her eyes.

Meseguer then said, "Nicolas, I would now like to introduce you to my wife, Natalia." Natalia was still hugging Meseguer's arm tightly and she smiled shyly, as she quickly glanced at Nicolas, then returned her glance toward Meseguer, as if looking for his approval.

"Sit," Meseguer demanded and pointed to a chair while looking at Nicolas. Nicolas did as he ordered. He sat on the chair and looked around the room.

There was a fire in the fireplace. The mantle had the same etchings of faces of agony on the pillars at the entrance of the house. He saw a door open to the patio. There was also an open door, which appeared to lead to the back of the house and through the doorway. All he saw was darkness.

Nicolas rested his arms on his legs and then placed his hands over his face. He wiped the perspiration from his brow. When he looked up he realized he was now alone with Sr. Meseguer. He hadn't heard the women leave.

Nicolas looked at his watch and realized it was 2:00 a.m. He told Meseguer they must hurry. He knew Mia would not last long. He knew he needed to catch a plane to the states as soon as possible.

Meseguer smiled and said, "Everything will be fine, you will have enough time to arrive and save her, my son."

Mesesguer began to speak slowly in an almost inaudible tone. "Nicolas, there is something I must tell you." Nicolas looked at Meseguer waiting for him to begin, while straining to hear him speak. In a whisper like tone, he began, "Nicolas, I will save your beloved Mia, at one cost."

Nicolas sat up straight in his chair and desperately replied, "I will pay you anything to save her. Please tell me Sr. Meseguer, what must I do?"

Meseguer then looked deeply into Nicolas' eyes and said strongly, "Nicolas, I will save Mia but you must promise me one thing." Nicolas said, "Yes, Meseguer, yes, anything, please I am desperate."

Sr. Meseguer continued, "You will give to me your and Mia's first born daughter when she reaches 17 years of age."

"What?" Nicolas shouted as he began to rise from his seat. Nicolas was shocked. How could Meseguer ask this of him? Nicolas asked, "Why do you want my daughter?" Meseguer answered, "She will wed my son."

"Son?" Nicolas asked then looked toward Meseguer's wife as she appeared from the darkened entrance, where she remained in the doorway. She looked at Meseguer then turned away with a sorrowful look.

Nicolas could not agree. He would not agree. How could he give his daughter to this man? How could he promise something so horrible?

"No!" he shouted, as he wiped his hands over his face. Nicolas sat back in the chair and threw his head backward in desperation. Then he remembered Mia could not have more children because of her illness and what she was carrying now were twins. The twins were boys.

"Boys," Nicolas whispered to himself, knowing this would be his only chance to save Mia. "Yes! I can promise him this," he thought, reassuring himself he would never have to comply with this promise. For he had seen with his very eyes they were both boys and the doctor had explained they shared the same amniotic sac. As he hesitated to give Meseguer an answer, he again recalled the ultrasound, and remembered seeing for himself that both his children were boys.

They would not have more children, as to not endanger Mia if she were to live. Nicolas knew he would not have to fulfill his promise, because he and Mia would never have a daughter. Nicolas then said, desperately, "Yes, I promise my first born daughter as payment for saving the life of Mia."

Meseguer smiled an evil smile and turned toward a shelf with books. He took the only book that lay on the top shelf and opened it. He pulled out a sheet with writing in calligraphic lettering. In the book was a very small compartment which protected a small silver dagger. Meseguer lifted the small dagger and turned toward Nicolas. He told Nicolas he must prick his fingertip and press it to the paper acknowledging the agreement with his blood. Meseguer held the dagger as he spoke to Nicolas, slowly sliding his fingers over the blade, from the base of his fingers to the tip. He handed the dagger to Nicolas and told him the dagger would be the instrument to prick his finger.

Nicolas took the dagger and pushed the point into his thumb on his left hand. When Sr. Meseguer saw the blood slowly push its way out, he placed the written form on the table in front of Nicolas and pointed to the spot Nicolas must place his bloodied fingerprint. Nicolas pushed his thumb onto the paper, then lifted it and saw the blood imprint that sealed the agreement to save Mia's life. He placed the silver etched dagger on the desk after wiping his bloody finger on his pants. Meseguer then took the paper and filed it in the book, and returned the book to the top shelf of the bookcase, from where he had taken it. Nicolas watched Meseguer as he carefully placed the book on the shelf.

Meseguer then turned to Nicolas. Nicolas looked into his eyes, which were completely black and hypnotizing.

Nicolas stepped back, then placed his hand to his head, he had become dizzy and grabbed the chair at his side to balance himself so he would not fall to the floor.

What Nicolas then heard, as if he were reliving the experience, were Mia's screams. The blood curdling screams he had heard in the dream. He recalled Mia looking into the darkness where those eyes, so evil, had appeared and now, those very eyes were upon him. The screams echoed in his brain. Why? Should he turn back... could he turn back?

Meseguer then pushed a silver chalice toward Nicolas and ordered him to drink. Nicolas obeyed. As he slowly drank the thick liquid, memories played out in his mind. Memories, of what seemed to be every moment he shared with Mia, flashed through his mind like a film played in fast forward. Meseguer stood over Nicolas as he drank. When Nicolas looked up, he saw Meseguer smile.

The same smile he had seen in the dream, and from the smile appeared dagger like teeth. Meseguer pulled Nicolas close, as Nicolas tried to push his way free. He fought Meseguer's grasp, which was much stronger than his own, even with his desperate twisting and turning to break free, he could not. Meseguer then pulled Nicolas forcefully toward him and bit down on his neck, slowly sinking his teeth into his warm flesh.

Nicolas continued to struggle for a moment, then felt his body falling limp. He felt as if the life was slowly being drained from his body. His body turned ice cold as

Meseguer sucked the blood from him. He was left with no energy to fight.

Nicolas saw the blood on Meseguer's mouth as he felt his body falling slowly to the floor. Nicolas, again, felt as if time were standing still and each second seemed like a lifetime as he felt himself fall. His mind was filled with jumbled memories, of each and every moment he shared with Mia, flashing before him. Every sensation he had ever felt with her ran through his body as he fell lifeless onto the cold marble floor.

He lay there, his mind lost in confusion, as memories of his life played in his mind. In his memories, he was a bystander, seeing himself as a child running toward the beach. He heard his parents' voices. He saw every moment of his life pass before his eyes, and felt every sensation he had once felt, as if he were reliving it, only each experience or memory was intensified.

Suddenly Mia's face appeared, she was smiling at him. In the distance, he heard her sing the song she always sang. It rang in his ears loudly. Her laughter, her eyes, her smile, he could only see her.

Her face, so beautiful, innocently laughing, then turning to a horrible scream-like laughter. Her face converted from an angelic stare to pure evil, laughing hysterically as she looked into his eyes.

Her stare was blank then quickly turned angry as she looked at Nicolas, almost as though she wanted to kill him. There was hatred in her eyes. Nicolas could not turn from the horridness her face had now become. He cried out and then began to shake in spasms on the floor. His back arched. He reached out as he tried to grasp the cold floor beneath him. He reached out for something, anything to support him as he tried to lift himself. He screamed loudly.

He knew not what was happening to him, but deep inside he knew what this meant.

Nicolas knew he was dying.

The cold entered his body slowly. He felt it creep into him slowly, like a million bugs running wildly through his skin. It began in his feet, then slowly made its way up his legs, crawling up to his groin then to his stomach, filling his chest, his neck, and then his head. As it reached the top of his body, he felt his soul escape from his once, life filled body. Empty, hollow, cold, is what he felt as the life he once knew, slowly lifted from him.

He lay on the floor with his eyes open. He watched his soul as it seemed to be lifted toward the painting on the ceiling. And, from his lifted soul, he saw himself lying on the floor. His soul floated above looking down at his body, while he stared at himself, floating above. There were two entities, one looking down at the lifeless body. The other stared at his soul hovering above.

The two were separated, staring each other in the face. The being that lay on the floor was a part of him that remained alive so deep inside the walls of his mind where his memories echoed loudly.

The being above was the empty hollows of what his life would now become. Smells, feelings, sounds echoed in the hallways of his mind, as his spirit hovered above, protecting a part of him that would never be compromised, his soul and his heart.

A broken man, separated from his soul, he shouted with pain filled howls. His eyes widened as he saw his shadowed soul lower to the hollow body that was him, laying lifeless on the floor. Slowly, he felt his soul reenter his body. Nicolas knew his body was awakening from the cold dcath he had only felt minutes before. His body convulsed as his soul slowly reentered. He was alive.

He suddenly weakened and fell unconscious. In the instant before his soul entered and what he knew must be death, Meseguer released him.

Nicolas, not realizing he had been in Meseguer's arms, fell back, and his eyes opened widely. His body was filled with the agony of a thousand years. He yelled in utter pain as his body twisted trying to release all he was becoming. Nicolas lay on the floor with vivid pictures of the sun rising, the clouds sweeping through the sky, turning day into night, which left him in complete confusion.

He pressed his hands to his head and he slightly lifted it off the floor. He could not control the vivid thoughts that went through his mind. He let his head fall and became still as he looked up at the paintings on the ceiling. Paintings of small children playing seemed to come to life, as he lay weakened on the cold hard floor.

Nicolas was lost in the scene of the mural on the ceiling. The images had come to life. He heard the laughter of the children, and then a song in the far off distance. A song he recognized so well. It was the song Mia so often sang. Nicolas fell deeper into the trance of children playing as the song consumed his mind.

Meseguer then took another small dagger from his pocket and pressed it into his wrist. He lowered his wrist onto Nicolas' mouth. "Drink so you will live." Nicolas drank feverishly, feeling his body strengthen with the thick liquid that entered his body. The floor no longer felt cold as Nicolas slowly regained what he knew was consciousness. He felt stronger than he had ever felt before as his body was brought back to life.

Meseguer stood above him, his fingertips brushed and smeared what seemed to be blood from his lips. A smile formed on his face as his looked into Nicolas' eyes and said "Remember, Nicolas, what you promised. Do not forget. Your first born daughter on her 17th birthday will belong to me."

Nicolas looked into his hungry eyes then quickly looked away as he nodded in agreement. Nicolas knew he would never be obligated to comply.

Nicolas stood up, wiped his face of the cold perspiration. He felt different. He felt strong. And now, more than ever, he knew Mia would not die, not ever. He did not know what had happened, but he knew this was the answer to saving Mia's life.

Meseguer told him. "Go now, save her. You have 24 hours to complete the process of saving her. There is a private jet waiting to take you to her. When she is well, you will then come to me and I will guide you both on your new journey."

He handed Nicolas a small book and said, "You must read this on your trip tonight. It will guide you in saving Mia. Do exactly as it says. After Mia is cured, continue to read, and you will know what you will need and how you will live. This book will be your guide, until you become accustomed to our way of life. The book will tell you all you need to know until we meet again. Remember, you can only read it once, you must remember what is written in this book, and if forgotten or not obeyed, it will cause hardship in your lives." Nicolas wondered what he meant and slipped the book into his coat pocket.

Nicolas ran from the house knowing he would never return. As he ran, he felt the stares of a thousand hungry eyes upon him. He knew the stares came from the faces of the etchings on the pillars of the Meseguer Villa. The very faces who had warned him of entering the villa were now pushing him to run. To run as far away as he could, and to never turn back.

Nicolas ran faster trying to escape the stares, which felt like a thousand daggers piercing every inch of his body. As he ran, he heard laughter turning to loud sorrowful cries in the darkness. Nicolas tried to drown out the sounds as he ran faster. When he finally reached the outskirts of the darkened city, they stopped.

He lingered before he began to walk down the dark narrow streets. He was uneasy and felt something lurking deep in the shadows. He remembered having the same feeling the night he was alone in the streets, before meeting Meseguer. He sensed the same stares, which came from the shadows, had returned. He knew he was not alone. What he sensed now was stronger. He was unsure if what was enveloped, by the darkness, was now there to help or to hurt him.

Nicolas felt strong and pushed forward. He knew he was no longer the same. He also knew nothing could stop him from saving her. He had no doubt what had happened to him tonight would help him save Mia's life.

Nicolas turned a corner, and came upon the bar where he met Meseguer. A woman whose face was covered by a veil stood by the coach that had taken him to Meseguer's villa. She motioned to him and said time was running out and they would take him where he needed to catch his plane.

Nicolas got into the coach. It drove quickly through the city and stopped in front of his apartment. He took the stairs up to the apartment and quickly packed his belongings and locked up the apartment. He went downstairs and saw the Mercedes he had seen at the tattoo shop, which was now waiting for him where the coach had been. Joaquin, the driver, was in the Mercedes and nodded as Nicolas got in. Joaquin shook Nicolas' hand and Nicolas said, "You drive for everyone don't you? Joaquin grinned and drove without saying a word.

They arrived at the airport quickly. There was a private jet waiting for Nicolas. He noticed it was dark inside as he approached. When he entered, it smelled of jasmine, just as the home of Meseguer had smelled. The cabin was dimly lit. The plane had four seats. They were upholstered with the finest Italian leather. He looked around, and although the jet was one of the latest models, the décor was from another era, similar to Meseguer's home.

Nicolas pressed his head into the seat back and closed his eyes. He was alone. He heard footsteps approach him and he opened his eyes. He saw a tall, thin gentleman leaving the cockpit, closing the door behind him. The man spoke softly saying, "I am Philipe and am here to serve you."

Before Philipe could finish, the captain spoke over the intercom and informed them they would be leaving shortly. The captain also said they would be landing in Miami in 10 hours

Philipe then said, "You will be very hungry, and I will serve you your cocktail, which will satisfy the hunger you will feel."

Philipe went to the back of the plane and returned with a heavy wine glass filled with a dark wine colored liquid. Nicolas lifted the glass to his mouth, and as he pushed it closer, he smelled what was not wine. What he did smell was the best smell he could ever remember smelling. What could this be? He wondered. His mouth watered. He placed the glass to his lips and before drinking he touched the liquid with his tongue then savagely drank the thick dark liquid he would soon realize was blood.

He spit the liquid from his mouth then threw the glass toward the floor shattering it while remnants of blood splattered throughout the cabin. Nicolas forcefully wiped his mouth then looked at his bloodstained sleeve wondering why he had been given blood to drink. He stood up and looked at Philipe and yelled, "What are you doing to me?"

"Sir, please calm down. You must realize this is what will now nourish you." Nicolas turned toward the broken glass and as he looked at the droplets of blood that now covered the seats near him, he felt a deep insatiable craving in the deepest part of his stomach. He wanted more, even as the thought of it caused such repugnance in him.

As he turned toward Philipe, he saw Philipe had already filled another glass. Nicolas grabbed the glass and pushed back his head, emptying the contents of the glass into his mouth. It poured freely into his throat, satiating his hunger. "Philipe, get me more," he ordered! Philipe did as Nicolas asked and returned with more. After an hour of drinking one glass after another, Nicolas sat back in the chair, satisfied. The repugnance he had initially felt was no longer evident.

Nicolas sat back. He looked at the time. 7:00 a.m. He wondered where the time had gone. He felt as if he had only been at Meseguer's for minutes. Nicolas looked toward the windows and saw the sun was rising. The windows were darkened with a film of tint and the sun appeared to be a ball of fire in the midst of the open skies. Nicolas hypnotically stared at it.

He placed his head back into the seat, as he felt the rush of the plane thrusting forward into the clouds. He closed his eyes.

He tried to remember what had happened the night before. He remembered the vision of the mural as it came to life, and how vivid the children were as they danced and played. He also remembered the image of a little girl in a white nightgown playing near a farmhouse. He remembered it being very similar to the painting won at the auction by the mysterious man. The same painting that had been given to them on their wedding day.

He remembered the little girl dancing under the moon singing the song Mia so often hummed. There were lyrics in the song, not just the humming Mia did. He could not remember the words the little girl sang, but remembered it was almost bewitching.

He searched deeper into his memory and suddenly remembered Mia's face as it turned from the beautiful face he so loved, to a hungry monster he feared. What did this have to do with Mia, what was the song he wondered, and what was the connection to Mia? There were too many similarities and he had to know.

He kept his eyes closed, in search of sleep. He knew he should be feeling exhausted due to lack of sleep over the last few days as well as what had happened the night before.   But what he felt now was the most energy and the strongest he had ever felt.   He sat further back into his seat.

Visions of Meseguer's eyes would not leave his thoughts. He remembered the smile and the teeth, which protruded before he lost consciousness. What had happened? He remembered feeling as if he were dying.   He remembered the pain he felt as he lay dying on the floor.

He remembered the visions that filled his mind. The visions of his life and the people he loved, played out so vividly in his memory. He could not understand how, with each memory, he felt he was reliving each moment he had once lived only the sensations were intensified. What had Meseguer done to him?   And why was he now drinking blood?

He tried to make sense of it all and remembered the dream like, frozen state he felt as he lay on the floor. He remembered he had not only seen himself on the floor but he also watched himself hovering above.   It reminded him of what he had often heard when people talked about out of body experiences.   No, this is not what happened to him. It was a dream he thought. Because, he knew, he was not dead.   Could it have been a near death experience like he had read or heard about?   Nicolas did not understand.

He began to feel nervous. Because of the promise he made to Meseguer, he worried about Mia and his children.   He stood and approached Philipe. Nicolas asked if there was a way to communicate with land.

Philipe brought him the phone. Nicolas returned to his seat and dialed the hospital. He was immediately connected with Mia's room. His mother answered and asked him why he had not called sooner.

"Nico, I couldn't reach you, I had to make a decision without you," she said. The babies were delivered at 4:12 a.m."

"What about Mia? How is she? I'm sorry, I was busy and it was impossible for me to call. How are the babies?" Nicolas continued.

She said, "They are so precious. They are small but they will be ok." Nicolas then asked, "And Mia, how is she?"

His mother quietly replied and with a lack of optimism in her voice, she said, "She is not doing well. She keeps calling for you. The doctors don't think she will make it another 24 hours. You must hurry, son, we are losing her."

Nicolas then told her he would be there in five hours. "Please let me talk to Mia. Mom, she needs to hang on, keep talking to her, let her know I am coming." His mother placed the phone near her ear and said, "ok, you can talk now, she is listening."

"Mia, Mia, my love. It's me, Nicolas. I'm coming home. Please wait for me. I will make everything ok. And yes, baby, we will be together… forever. Don't worry my love, you will never have to worry again, I promise."

Mia's breathing was shallow and she whispered into the phone, "I love you Nico. Come home soon, I need you."

"I'm almost home Mia, I'm almost home and everything is going to be all right, I promise."

Sofia took the phone and said, "She has very little strength and can't talk." Nicolas told his mother, "I'll be there soon. Kiss her for me. And tell her I love her."

Nicolas hung up and sat back in the chair. He knew everything would be ok, once he got there. But just as he thought that, he realized he had no way of making her better. He realized Meseguer had not given him anything to save her. What was he going to do?

He stood up, and went to Philipe. Before Nicolas could say anything, Philipe said, "In your pocket is the answer."

He reached into his pocket and found the book and vaguely remembered Meseguer had given it to him. What he did remember was Meseguer telling him to read it and memorize it and it would help him until the next time they met.

The book was small. The cover was faded red leather and it held no more than 10 pages. He opened it.

And began to read.

~~Read this, and memorize it. You will only read it once, and you must live as you are told."

"You are no longer mortal. You are now immortal. You will live forever, as long as you follow the law."

"You must not go into the sun without dark glasses. The rays of the sun will blind you for eternity and once you are blinded the rays of the sun will creep into your soul and will kill you slowly and painfully. You can go into the sun with covered eyes. You must remember to cover your skin from direct sunlight between the hours of 10 a.m. and 2 p.m., when the sun's rays are strongest. They will weaken you and after long exposure may take your life."

"You must learn to rest during the day. The nights will be yours. You will feed off blood. You may eat as you once ate, but this will not suffice to keep you alive. You may drink, but this will only be for purposes of fitting in. You will get your nourishment from either humans or from animals or the now famous synthetic blood for our kind. If you feed off a human, there may be consequences to pay, as they will die. This may bring suspicion to you and to our kind. Yes, there are more. It is best to keep to yourself and keep away from others like us.

You must control your desires. Your desire for sex will be insatiable yet controllable. The decision is yours if you should take more than one mate.

You must not turn another without the consent of your maker. You will turn your wife, who is dying. She will be your eternal mate. You will do this by following my instructions.

You must bite the artery of her neck and drink her blood. You will drink until you feel the life leaving her. Then you must stop. There is a chance you will not be able to stop, as this is your first human blood. You must stop or she will die. When she is close to death, you must then feed her your blood. Your blood must enter her blood stream or she will die within minutes. If she is too weak to suck your blood, you must cut your wrist and feed it into her blood stream. This will bring her back to life and she will live eternally as you will do as well.

Also, remember, the agreement you have made and you stake your life as you have confirmed by your bloody print placed on the scroll of our kind.

When you have finished, you will then come to me and I will guide you on your journey as immortals. There are specific rules you must follow and because I am your maker, I am responsible to teach you the way we immortals shall live.

When I have taught you all there is to know of our kind, then you can live on your own until we meet on the day of your daughter's 17th birthday.

And, on your daughter's 17th birthday, she will be delivered to me, to a specific location I will provide to you, as the day gets closer. This is when your debt to me will be paid in full. ~~

Nicolas closed the book, and held it tightly in his hands. He had read enough. He pushed his head into the chair back and closed his eyes.

He knew he would never see Meseguer again. He was as sure of this as he was sure of never having a daughter, and therefore never having to comply with the agreement made with Meseguer. He slowly fell into a sleep like state as he thought of his eternal life with Mia.

About 30 minutes before landing, Philipe touched Nicolas on the shoulder. "Sir, we will be landing in approximately 30 minutes." You may want to prepare for the landing." "You must also nourish yourself, as you will be near humans and can not be hungry as this may ruin all you've come to accomplish."

Philipe handed Nicolas three bags of blood. He took the first and filled the wine glass and watched Nicolas drink. He repeated this with the remaining two bags then began to explain.

"Nicolas, in your car there is a cooler already installed, filled with bags of blood to nourish you and Mia. A locked refrigerator has also been placed in your garage, and the key is in your pocket. This will nourish you until you meet with Señor Meseguer and it is then that he will inform you where you will get your nourishment.

Nicolas, feeling weak, looked out toward the far away lights. Philipe brought Nicolas another glass of blood. Nicolas drank it quickly, and by the time he was placing the glass down, Philipe had another for him. He drank another four glasses, and with each he felt stronger.

Nicolas thought of what Philipe said about the cooler and refrigerator filled with blood. He then began to worry how he would find blood after he finished what was supplied for them. He knew he wouldn't meet with Meseguer, but he worried how he would find blood, knowing he could never harm an innocent person.

He also knew he would do everything possible to keep his family away from Meseguer and would do whatever it took to save his family.

Just as he thought that, he felt the plane touch down. He stood up as the plane parked on the runway. He grabbed his bags and waited impatiently for the door to open. He walked down the stairs and parked next to the plane was a black Mercedes truck, just like the one in Spain. He was hesitant to approach, but did because he knew it would be the fastest way to get to Mia. He didn't have time to have his father pick him up, and he hadn't brought his truck to the airport.

He got into the truck and the man driving was a middle-aged man. The gentleman did not say a word. He drove speedily to the hospital, parked at the entrance and got out to open the door for Nicolas. Nicolas got out and thanked him. The driver said nothing and closed the door.

Nicolas stood outside looking up toward her second floor window just like he had always done before entering the hospital since she got sick. He remembered how he would park at night and when her window was open he would first whistle then yell out, "Juliet, I am here, your Romeo is here."

He remembered, when she had energy she would go to the window, and he would say, "Mia, Mia, let down your hair down from the tower and I will climb up." They'd laugh and he'd run into the hospital. When he would enter the room, Mia would playfully say, with her eyes closed, "Where art thou my Romeo?" That is when he would kiss her on the lips. It was just one of the many games they played. Nicolas did not smile as he looked up toward the window. He felt a sense of sadness and hoped she would still be alive.

Nicolas shook his head to clear his mind and walked quickly into the building. Two nurses were standing at the desk when he walked in. They looked at him with hunger in their eyes. Nicolas smiled and they turned to follow him. He looked at them curiously, as they asked if they could help him. Their eyes fixated on him as they spoke. Their movements and tone were almost trancelike. He said he was there to see his wife, thanked them, and got into the elevator. The elevator rose to the 2nd floor. He walked toward her room.

When he approached her room he saw her through the window. She was now on the opposite side of the hall in the intensive care unit. Nicolas saw the doctor, two nurses and his mother at her side. His mother was crying, and as she lifted her hand to wipe her eyes, she saw Nicolas.

Had he arrived too late? Was the love of his life gone? He felt weak as he reached for the door. Frantically, he pulled the door open and rushed to her. She was so frail. Her complexion was pale, almost deathlike. She was so thin, thinner than when he left. But, she was alive.

He looked toward his mom and she managed to say through her sobs, "We are losing her, son." "No!" he shouted. "You must all leave. I need to be alone with her."

The nurses looked at the doctor, as his mother walked toward the door. The doctor nodded and turned to leave, the nurses followed behind. Nicolas went to the window and pulled the thick curtain-like liner closed to cover the window.

He walked over to her and touched her face gently. He bent closer to her and kissed her firmly on the mouth, and said, "Mia, baby, I am here." Her lips turned upward slightly into a weakened smile. Tears welled up in his eyes as he looked into her eyes. She was dying. Her eyes, cloudy and distant, looked toward him, but he knew she was not seeing him, as they stared blankly and did not focus on him. She whispered, "You're home… Nico please hold me, I am cold, please keep me warm."

"Hang on baby, I'm here." He worked quickly, knowing exactly what to do, yet questioned how he remembered. What if he drank too much, she would die? What if he could not control his hunger? He had to control it, he could not lose her, not ever.

He first stopped the drip on the IV bag. He had to be careful not to give her blood until he bit her and sucked the remaining life from her. He would release the drip as soon as it was time for her to receive his blood.

He quickly lowered the stand where the IV hung and he opened the bag. He took the knife from his pocket and cut his wrist. He cut the opening of the bag and placed his wrist above the bag and his blood dripped into the bag slowly. The IV bag began to fill with blood.

The clear liquid slowly turned pink and then it became redder and redder as his blood filled the bag. He pulled his wrist away and wrapped it with a towel.

Mia's breathing became more shallow. He knew he was close to losing her. It was now time to drain her of her blood. He saw the veins on her neck pulsing. "How was he going to do this?" he asked himself, "She is so close to death." He kissed her lips then kissed his way down to her throat. He heard her moan and quietly whisper "I love you, my Nico."

Mia opened her eyes and looked up toward Nicolas. It appeared she was now seeing him clearly. She smiled, and when Nicolas smiled back, she saw his now sharpened teeth as they protruded from his mouth.

Nicolas saw the fear in Mia's eye and with her last breath, she gasped, pushing out the words "Nico, No!" He placed his mouth on her thin neck and bit down. He felt the pulsing of her heart through her veins. He sucked on her neck and slowly drained her of the infected blood that was killing her.

Suddenly, her eyes opened widely and her body went into spasms. He sucked until he felt he was losing her. The tears fell from his eyes as he felt her frail body weaken in his arms as he sucked the remaining life from her.

He pulled his mouth away forcefully, stood up and fell against the wall. She lay there, lifeless. He pushed himself forcefully from where he had fallen and rushed to her. He held her head in his hands as he looked down at her. The last teardrops had escaped from her closed eyes and ran down to his hands.

He lost her. Mia was dead.

He began to sob loudly and tightly held her close to his body. He shook with anger and with regret. He had lost Mia. He knew he had drank more blood than he should have. He lay on the bed next to her, and ran his fingers through her hair as she lay lifeless.

Then he remembered the IV bag, he hadn't let the liquid enter her body. He jumped from the bed and let the flow begin. He saw it creeping toward her body. Had he waited too long to release the blood? He knew she had to have some life left in her in order for the blood to enter her body and bring her back to him. Then he saw tears as they wet her lashes, they were the first sign of life. He knew it.

He suddenly raised the IV bag higher, with the now darkened liquid, and watched it as it dripped its way into her veins more quickly. His blood, her new life source was approaching the entrance to her body.

Nico's blood entered slowly. Mia lay there motionless. Then he saw the vein in her neck began to swell and pulse stronger. Mia shook and sat up quickly gasping for air. She reached out, searching for something to grab. She grabbed the blankets at her side and fell back onto the bed and began to breathe deeper and more steadily, the color came back to her face and she opened her eyes. Her face was now the face he first fell in love with, her hair was vibrant, her cheeks had regained their color, even her hair seemed to come to life. She was beautiful.

Her head fell backward. Her body tightened and began to convulse wildly as she began to scream. Her nails entered his body as he grabbed her closely to comfort her and to muffle her screams. Nicolas then reached into his pocket and he pulled out a tiny silver dagger. He placed the dagger on his other wrist and pressed down, the blood began to flow slowly from his wrist. He placed his wrist above her mouth and said, "Drink my love. Live, my love!" Mia began to suck his blood ravenously.

He then pulled out a syringe and slid the needle into her arm. The syringe contained a serum to make her sleep. He knew she had to sleep until the following evening when he would then take her out of there. She looked into his eyes. Her eyes were filled with fear, as her mouth opened slightly and a whisper of "no" escaped before she fell unconscious. He held her tightly.

CHAPTER XXIV

As Mia slept, Nicolas cleaned the area leaving no trace of what he had done. He could hear two women talking in the distant hallway. One was his mother, and the other was an unfamiliar voice. Although they were down the hall he heard their words as if they were standing next to him. The voices grew louder as they approached the room.

He took Mia's hand in his, sat back in the chair and acted as if he were sleeping. When the women entered the room, they were astonished by the change in Mia. She was no longer the weak, dying woman they had seen only an hour before. They looked at Mia in disbelief. Mia was healthy and vibrant. Sofia thought she looked even more healthy than the first time she met her. She was beautiful. Her skin was pale, with only a hint of pink on her lips and cheeks. Her hair seemed to have thickened and grown. Sofia recalled how thin it had gotten during her illness. What could have happened, she wondered.

Sofia shook Nicolas forcefully. "Nico, Nico, wake up!! Mia is getting better!" Nico appeared to wake slowly. He did not want anyone to realize he had not been sleeping. The nurse took Mia's pulse and blood pressure and everything appeared to be strong, then she quickly ran out of the room and called for the doctor.

The doctor entered the room followed by the head nurse. He verified Mia's vitals, not once, but twice. The doctor stood over Mia frowning, slowly shaking his head. The nurses and Sofia watched Mia as she slept, wondering what could have happened to make her change so drastically in only a few minutes. No one could believe the change she had taken. They had never seen anything like it before.

Nicolas stood at her side, touching her hair as he looked down at her. He did not want to make eye contact with the others in the room. He smelled them and even felt he could feel their hearts beat. But, because he had not been near humans, he was afraid of how he could react. He remained near Mia, softly talking to her.

Sofia looked at Nico with a questioning look and whispered, "What did you do?" He smiled and looked at her and said he had held her and he prayed. His mother hugged him and uttered, "It's a miracle, Nico, a true miracle!"

While the doctor continued to examine Mia, Sofia pulled Nicolas aside. "Nico, what did you do? Did you find the cure? She was so close to death." Nico said, "Yes Mom, she is going to be ok, everything is going to be ok, now." Sofia hugged him tighter, somehow knowing Nicolas was right.

They stood over Mia watching her sleep, as the head nurse and doctor stood toward the back of the room astonished by what could only be called a miracle.

Sofia nudged Nicolas and said, "Lets go to the nursery, you still have not seen the babies. They are beautiful! They were born early this morning." He nodded slowly and looked at Mia, who was sleeping soundly. He somehow knew she would be ok and agreed to go to the nursery. Nicolas had gotten so caught up in saving Mia and making sure she would be ok, that he had forgotten to ask about their boys.

He walked toward the nursery, hugging his mom closely. They arrived at the nursery window and inside were 6 babies, who were sleeping. Nicolas looked into the room, worried, as he did not know which were his sons.

"Nico, honey, look at them, they are perfect." Sofia tapped on the window and the nurse looked up and smiled. She went to the babies' beds and rolled them toward the window. They both had blue caps on. They each had a card on the foot of the bed. Diaz Boy 1. Diaz Boy 2. "Boys!" he whispered to himself. He wiped the tear that fell from his eye, as he confirmed to himself, he had nothing more to worry about.

The nurse motioned to them, asking if they would like to hold the babies. Sofia nodded and the nurse brought out the first baby and handed him to Nicolas. Then returned for the second baby and placed him in Nicolas' second arm.

He was so excited. He couldn't believe his eyes. His boys were perfect. He asked who was born first. The nurse pointed toward the baby in his right arm. He looked at his son and said, "Hi Michel, your mommy and I chose the name Michel for you. And your brother's name is Angelo." As he looked at his second son, in his left arm, and who was now awake.

Nicolas looked at his boys, trying to find differences in them and couldn't. Their eyes were big and brown. They reminded him of Mia's eyes. The little hair they had was dark and lay flat on their heads. He looked at their fingers and their feet and was amazed at how much they looked alike. He thought it seemed as if he held the same baby in both arms.

They looked so much like Mia, he thought, yet he could see himself in them as well. Maybe the nose he thought, or was it the lips? He smiled then asked the nurse how they would tell them apart. They were identical. The nurse said, "You can start by looking at their bracelets, then as time goes by, you will tell them apart by their personalities and looks as well, it won't be difficult. Baby A, is Michel, the firstborn and Baby B is Angelo, who was second. They are 12 minutes apart."

As the nurse finished talking, Angelo began to cry. Nicolas pushed his face between his boys, and held them closely and softly hummed Mia's song, trying to soothe Angelo and stop him from crying, and also hoping he wouldn't wake Michel.

"Wow, this is truly a miracle," Nico said, and looked at his mother. Sofia nodded in agreement and laughed at the fear she saw painted on Nicolas' face while he awkwardly tried to calm Angelo, while also trying to keep Michel calm.

Michel was now awake. He cooed gently with his eyes fixated on Nico.

Sofia took Angelo from Nico's arm and said "Angelo is definitely the feisty one." She rocked Angelo slowly and he continued to whimper softly. They laughed at his cry.

Nicolas looked down at his boys and began to cry. He held Michel close. He could not hold his tears back as he realized he had saved Mia and they had two healthy baby boys and he would never have to deal with Señor Meseguer again.

Just as Angelo quieted down, the head nurse pushed the door open and announced Mia was awake and was asking for them. Nico knew she would be hungry in a few hours and he had to be close to her to make sure nothing went wrong. Somehow he knew she would be ok until morning, when she would need more blood.

He remembered Philipe told him about the cooler in his truck. He asked his mother if his father had taken the truck. She said no, it had been brought to the hospital for him. Nicolas was relieved.

Nicolas held Michel and his mother held Angelo, who was now asleep. They walked toward Mia's room. They walked down the long hall and as they passed the elevator, the door opened and Ana got off.

When she saw Nicolas, she ran to him. She hugged him and told him how happy she was to see him home. She held onto his arm, and began to cry as she talked about how sick Mia was. Nicolas soothed her and said, "Everything is going to be ok, please don't cry." Ana shook her head, because she knew they were losing her and there was no way to save her.

Sofia entered the room first, with Nicolas and Ana behind her. Ana wiped her eyes and looked toward Mia. When she saw her, she took a step back, grabbed onto the door and gasped. She could not believe her eyes. This was not Mia and definitely not the same person who she had left only an hour before.

She remained at the door, pale from the shock of seeing Mia healed. She grabbed the chair to support herself and said "No, this can't be! What have you done Nicolas?" She looked at him, frighteningly. Nico said, "I found a cure and everything will be ok."

Mia slightly lifted her head, she was still very groggy, but she looked beautiful Nico thought, as he walked into the room. Her hair was long, and thick and wavy, not the same thinned out hair she had, only hours before.

He loved her more than life itself. Her face was whiter than he remembered, but her cheeks had a small hint of pink painted across them. It reminded him of the first time they made love. He remembered noticing the redness in her cheeks when he held her in his arms that day.

They walked toward the bed and the nurse helped Mia sit up. Mia looked at Nicolas and Sofia and said, "I want my babies, I've missed them."

They placed the boys in her arms, and she kissed each one on their tiny lips. She called each one by name without looking at their bracelets, telling them just how much she loved them.

She looked up at Nicolas and said "They are perfect, just like we knew they'd be." Nicolas smiled and leaned down to kiss her. She kissed him back and then she looked around the room, as if she was looking for something. She looked at each person in the room. Everyone, still in shock at the change in her, just smiled.

She then looked directly at her grandmother and lifted her shoulders, as if she were asking her grandmother something. Her grandmother kept her hand over her mouth and sadly looked at Mia.

Then the door opened slowly and everyone turned.

A beautiful nurse, dressed in a blue outfit, unlike the others in white, walked into the room slowly. In her arms, she held a baby wrapped in the same white blanket as the boys. The baby cooed and the nurse was entranced with the little baby in her arms. She looked at the baby lovingly.

Nico looked at the nurse, and said, "You're in the wrong room, we have our babies." She smiled eerily at Nico and walked toward Mia and placed the baby between Michel and Angelo.

Mia looked up at Nico and said, "Surprise my love, let me introduce you to our beautiful daughter, Lana."

Nico stumbled backwards, grabbing his head then reaching for something to keep him from falling.

He fell to his knees and tightly clenched his face with his hands. He shook his head as he looked toward the ceiling, then slammed his fists onto the floor and yelled…
"Noooooo!!!!! Nooooo!!!!"

THE END

www.ingramcontent.com/pod-product-compliance
Lightning Source LLC
Chambersburg PA
CBHW051229260626
47162CB00002B/344